S   Dunlap, Susan
Dunlap
2001
           The celestial buffet
           and other morsels of

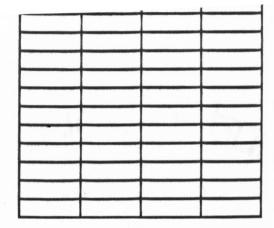

DEMCO

SUSAN DUNLAP
(Photograph © by Newell Dunlap)

the celestial buffet

AND OTHER
MORSELS OF MURDER

SUSAN DUNLAP

DEACCESSIONED

Crippen & Landru Publishers
Norfolk, Virginia
2001

Cover painting by Carol Heyer

Cover design by Deborah Miller

Crippen & Landru logo by Eric D. Greene

ISBN (limited edition): 1-885941-53-6
ISBN (trade edition): 1-885941-54-4

FIRST EDITION

10 9 8 7 6 5 4 3 2 1

Crippen & Landru Publishers
P. O. Box 9315
Norfolk, VA 23505
USA

www.crippenlandru.com
CrippenL@Pilot.Infi.Net

To Jacque and Ron Lynn, with love

CONTENTS

INTRODUCTION

I love writing short stories. For the writer of series novels, short stories are a vacation. You get to go anywhere you want, try different styles, tones, locales. The brevity allows a playfulness, a wry look at a problem. It's a chance to put personal failings to work. I've mined many of my own. (And in this case there's no chance of going back to the well once too often. This well never runs dry.)

And then there's revenge. In life there are a number of petty-seeming grievances for which the score is never settled. (Bad enough to have a grievance, but to know it's petty, to have it *called* petty, well, that's insult added firmly to injury.) When I'm about to write a short story the driver who cuts me off, or the person who doesn't return a phone call for days, becomes not an irritant but an inspiration. Revenge is mine (and in this book, yours).

Another of the pleasures of writing short stories is I can create a new character whom I will never see again. With those characters I can do whatever I please, with no telltale after-affects. They exist only for that one story.

The flip side of that, is the short story which features a series character. In some ways, it's an easier story for me to write because I already know Jill Smith and Kiernan O'Shaughnessy. With them, I understand how a specific concept will work, and for which one of them it will work. But I have a 'contract' with you, the reader, concerning these characters. Whatever I write about them, wherever it is published, becomes part of their lives. So, for instance, "Ott on a Limb" revealed a secret about Herman Ott which hadn't come up in any of the Jill Smith books. But after the story was published, it became part Ott's life, and had to be taken into account even for readers who might not have read the story. You could read the books and not know this particular fact and it wouldn't make too much difference, but if I had a short story in which Jill Smith decided to move to Australia . . . well, you can see the problem.

And, you can see the attraction of no-accountability in the one-shot story. At the end of a one-shot the hero can move to the South Pole and open a sun-tanning parlor and I'm not left with a problem explaining poor choices in customer-base predictions.

This volume contains about two-thirds of my short stories, the earlier ones. And I have to say, rereading them all-together surprised me. I did know that I like speculating about different locales, but I hadn't quite realized how often those locales are 'the afterlife' or, more accurately, the after*lives*, because the place changes from story to story in which death is not the end — not hardly.

I've arranged the stories not in chronological order, but as I would want to read them. I hope you'll enjoy them.

Susan Dunlap
Albany, California
September 8, 2000

Twice in my writing career a piece has just about written itself. One was the first chapter of An Equal Opportunity Death, *and the other was this story. I wrote "The Celestial Buffet" one afternoon while the friends I was visiting were at work. I sent it to magazines. It didn't sell. I submitted it to other magazines. Still, no sale. And so it resided in the closet until a writer friend read it and said, "It needs another twist." So I twisted, and resubmitted. It sold and won an Anthony Award. It's nice to have friends.*

THE CELESTIAL BUFFET

I hadn't stepped onto the celestial escalator with the escort of two white-suited angels like I had seen in the 1940's movies, but I did have the sense that I had risen up. I was very aware of the whole process, which is rather surprising considering what a shock my death was. I hadn't been sick, or taken foolish chances. I certainly didn't plan on dying — not ever, really — but in any case not so soon.

I looked down from somewhere near the ceiling and saw my body lying on the floor. I should have been horrified, overwhelmed by grief, more grief than I'd felt at the sight of any other body, but I really felt only a mild curiosity. My forty year old body was still clad in a turquoise running suit. It was, as it had been for most of its adult life, just a bit pearshaped around the derriere. It could have stood to lose five pounds (well, too late now). It was lying on the living room floor, its head about six inches from the coffee table, the stool overturned by its feet. How many times had Raymond told me not to stand on that stool to change the light bulb? If he had seen me holding the last, luscious bite of a Hershey bar in my left hand he would have said, "One of these days, you'll fall and kill yourself." And, of course, he would have been right. Now, I recalled wavering on that rickety stool, knowing I should reach up and grab onto the light fixture, hesitating, unwilling to drop the chocolate. It was still there, in my hand, clutched in a cadaveric spasm. How humiliating! I could almost hear Raymond's knowing cackle. At least that infuriating cackle was not the last sound I'd heard in life. If I had felt anything at all for that body on the floor I would have hoped Raymond wouldn't tell anyone how it died.

But the body and the possibility of its being ridiculed didn't hold my attention for long. I left it there on the floor and rose up. Exactly how I rose is unclear. I didn't take a white escalator, or a shimmering elevator, or any more sophisticated conveyance, I just had the sense of ascending till I reached a sort of landing.

I can no more describe the landing than I can the means of reaching it. There were no clear walls or floor, no drapes, no sliding gossamer doors, no pearly gates or streets paved with gold. Nothing so obvious. Just a sense, a knowing that this was the antechamber, the place of judgment. I stood, holding my breath (so to speak). Somewhere in the Bible it speaks of the moment of judgment when the words each of us has whispered in private will be broadcast aloud.

A distinctly uncomfortable thought. I had rather hoped that if that had to happen it would be at a mass event with a lot of babble and confusion, and everyone else as embarrassed at his own unmasking as I was. But here I was, alone, surrounded by silence. I waited (what choice had I?) but no public address system came on. So, the celestial loud speaker, at least, was a myth.

But even with that out of the way, I still knew (knew, rather than was told, for it was apparent to me now that communication in this place was not verbal or written — things simple were known) that there was a heaven and, God forbid, a hell, and this was the last neutral ground between the two. In a short time I would know which I was to reside in. Forever.

But I had led a decent life. There was no reason to worry. I had worked hard . . . well, hard enough. I'd voted, even in off-year elections. I'd spent Christmas every other year with my parents when they were alive. (Weren't my parents supposed to be here to meet me? Surely their absence wasn't because they were not in heaven? No. More likely, the greetings by all those who had gone on before was another myth.) I realized that my conception of this place was as ephemeral as the room itself. I hadn't given it more than the most cursory of thoughts, being sure that, at worst, I had years to form an idea of it. So what expectations I did have came mostly from Sunday school, and of course, 1940s movies.

The waiting was making me uneasy. Couldn't I move on to eternal bliss now? Why the delay? I had been a good person. I had followed the Ten Commandments, as much as was reasonable for someone living in San Francisco. I had honored my mother and father on those Christmases, and long distance after five and on Saturdays. I had kept the sabbath when I was a child, before I got hooked on football games on TV, which is all that could be legitimately expected. I had even gone to a series of meditation lectures on Sundays a year or two ago.

13   The Celestial Buffet

But my parents and the sabbath were only two commandments. What of the other eight? What *were* the other eight? That was a question I had considered only in connection with the Seven Dwarfs or the eight reindeer. Commandments? Ah, taking the name of the Lord in vain. Oh, God! Whoops! Admittedly, I'd been less than pure here, but who hadn't? If that commandment had been pivotal there would be no need for this room at all. The escalator would only go down.

Regardless, I felt distinctly uncomfortable. I looked around, searching for walls, for a bench, for something solid, but nothing was more substantial than a suggestion, a fuzzy conception way in the back of my mind.

Then, suddenly, there were double doors before me. With considerable relief, I pushed them open and walked into a large room, a banquet hall. To my right were the other guests. I couldn't make out individuals, but I knew they were seated at festively decorated tables, with full plates before them and glasses of Dom Perignon waiting to be lifted. No words were distinct, but the sounds of gaiety and laughter were unmistakable. Maybe the welcoming of those who had gone on before was not a myth. A welcoming dinner!

To my left was a buffet table.

It had been a long time since that fatal chocolate bar. The whole process of dying had taken a while, and the Hershey's had been a preprandial chocolate. Now that I was no longer distracted by apprehension, I realized I was famished. And I couldn't have been in a better place. I was delighted that this was not to be a formal dinner with choice limited to underdone chicken breast or tasteless white fish, and a slab of neapolitan ice cream for dessert. For me a buffet was the perfect welcome.

The buffet table was very long and wonderfully full. Before me were bowls of fruit. Not just oranges or canned fruit cocktail, but slices of fresh guavas and peaches, of mangoes and kiwi fruit, hunks of ripe pineapple without one brown spot, and maraschino cherries that I could gorge on without fear of carcinogens. As I stood pleasantly salivating, I knew that here at the celestial buffet I could eat pineapple and ice cream without getting indigestion, mountains of coleslaw or hills of beans without gas. And as much of them as I wanted. Never again the Scarsdale Diet. No more eight glasses of water and dry meat. Never another day of nine hundred or fewer calories. I could consume a bunch of banana, thirty Santa Rosa plums, enough seedless grapes to undermine the wine industry, and remain thin enough for my neighbor's husband to covet me.

But that was a topic I did not want to consider in depth. Surely, in business, in the twentieth century, in California, a bit of extramarital coveting was taken for granted. I hadn't, after all, coveted my neighbor's husband (he was sixty, and *he* only coveted a weed-free lawn.) I hadn't really coveted Amory as much as I did his ability to make me district manager. After the promotion I hadn't coveted him at all. And his wife never knew, and Raymond only half suspected, so that could hardly be considered Mortal Coveting. Besides, there wouldn't be guavas in hell.

A plate, really more of a platter than a mere one-serving plate, hovered beside me as if held up on the essence of a cart. Balancing the plate and the cup and holding the silver and napkins was always such a nuisance at buffets (and balancing, as I had so recently been reminded, was not my strong skill). So this floating platter was a heavenly innovation. I was pleased that things were so well organized here. I scooped up some guava, just a few pieces, not wanting to appear piggish at my welcoming dinner. I added a few more, and then a whole guava, realizing with sudden sureness that at this banquet greed was not an issue. I heaped on cherries, berries, and peeled orange sections soaked in Grand Marnier. Had this been an office brunch I would have been ashamed. But all the fruit fit surprisingly well on the platter and, in truth, hardly took up much of the space at all. It must have been an excellent platter design. Each fruit remained separate, none of the juices ran together, and I knew instinctively that the juices would never run into any of the entrees to come.

I moved along and found myself facing lox, a veritable school of fresh pink lox, accompanied by a tray of tiny, bite-size bagels, crisp yet soft, and a mound of cream cheese that was creamy enough to spread easily but thick enough to sink my teeth into. And there was salmon mousse made with fresh dill weed, and giant prawns in black bean sauce, and a heaping platter of lobster tails, and Maryland soft shell crab, and New Jersey blue fish that you can't get on the west coast, and those wonderful huge Oregon clams. I could have made a meal of any of them. But meal-sized portions of each fitted easily onto the platter. More than I ever coveted.

Coveting again. I may have coveted my neighbor's goods, but I had certainly not broken into his house and taken them. Oh, there had been the note pads and pens from the office, a few forays into fiction on my tax returns, but no one fears eternal condemnation for that. And there was the money from Consolidated Orbital to alter the environmental survey, but that was a gift, not stolen, regardless of what the environmentalists might have said. No, I could rest assured on the issue of coveting my neighbor's goods.

I adore quiche and for the last three years it has given me indigestion. But there is no need for plop plop fizz fizz amongst the heavenly host. And the choice of quiche here was outstanding. Nearest me was Italian Fontina with chanterelle mushrooms, New Zealand spinach, and — ah! — Walla Walla onions that were in and out of season so fast that a week's negligence meant another year's wait. Beside it, bacon. Bacon throughout the quiche and crisp curls decorating the top! The smell made me salivate. I could almost taste it. Bacon loaded with fat and sodium and preservatives and red dyes of every number. I had forced myself to forego it for years. And crab quiche, and one with beluga caviar sprinkled, no, ladled over the top. I couldn't decide. I didn't have to. It was truly amazing how much fitted onto the platter. I was certainly glad I didn't have to hold it up. Had I even contemplated eating this much on earth I would have gained five pounds. Ah, heaven! On earth, I would have killed for this.

I smiled (subtly speaking, for my spiritual face didn't move but my essence shifted into the outward show of happiness.) *Thou Shalt Not Kill*. Well, I wasn't a murderer either. And that was a biggie. The closest I had come to a dead body was my own. I moved on to the meats — rare roast beef with the outside cuts ready for my taking, and crispy duck with no grease at all. Admittedly, Milt Prendergast, my predecessor as district manager had killed himself, but that was hardly my fault. I didn't murder him. He was merely overly attached to his job. I added some spare ribs to my platter. I could sympathize with Prendergast's attachment to the job. I had aimed for it myself, and there was a lot of money to be had through it. But still, suicide was hardly murder, even if he did tell me he would kill himself if I exposed him. And I had to do that or even with Amory's help I couldn't have gotten the job. Well, considering the shenanigans Prendergast had been involved in, at least I knew I wouldn't be running into him up here.

The roast turkey smelled wonderful, a lifetime of Thanksgivings in one inhalation. With that sausage stuffing my Mom used to make. And fresh cranberries. My whole body quivered with hunger at the smell. I took a serving, then another.

There was still room for the muffins and breads — steaming popovers, orange nut loaf, Mexican corn bread with cheese and chilies — and for the grand assortment of desserts beyond.

But I was too hungry to wait. The juices in my empty stomach swirled; and I found myself chomping on my tongue in juicy anticipation. I needed to eat *now*. And this was, after all, a buffet. I could come back — eternally.

I reached for my platter.

It slipped beyond my grasp.

I grabbed.

Missed!

I heard laughter. Those diners at the tables, they were laughing at me.

My stomach whirled, now in fear. Surely, this couldn't mean that I was in. . . I lunged. But the platter that had been right beside me was suddenly, inexplicably, three feet away. Too far to reach, but near enough for the sweet smell of pineapple to reach me. Despite my fear, my tastebuds seemed to be jumping up and down at the back of my tongue. The laughter from the tables was louder.

I didn't dare turn toward the diners. Judgment Day separated the sheep from the goats. And even I, a city person, knew that sheep don't laugh. And there was a definite billy-goat quality to that cackle.

I stood still, inhaling the salty aroma of the caviar, the full flavor of that freshest of salmon, the smell of the bacon, of the turkey dressing. The platter stayed still, too — still out of reach. The smell of the cranberries mixed with tangy aroma of the oranges. I inhaled it, willing it to take substance in my throbbing stomach. It didn't.

If I couldn't capture that platter . . . but I didn't want to think about the hellish judgment that would signify. But there was no point making another grab. The laughter was louder; it sounded strangely familiar.

Slowly I turned away from the platter, careful not to glance out at the diners, afraid of what I might see. Head down, shoulders hunched over, I took a shuffling step away from the food. I could sense the platter following me. I took another step. From behind me, the oranges smelled stronger, sweeter. I could almost taste them. Almost. I lifted my foot as if to take another step, then I whirled around and with both hands lunged for the food. The hell with the platter.

The laughter pounded at my ears.

Let them laugh. I'd come up with one hand full of cranberries and the other grasping a piece of caviar quiche. I had my food. Triumphantly, and with heavenly relief, I jammed half the quiche in my mouth. No eternal damnation for me!

The laughter grew even louder. I knew that laugh; it came from a multitude of mouths, but it was all the same cackling sound. I swallowed quickly, and poured the whole handful of cranberries into my mouth.

That cackle — Raymond's laugh!

I swallowed and pushed the rest of the quiche into my mouth. Then the oranges from the now-near platter, and the salmon, and the pineapple, the prawns in the black bean sauce, the turkey, and the Oregon clams, and the Walla Walla sweet onions.

17 The Celestial Buffet

But there was no silencing Raymond's knowing cackle. And there was no denying where I was — eternally. I'd got my food all right, but it all tasted exactly the same. It tasted like it had been burned in the fires of Hell.

This is the only solo Kiernan O'Shaughnessy short story, though she joins her one-summer roommate, Margaret Maron's Deborah Knott, in "What's a Friend For?". Kiernan featured in four novels: Pious Deception, Rogue Wave, High Fall, *and* No Immunity.

Kiernan O'Shaughnessy was a forensic pathologist, working for a county north of San Francisco before she was fired. After considering her options, she moved to La Jolla, just north of San Diego, bought a duplex on the ocean, and hired a former offensive lineman for the San Diego Chargers as her cook, housekeeper and dog walker of her beloved Irish Wolfhound, Ezra.   She apprenticed to a private investigator and then opened her own agency in which she handles cases that require her medical expertise.

When I was at a private investigators' convention, I asked a few of the P.I.'s what techniques they used for housebreaking. To a one, they said, "I would never break the law." They paused, then added with smiles, "But I've got a friend who loves doing whatever it takes." Kiernan O'Shaughnessy could be that friend.

DEATH AND DIAMONDS

"The thing I love most about being a private investigator is the thrill of the game. I trained in gymnastics as a kid. I love cases with lots of action. But, alas, you can't always have what you love." Kiernan O'Shaughnessy glanced down at her thickly bandaged foot and the crutches propped beside it.

"Kicked a little too much ass, huh?" The man in the seat beside her at the Southwest Airlines gate grinned.   There was an impish quality to him. Average height, sleekly muscled, with the too-dark tan of one who doesn't worry about the future. He was over forty but the lines around his bright green eyes and mouth suggested quick scowls, sudden bursts of laughter, rather than the folds of age setting in. Amidst the San Diegans in shorts and T-shirts proclaiming the Zoo, Tijuana, and the Chargers, he seemed almost formal in his chinos and sports jacket and the forest green polo shirt. He crossed, then recrossed his long legs, and glanced impatiently at the purser standing guard at the end of the ramp.

The Gate 10 waiting area was jammed with tanned families ready to fly from sunny San Diego to sunnier Phoenix. The rumble of conversations was broken by children's shrill whines, and exasperated parents barking their names in warning.

We are now boarding all passengers for Southwest Airlines flight twelve forty-four to Oakland, through gate nine.

A mob of the Oakland-bound crowded closer to their gate, clutching their blue plastic boarding passes.

Beside Kiernan, the man sighed. But there was a twinkle in his eyes. "Lucky them. I hate waiting around like this It's not something I'm good at. One of the reasons I like flying Southwest is their open seating. If you move fast you can get whatever seat you want."

"Which seat is your favorite?"

"First row, aisle. So I can get off fast. *If* they ever let us *on*."

The Phoenix-bound flight was half an hour late. With each announcement of a Southwest departure to some other destination, the level of grumbling in the Phoenix-bound area had grown till the air seemed thick with frustration, and at the same time old and overused, as if it had held just enough oxygen for the scheduled waiting period, and now, half an hour later, the tired air only served to dry out noses, make throats raspy, and tempers short.

The loudspeaker announced the Albuquerque flight was ready for boarding. A woman in a rhinestone-encrusted denim jacket ran by racing toward the Albuquerque gate. Rhinestones. Hardly diamonds, but close enough to bring the picture of Melissa Jessup to Kiernan's mind. When she'd last seen her Melissa Jessup had been dead six months, beaten, stabbed, her corpse left outside to decompose. Gone were her mother's diamonds, the diamonds her mother had left her as security. Melissa hadn't yet been able to bring herself to sell them, even to finance her escape from a life turned fearful, and man who preferred them to her. It all proved, as Kiernan reminded herself each time the memory of Melissa invaded her thoughts, that diamonds are *not* a girl's best friend, that mother (or at least a mother who says "don't sell them") does *not* know best, and that a woman should never get involved with a man she works with. Melissa Jessup had made all the wrong decisions. Her lover had followed her, killed her, taken her mother's diamonds, and left not one piece of evidence. Melissa's brother had hired Kiernan, hoping with her background in forensic pathology she would find some clue in the autopsy report, or that once she could view Melissa's body she would spot something the local medical examiner had missed. She hadn't. The key that would nail

Melissa's killer was not in her corpse, but with the diamonds. Finding those diamonds, and the killer with them had turned into the most frustrating case of Kiernan's career.

She pushed the picture of Melissa Jessup out of her mind. This was no time for anger or any of the emotions that the thought of Melissa's death brought up. The issue now was getting this suitcase into the right hands in Phoenix. Turning back to the man beside her, she said, "The job I'm on right now is babysitting this suitcase from San Diego to Phoenix. This trip is not going to be 'a kick'."

"Couldn't you have waited till you're were off the crutches?" he said, looking down at her bandaged right foot.

"Crime doesn't wait." She smiled, focusing her full attention on the conversation now. "Besides, courier work is perfect for a hobbled lady, don't you think, Mr. uh?"

He glanced down at the plain black suitcase, then back at her. "Detecting all the time, huh?" There was a definite twinkle in his eyes as he laughed. "Well, this one's easy. Getting my name is not going to prove whether you're any good as a detective. I'm Jeff Siebert. And you are?"

"Kiernan O'Shaughnessy. But I can't let that challenge pass. Anyone can get a name. A professional investigator can do better than that. For a start, I surmise you're single."

He laughed, the delighted laugh of the little boy who's just beaten his parent in rummy. "No wedding ring, no white line on my finger to show I've taken the ring off. Right?"

"Admittedly, that was one factor. But you're wearing a red belt. Since it's nowhere near Christmas, I assume the combination of red belt and green turtleneck is not intentional. You're color blind."

"Well, yeah," he said buttoning his jacket over the offending belt. "But they don't ask you to tell red from green before they'll give you a marriage license. So?"

"If you were married, your wife might not check you over before you left each morning, but chances are she would organize your accessories so you could get dressed by yourself, and not have strange women like me commenting on your belt."

This is the final call for boarding Southwest Airline flight twelve forty-four to Oakland at gate nine.

Kiernan glanced enviously at the last three Oakland-bound passengers as

they passed through gate nine. If the Phoenix flight were not so late, she
would be in the air now and that much closer to getting the suitcase in the
right hands. Turning back to Siebert, she said, "By the same token, I'd guess
you have been married or involved with a woman about my size. A blonde."

He sat back down in his seat, and for the first time was still.

"Got your attention, huh?" Kiernan laughed. "I really shouldn't show off
like that. It unnerves some people. Others, like you, it just quiets down.
Actually, this was pretty easy. You've got a tiny spot of lavender eye shadow
on the edge of your lapel. I had a boyfriend your height and he ended up
sending a number of jackets to the cleaners. But no one but me would think
to look at the edge of your lapel, and you could have that jacket for years and
not notice that."

"But why did you say a blonde?"

"Blondes tend to wear violet eye shadow."

He smiled, clearly relieved.

*Flight seventeen sixty-seven departing gate 10 with service to Phoenix will begin
boarding in just a few minutes. We thank you for your patience.*

He groaned. "We'll see how few those minutes are." Across from them
a woman with an elephantine carry-on bag pulled it closer to her. Siebert
turned to Kiernan, and giving her that intimate grin she was beginning to
think of as *his look*, Siebert said, "You seem to be having a good time being a
detective."

The picture of Melissa Jessup popped up in her mind. Melissa Jessup had
let herself be attracted to a thief. She'd ignored her suspicions about him until
it was too late to sell her mother's jewels and she could only grab what was at
hand and run. Kiernan pushed the thought away. Pulling her suitcase closer,
she said, "Investigating can be a lot of fun if you like strange hours and the
thrill of having everything hang on one maneuver. I'll tell you the truth, it
appeals to the adolescent in me, particularly if I can pretend to be something
or someone else. It's fun to see if I can pull that off."

"How do I know you're not someone else?"

"I could show you I.D., but, of course, that wouldn't prove anything." She
laughed. "You'll just have to trust me, as I am you. After all *you* did choose
to sit down next to me."

"Well that's because you were the best looking woman here sitting by
herself."

"Or at least the one nearest the hallway where you came in. And this is the only spot around where you have room to pace. You look to be a serious pacer." She laughed again. "But I like your explanation better."

Shrieking, a small girl in yellow raced in front of the seats. Whooping gleefully, a slightly larger male version of her sprinted by. He lunged for his sister, caught his foot on Kiernan's crutch, and sent it toppling back as he lurched forward, and crashed into a man at the end of the check-in line. His sister skidded to a stop. "Serves you right, Jason. Mom, look what Jason did!"

Siebert bent over and righted Kiernan's crutch. "Travel can be dangerous, huh?"

"Damn crutches! It's like they've got urges all their own," she said. "Like one of them sees an attractive crutch across the room and all of a sudden it's gone. They virtually seduce underage boys."

He laughed, his green eyes twinkling impishly. "They'll come home to you. There's not a crutch in the room that could hold a *crutch* to you."

She hesitated a moment before saying. "My crutches and I thank you." This was, she thought, the kind of chatter that had been wonderfully seductive when she was nineteen. And Jeff Siebert was the restless, impulsive type of man who had personified freedom then. But nearly twenty years of mistakes — her own and more deadly ones like Melissa Jessup's — had shown her the inevitable end of such flirtations.

Siebert stood up and rested a foot against the edge of the table. "So what else is fun about investigating?"

She shifted the suitcase between her feet. "Well, trying to figure out people, like I was doing with you. A lot is common sense, like assuming that you are probably not a patient driver. Perhaps you've passed in a No Passing zone, or even have gotten a speeding ticket."

He nodded, abruptly.

"On the other hand," she went on, "sometimes I know facts beforehand, and then I can fake a Sherlock Holmes and produce anything-but-elementary deductions. The danger with that is getting cocky and blurting out conclusions before you've been given 'evidence' for them."

"Has that happened to you?"

She laughed and looked meaningfully down at her foot. "But I wouldn't want my client to come to that conclusion. We had a long discussion about whether a woman on crutches could handle his delivery."

"Client?" he said, shouting over the announcement of the Yuma flight at the next gate. In a normal voice, he added, "In your courier work, you mean? What's in that bag of your client's that so very valuable?"

She moved her feet till they were touching the sides of the suitcase. He leaned in closer. He was definitely the type of man destined to be trouble, she thought, but that little-boy grin, that conspiratorial tone was seductive, particularly in a place like this where any diversion was a boon. She wasn't surprised he had been attracted to her; clearly, he was a man who liked little women. She glanced around, pleased that no else had been drawn to this spot. The nearest travelers were a young couple seated six feet away and too involved in each other to waste time listening to strangers' conversation. "I didn't pack the bag. I'm just delivering it."

He bent down, ear near the side of the suitcase. "Well, at least it's not ticking." Sitting up, he said, "But seriously, isn't that a little dangerous? Women carrying bags for strangers, that's how terrorists have gotten bombs on planes."

"No!" she snapped. "I'm not carrying it for a lover with an M-1. I'm a bonded courier."

The casual observer might not have noticed Siebert's shoulders tensing, slightly, briefly, in anger at her rebuff. Silently, he looked down at her suitcase. "How much does courier work pay?"

"Not a whole lot, particularly compared to the value of what I have to carry. But then there's not much work involved. The chances of theft are minuscule. And I do get to travel. Last fall I drove a package up north. That was a good deal since I had to go up there anyway to check motel registrations in a case I'm working on. It took me a week to do the motels and then I came up empty." An entire week to discover that Melissa's killer had not stopped at a motel or hotel between San Diego and Eureka. "The whole thing would have been a bust if it hadn't been for the courier work."

He glanced down at the suitcase. She suspected he would have been appalled to know how obvious was his covetous look. Finally he said, "What was in that package, the one you delivered?"

She glanced over at the young couple. No danger from them. Still Kiernan lowered her voice. "Diamonds. Untraceable. That's really the only reason to go to the expense of hiring a courier."

"Untraceable, huh?" he said, grinning. "Didn't you even consider taking off over the border with them?"

"Maybe," she said slowly, "if I had known they were worth enough to set me up for the rest of my actuarial allotment, I might have."

We will begin pre-boarding Southwest Airlines Flight seventeen sixty-seven with service to Phoenix momentarily. Please keep your seats until pre-boarding has been completed.

She pushed herself up, and positioned the crutches under her arms. It was a moment before he jerked his gaze away from the suitcase and stood, his foot tapping impatiently on the carpet. All around them families were hoisting luggage and positioning toddlers for the charge to the gate. He sighed loudly. "I hope you're good with your elbows."

She laughed and settled back on the arm of the seat.

His gaze went back to the suitcase. He said, "I thought couriers were handcuffed to their packages."

"You've been watching too much TV." She lowered her voice. "Handcuffs play havoc with the metal detector. The last thing you want in this business is buzzers going off and guards racing in from all directions. I go for the low key approach. Always keep the suitcase in sight. Always be within lunging range."

He took a playful swipe at it. "What would happen if, say, that bag were to get stolen?"

"Stolen!" She pulled the suitcase closer to her. "Well for starters, I wouldn't get a repeat job. If the goods were insured that might be the end of it. But if it were something untraceable" — she glanced at the suitcase — "it could be a lot worse." With a grin that matched his own, she said, "You're not a thief are you?"

He shrugged. "Do I look like a thief?"

"You look like the most attractive man here." She paused long enough to catch his eye. "Of course, looks can be deceiving." She didn't say it, but she could picture him pocketing a necklace carelessly left in a jewelry box during a big party, or a Seiko watch from under a poolside towel. She didn't imagine him planning a heist, but just taking what came his way.

Returning her smile, he said, "When you transport something that can't be traced don't they even provide you a back-up?"

"No! I'm a professional. I don't need back-up."

"But with your foot like that?"

"I'm good with the crutches. And besides, the crutches provide camouflage. Who'd think a woman on crutches carrying a battered suitcase had anything worth half a mi— Watch out! The little girl and her brother are loose again." She pulled her crutches closer as the duo raced through the aisle in front of them.

We are ready to begin boarding Southwest Airlines Flight number seventeen sixty-seven to Phoenix. Any passengers traveling with small children, or those needing a little extra time may begin boarding now.

The passengers applauded. It was amazing, she thought, how much sarcasm could be carried by a non-verbal sound.

She leaned down for the suitcase. "Pre-boarding. That's me."

"Are you going to be able to handle the crutches and the suitcase?" he asked.

"You're really fascinated with this bag, aren't you?"

"Guilty." He grinned. "Should I dare to offer to carry it? I'd stay within lunging range."

She hesitated.

In the aisle a woman in cerise shorts, carrying twin bags herded twin toddlers toward the gate. Ahead of her an elderly man leaned precariously on a cane. The family with the boy and girl were still assembling luggage.

He said, "You'd be doing me a big favor letting me pre-board with you. I like to cadge a seat in the first row on the aisle."

"The seat for the guy who can't wait?"

"Right. But I got here so late that I'm in the last boarding group. I'm never going to snag a first row seat. So help me out. I promise," he said grinning, "I won't steal."

"Well . . . I wouldn't want my employer to see this. I assured him I wouldn't need any help. But . . ." She shrugged.

"No time to waver now. There's already a mob of pre-boarders ahead of us." He picked up the bag. "Some heavy diamonds."

"Good camouflage, don't you think? Of course, not everything's diamonds."

"Just something untraceable?"

She gave him a half wink. "It may not be untraceable. It may not even be valuable."

"And you may be just a regular mail carrier," he said, starting toward the gate.

She swung after him. The crutches were no problem and the thickly taped right ankle looked worse than it was. Still, it made things much smoother to have Siebert carrying the suitcase. If the opportunity arose, he might be tempted to steal it, but not in a crowded gate at the airport with guards and airline personnel around. He moved slowly, staying right in front of her, running interference. As they neared the gate, a blond man carrying a jumpy toddler hurried in front of them. The gate phone buzzed. The airline rep. picked it up and nodded at it. To the blond man and the elderly couple who had settled in behind him, Kiernan and Siebert, he said, "Sorry folks. The cleaning crew's a little slow. It'll just be a minute."

Siebert's face scrunched in anger. "What's 'cleaning crew' a euphemism for? A tire fell off and they're looking for it? They've spotted a crack in the engine block and they're trying to figure out if they can avoid telling us?"

Kiernan laughed. "I'll bet people don't travel with you twice."

He laughed. "I just hate being at someone else's mercy. But since we're going to be standing here a while, why don't you do what you love more than diamonds, Investigator: tell me what you've deduced about me."

"Like reading your palm?" The crutches poked into her armpits; she shifted them back, putting more weight on her bandaged foot. Slowly she surveyed his lanky body, his thin agile hands, con man's hands, hands that were never quite still, always past *Ready,* coming out of *Set.* "Okay. You're travelling from San Diego to Phoenix on the Friday evening flight, so chances are you were here on business. But you don't have on cowboy boots, or a Stetson. You're tan, but it's not that dry tan you get in the desert. In fact you could pass for a San Diegan. I would have guessed that you travel for a living, but you're too impatient for that, and if you'd taken this flight once or twice before you wouldn't be surprised that it's late. You'd have a report to read, or a newspaper. No, you do something where you don't take orders, and you don't put up with much." She grinned. "How's that?"

"That's pretty elementary, Sherlock," he said with only a slight edge to his voice. He tapped his fingers against his leg. But all in all he looked only a little warier than any other person in the waiting area would as his secrets were unveiled.

Southwest Airlines flight number seventeen sixty-seven with service to Phoenix is now ready for pre-boarding.

"Okay, folks," the gate attendant called. "Sorry for the delay."

The man with the jittery toddler thrust his boarding pass at the gate attendant and strode down the ramp. The child screamed. The elderly coupled moved haltingly, hoisting and readjusting their open sacks with each step. A family squeezed in in front of them causing the old man to stop dead and move his bag to the other shoulder. Siebert shifted foot to foot.

Stretching up to whisper in his ear, Kiernan said, "It would look bad if you shoved the old people out of your way."

"How bad?" he muttered grinning, then handed his boarding pass to the attendant.

As she surrendered hers, she said to Siebert, "Go ahead, hurry. I'll meet you in row one."

"Thanks." He patted her shoulder.

She watched him stride down the empty ramp. His tan jacket had caught on one hip as he balanced her suitcase and his own. But he neither slowed his pace nor made an attempt to free the jacket; clutching tight to her suitcase he hurried around the elderly couple, moving with the strong stride of a hiker. By the time she got down the ramp the elderly couple and a family with two toddlers and an infant that sucked loudly on a pacifier crowded behind Siebert.

Kiernan watched irritably as the stewardess eyed first Siebert then her big suitcase. The head stewardess has the final word on carry on luggage, she knew. With all the hassle that was involved with this business anyway, she didn't want to add a confrontation with the stewardess. She dropped the crutches and banged backward into the wall, flailing for purchase as she slipped down to the floor.

The stewardess caught her before she hit bottom. "Are you okay?"

"Embarrassed," Kiernan said, truthfully. She hated to look clumsy, even if it was an act, even if it allowed Siebert and her suitcase to get on the plane unquestioned. "I'm having an awful time getting used to these things."

"You sure you're okay? Let me help you up," the stewardess said. "I'll have to keep your crutches in the hanging luggage compartment up front while we're in flight. But you go ahead now; I'll come and get them from you."

"That's okay. I'll leave them there and just sit in one of the front seats," she said, taking the crutches and swinging herself on board the plane. From the luggage compartment it took only one long step on her left foot to get to row 1. The plane was old, small, with only two seats on either side of the aisle. All seats faced the cockpit. She swung around Siebert, who was hoisting his own suitcase into the overhead bin beside hers, and dropped into 1D, by the window. The elderly couple was settling into 1A and B. In another minute Southwest would call the first thirty passengers, and the herd would stampede down the ramp, stuffing approved carry-ons in overhead compartments, and grabbing the thirty most prized seats.

"That was a smooth move with the stewardess," Siebert said, as he settled into his coveted aisle seat.

"That suitcase is just about the limit of what they'll let you carry on. I've had a few hassles. I could see this one coming. And I suspected that you" — she patted his arm — "were not the patient person to deal with that type of problem. You moved around her pretty smartly yourself. I'd say that merits a drink from my client."

He smiled and rested a hand on hers. "Maybe," he said, leaning closer, "we could have it in Phoenix."

For the first time she had a viscerally queasy feeling about him. Freeing her hand from his she gave a mock salute. "Maybe so." She looked past him at the elderly couple.

Siebert's gaze followed hers. He grinned as he said, "Do you think they're thieves? After your loot? Little old sprinters?"

"Probably not. But it pays to be alert." She forced a laugh. "I'm afraid constant suspicion is a side effect of my job."

The first wave of passengers hurried past. Already the air in the plane had the sere feel and slightly rancid smell of having been dragged through the filters too many times. By tacit consent they watched the passengers hurry on board, pause, survey their options, and rush on. Kiernan thought fondly of that drink in Phoenix. She would be sitting at a small table, looking out a tinted window, the trip would be over, the case delivered into the proper hands, and she would feel the tension that knotted her back releasing with each swallow of scotch. Or so she hoped. The whole frustrating case depended on this delivery. There was no fall back position. If she screwed up, Melissa Jessup's murderer disappeared.

That tension was what normally made the game fun. But this case was no longer a game. This time she had allowed herself to go beyond her regular rules, to call her former colleagues from the days when she had been a forensic pathologist, looking for some new test that would prove culpability. She had hoped the lab in San Diego could find something. They hadn't. The fact was that the diamonds were the only "something" that would trap the killer, Melissa's lover, who valued them much more than her, a man who might not have bothered going after her had it not been for them. Affairs might be brief, but diamonds, after all, are forever. They would lead her to the murderer's safe house, and the evidence that would tie him to Melissa. *If* she was careful.

She shoved the tongue of the seat belt into the latch and braced her feet as the plane taxied toward the runway. Siebert was tapping his finger on the armrest.

The engines whirred, the plane shifted forward momentarily, then flung them back against their seats as it raced down the short runway.

The *fasten seat belt* sign went off. The old man across the aisle pushed himself up and edged toward the front bathroom. Siebert's belt was already unbuckled. Muttering, "Be right back," he jumped up, stood hunched under the overhead bin while the old man cleared the aisle. Then Siebert headed full-out toward the back of the plane. Kiernan slid over and watched him as he strode down the aisle, steps firmer, steadier than she'd have expected of a man racing to the bathroom in a swaying airplane. She could easily imagine him hiking in the redwood forest with someone like her, a small, slight woman. The blond woman with the violet eye shadow. She in jeans and one of those soft Patagonia jackets Kiernan had spotted in the L.L. Bean catalog, violet with blue trim. He in jeans, turtleneck, a forest green down jacket on his rangy body. Forest green would pick up the color of his eyes, and accent his dark, curly hair. In her picture, his hair was tinted with the first flecks of autumn snow and the ground still soft like the spongy airplane carpeting beneath his feet.

When he got back he made no mention of his hurried trip. He'd barely settled down when the stewardess leaned over him and said, "Would you care for something to drink?"

Kiernan put a hand on his arm. "This one's on my client."

"For that client who insisted you carry his package while you're still on crutches I'm sorry it can't be Lafitte Rothschild. Gin and tonic will have to do." He grinned at the stewardess. Kiernan could picture him in a bar, flashing that grin at a tall redhead, or maybe another small blonde. She could imagine him with the sweat of a San Diego summer still on his brow, his skin brown from too many days at an ocean beach that is too great a temptation for those who grab their pleasures.

"Scotch and water," Kiernan ordered. To him, she said, "I notice that while I'm the investigator, it's you who are asking all the questions. So what about you, what do you do for a living?"

"I quit my job in San Diego and I'm moving back to Phoenix. So I'm not taking the first Friday night flight to get back home, I'm taking it to get to my new home. I had good times in San Diego: the beach, the sailing, Balboa Park. When I came there a couple years ago I thought I'd stay forever. But the draw of the desert is too great. I miss the red rock of Sedona, the pines of the Mogollon Rim, and the high desert outside Tucson." He laughed. "Too much soft California life."

It was easy to picture him outside of Show Low on the Mogollon Rim with the pine trees all around him, some chopped for firewood, the axe lying on a stump, a shovel in his hand. Or in a cabin near Sedona lifting a hatch in the floorboards.

The stewardess brought the drinks and the little bags of peanuts, giving Jeff Siebert the kind of smile Kiernan knew would have driven her crazy had she been Siebert's girlfriend. How often had that type of thing happened?

Had his charm brought that reaction so automatically that for him it had seemed merely the way women behave? Had complaints from a girlfriend seemed at first unreasonable, then melodramatic, then infuriating? He was an impatient man, quick to anger. Had liquor make it quicker, like the rhyme said? And the prospect of unsplit profit salved his conscience?

He poured the little bottle of gin over the ice and added tonic. "Cheers."

She touched glasses, then drank. "Are you going to be in Phoenix long?"

"Probably not. I've come into a little money and I figure I'll just travel around, sort of like you do. Find some place I like."

"So we'll just have time for our drink in town then?"

He rested his hand back on hers. "Well now, I may have reason to come back in a while. Or to San Diego. I just need to cut loose for a while."

She forced herself to remain still, not to cringe at his touch. *Cut loose* — what an apt term for him to use. She pictured his sun-browned hand wrapped around the hilt of a chef's knife, working it up and down, up and down, cutting across pink flesh till it no longer looked like flesh, till the flesh mixed with the blood and the organ tissue, till the knife cut down to the bone and the metal point stuck in the breastbone. She pictured Melissa Jessup's blond hair pink from the blood.

She didn't have to picture her body lying out in the woods outside Eureka in northern California. She had seen photos of it. She didn't have to imagine what the cracked ribs and broken clavicle and the sternum marked from the knife point looked like now. Jeff Siebert had seen that too, and had denied what Melissa's brother, and the Eureka Sheriff all knew — knew in their hearts but could not prove — that Melissa had not gone to Eureka camping by herself as he'd insisted, but had only stopped overnight at the campground she and Jeff had been to the previous summer because she had no money, and hadn't been able to bring herself to sell the diamonds her mother had left her. Instead of a rest on the way to freedom, she'd found Siebert there.

Now Siebert was flying to Phoenix to vanish. He'd pick up Melissa's diamonds wherever he'd stashed them, then he'd be gone.

"What about your client?" he asked. "Will he be meeting you at the airport?"

"No. No one will meet me. I'll just deliver my goods to the van, collect my money and be free. What about you?"

"No. No one's waiting for me either. At least I'll be able to give you a hand with that bag. There's no ramp to the terminal in Phoenix. You have to climb down to the tarmac there. Getting down those metal steps with a suitcase and two crutches would be a real balancing act."

All she had to do was get it in the right hands. She shook her head. "Thanks. But I'll have to lug it through the airport just in case. My client didn't handcuff the suitcases to me, but he does expect I'll keep hold of it."

He grinned. "Like you said, you'll be in lunging range all the time."

"No," she said firmly. "I appreciate your offer, Jeff; the bag weighs a ton. But I'm afraid it's got to be in my hand."

Those green eyes of his that had twinkled with laughter narrowed, and his lips pressed together. "Okay," he said slowly. Then his face relaxed almost back to that seductively impish smile that once might have charmed her, as it had Melissa Jessup. "I want you to know that I'll still find you attractive even if the bag yanks your shoulder out of its socket." He gave her hand a pat, then shifted in his seat so his upper arm rested next to hers.

The stewardess collected the glasses.

The plane jolted and began its descent. Kiernan braced her feet. Through his jacket, she felt the heat of his arm, the arm that had dug that chef's knife into Melissa Jessup's body. She breathed slowly and did not move.

To Kiernan, he said, "There's a great bar right here in Sky Harbor Airport, the Sky Lounge. Shall we have our drink there?"

She nodded, her mouth suddenly too dry for speech.

The plane bumped down and in a moment the aisles were jammed with passengers ignoring the stewardess' entreaty to stay in their seats. Siebert stood up and pulled his bag out of the overhead compartment and then lifted hers onto his empty seat. "I'll get your crutches," he said, as the elderly man across the aisle pushed his way out in front of him. Siebert shook his head. Picking up both suitcases, he maneuvered around the man and around the corner to the luggage compartment.

Siebert had taken her suitcase. *You don't need to take both suitcases to pick up the crutches.* Kiernan stared after him, her shoulders tensing, her hands clutching the armrests. Her throat was so constricted she could barely breath. For an instant, she shared the terror that must have paralyzed Melissa Jessup just before he stabbed her.

"Jeff!" she called after him, a trace of panic evident in her voice. He didn't answer her. Instead, she heard a great thump, then him muttering and the stewardess's voice placating.

The airplane door opened. The elderly man moved out into the aisle front of Kiernan, motioning his wife to go ahead of him, then they moved slowly toward the door.

Kiernan yanked the bandage off her foot, stepped into the aisle. "Excuse me," she said to the couple. Pushing by them as Siebert had so wanted to do, she rounded the corner to the exit.

The stewardess was lifting up a garment bag. Four more bags lay on the floor. So that was the thump she'd heard. A crutch was beside them.

She half-heard the stewardess's entreaties to wait, her mutterings about the clumsy man. She looked out the door down onto the tarmac.

Jeffrey Siebert and the suitcase were gone. In those few seconds he had raced down the metal steps, and was disappearing into the terminal. By the time she could make it to the Sky Lounge he would be halfway to Show Low, or Sedona.

Now she felt a different type of panic. *This* wasn't in the plan. She couldn't lose Siebert. She jumped over the bags, grabbed one crutch, hurried outside to the top of the stairs, and thrust the crutch across the hand rails behind her to make a seat. As the crutch slid down the railings, she kept her knees bent high into her chest to keep from landing and bucking forward onto her head. Instead the momentum propelled her on her feet, as it had in gymnastics. In those routines, she'd had to fight the momentum, now she went with it and ran, full out.

She ran through the corridor toward the main building, pushing past businessmen, between parents carrying children. Siebert would be running ahead. But no one would stop him, not in an airport. People run through airports all the time. Beside the metal detectors she saw a man in a tan jacket. Not him. By the luggage pick-up another look-alike. She didn't spot him till he was racing out the door to the parking lot.

Siebert ran across the roadway. A van screeched to a halt. Before Kiernan could cross through the traffic, a hotel bus eased in front of her. She skirted behind it. She could sense a man following her now. But there was no time to deal with that. Siebert was halfway down the lane of cars. Bent low, she ran down the next lane, the hot dusty desert air drying her throat.

By the time she came abreast of Siebert, he was in a light blue Chevy pick-up backing out of the parking slot. He hit the gas, and, wheels squealing, drove away.

She reached toward the truck with both arms. Siebert didn't stop. She stood watching as Jeffrey Siebert drove off into the sunset.

There was no one behind her as she sauntered into the terminal to the Sky Lounge. She ordered the two drinks Siebert had suggested, and when they came, she tapped "her" glass on "his," and took a drink for Melissa Jessup. Then she swallowed the rest of the drink in two gulps.

By this time Jeff Siebert would be on the freeway. He'd be fighting to stay close to the speed limit, balancing his thief's wariness of the highway patrol against his gnawing urge to force the lock on the suitcase. Jeffrey Siebert was an impatient man, a man who had nevertheless made himself wait nearly a year before leaving California. His stash of self-control would be virtually empty. But he would wait awhile before daring to stop. Then he'd jam a knife between the top and bottom of the suitcase, pry and twist it till the case fell open. He would find diamonds. More diamonds. Diamonds to take along while he picked up Melissa Jessup's from the spot where he'd hidden them.

She wished Melissa Jessup could see him when he compared the two collections, and realized the new ones he'd stolen were fakes. She wished she herself could see his face when he realized that a woman on crutches had made it out of the plane in time to follow him and to point out the blue pick-up truck.

Kiernan hoisted "Jeff's" glass and drank more slowly. How sweet it would be if Melissa could see that grin of his fade as the surveillance team surrounded him, drawn by the beepers concealed in those fake diamonds. He'd be clutching the evidence that would send him to jail. Just for life, not forever. As Melissa could have told him, only death and diamonds are forever.

Life is filled with inconvenience, and never it is so apparent as when you're trying to do a job you didn't want, to begin with. And when others compound that problem by not-listening, it can be very frustrating, and leave one feeling quite helpless. Though, not always.

AN UNSUITABLE JOB FOR A MULLIN

"Can't do." Mullin regretted he'd answered the phone.

"He needs you."

"I don't work anymore."

"I said, *He* needs you." The voice was unfamiliar, but the tone and cadence were always the same. They never changed, these callers. Did a night school offer: *Speak Like the Godfather?*

"I'm retired."

"There's only one way you retire from this racket."

Mullin shook his head. Maybe there was another class: *Triteness Made Easy.* "Look, uh . . ." but of course the kid hadn't given him a name. He'd probably taken a Saturday seminar in *Identity Concealment for the Ambitious Thug.* "I can't —"

"You cross him, you're gonna be the one hit."

"Well, kid, we all gotta die."

"He'll get somebody else to do him, and then do you."

Mullin scratched his head.

But before he could come up with the next line, the kid hit him below the belt. "He knows you ain't worked in fifteen years. He knows you act like you can retire. He knows you, Mullin, and what yer gonna say. Here's what he says: He'll get someone else, someone not as good as you, someone messy. And when the mark's mooshed all over the sidewalk, he'll put out the word that you did the hit."

Mullin was offended, first, at the August *He* assuming Mullin still cared about his professional reputation, and second, that he did. Messy meant not merely a sanitation challenge, but a painful death for the victim, an angry crowd of the victim's relatives, friends, 'business associates,' all of them out for revenge. All of them looking to take the shine off his golden years.

Still, he couldn't . . . "I can't."

"Name's Maddis Esterbee Groom. Lives with his wife at two two seven Pacific Avenue, San Francisco." He added phone numbers. "His mug's in the society section of your paper out there today. All you gotta do is drive across town. It's an easy hit. *He* is flying in at five, your time. *He* don't want Groom to be around to meet him, y'understand?"

Mullin felt like the walls were closing in, walls two feet thick. But he couldn't do the hit. He sighed. He'd vowed never to admit the reason to anyone in the profession, much less the family back east. That was why he'd moved a continent away. But now he had no choice, "Look, I'm not kidding, I can't —"

But the kid had hung up.

He put down the receiver. Now he really had no choice. He wondered what the story on him was back east. Lost his nerve? Got religion? Or some shaking disease? Whatever they thought, it was fine with him. Just as long as they didn't dig up the truth — the one thing in the world he could not bring himself to do ever again.

Mullin, the hitman, didn't drive. Not anymore.

♣

Five o'clock! In his shock he hadn't dealt with that at all. Because he was focused on the driving thing, not the hit itself. It wasn't like he could have said "I don't drive anymore." Even if he could have stood the cackles of laughter coming over the phone lines, and the prospect of cackles all over the east coast. It wouldn't be long before *He* wondered what else would spook him, and how easy it would be for the feds to turn him. *His* solution to that problem Mullin knew only too well. Mullin was so flustered by the miserable situation he hadn't thought to ask the kid about payment, or even why, after fifteen years, *He* had tracked him down on this cold summer day in San Francisco. Jeez, he had been out of the business too long.

Or maybe not. "Look for the ray of sun in every cloud, Cornelius," his sainted mother had said. His ma was no meteorologist, but he took her point. He could see the yellow ray peeking out of this cloud.

Warn Groom, that's what he should do. Letting a mark go would have never crossed his mind when he was still working. He would have been insulted at the idea. A mark who escaped just upped the ante. But retirement gives a man time for reflection.

It felt good doing the right thing.

It felt wise. Virtuous.

He checked the paper. In the photo Maddis Esterbee Groom, 55, President of Groom Consulting, was a barrel-chested man with sharp features and a wiry ruff of brown hair. His hand was on the arm of his wife, Alice, while he talked intently with the man beside him.

Virtue was rewarded, right? Groom could afford to reward him. He called.

"Groom."

"Maddis Groom?"

"Right. What is this in regard to?"

A matter of life and death, Mr. Groom, he could have said. But there are some subjects unsuitable for the phone. This one called for a face-to-face. Pulling up from memory one of the credos of professional behavior — Lead with Greed — he said, "It's about the morgue photo —" Mullin stopped. What was wrong with him? Did he have a one track mind? He *had* been retired too long. "We need a better picture for the feature we're running tomorrow. A news photo."

"What?" Groom grumbled. "You need a new DeSoto?" His voice was muted.

"Could you speak louder?"

He didn't. But he was still talking. He hadn't stopped even for Mullin's question. His words were covered by squeaking noises. Groom's hand, he realized, was over the phone.

Mullin let out a sigh. He had expected a certain degree of awkwardness in this conversation. There was no delicate way to lead into: *Mr. Groom, I've been hired to murder you by five o'clock. Clean up your act, square with Him, leave town, whatever.* He'd assumed by now he'd have delivered the warning and be off the phone. But he was still listening to squeaks.

Groom's voice boomed at him. "Excuse me, Mr. er . . . , you were saying something about a new quota. I really —"

"Mr. Groom, I've been hired to —"

"Right, Taffy, get that mailing ready this morning." Maddis Groom's hand was only partly over the receiver. "Yeah, I want to see it before it goes out. And call Burns; tell him I'll be late for lunch."

A whoosh of noise smacked Mullin's ear.

"Now about the dues quota," Groom said, "I can't see why —"

"Mr. Groom, I've been hired to murder you."

Mullin waited for a gasp. A denial. A threat. It was a moment before he realized Groom's hand was back over the receiver and he saying something about Guaymas.

Mullin's face was red; he could tell. Sweat was running down his brow, his neck, his back. "Groom," he shouted. "I'm going to murder you.

Murder! Today! You hear me?"

But Mullin, the murderer, was on hold.

❖

In the old days Mullin had learned everything about his marks' movements, but nothing about *them*. He didn't want to know. He didn't watch the news of their deaths or read about their funerals. But now, since he was sticking his neck out to let this mark live, he was tempted. And just in case Groom didn't understand how grateful he should be, it would be good to know how to get to him, socially and economically speaking.

He paged through the phone book, for the library reference desk. Sure, call them and leave his phone number on their records? No. He'd drive over . . .

He groaned. Driving was like smoking: no matter how long you'd been clean, in your gut you were never a non-driver. So, okay, he could *walk* to Mission Street, wait for the bus to Market Street, transfer to a street car . . . Or he could walk to Twenty-fourth Street and take BART and hope there were no delays underground. Or he . . .

Forget the library. It was already quarter to twelve.

He'd just go across town to Pacific Heights and deal with Groom.

Well, not just . . . If he took the bus to Market and changed . . .

Hell, he'd splurge on a cab.

He hiked up to Market and Sanchez and scanned the street. No cabs. He tried around Castro and Market. One cab, grabbed by a guy with suit and briefcase. Mullin waited. He had to watch his pennies now; cabs were a luxury of the past. After all, there was no Hitman's Benevolent League, no group medical with riders for gunshot wounds, no disability coverage for those nasty mishaps so common to careless bombers. No Old Hitman's Home. He couldn't look forward to evenings in a rocker replaying the years' greatest hits.

It wasn't as if he was going to get paid for this job that he wasn't going to do.

He paced to the corner, checking all directions. Buses passed, trolleys passed, and street cars, pedicabs, motorcycles, bicycles, and a lone unicycle. No taxis.

He spotted the bus to Pacific Heights on the far side of Market — getting ready to pull out. The light was against him. But the wait for the next one would be what — half an hour? He raced into traffic, hand thrust out as if those few inches of pallid flesh would halt thousands of pounds of station wagon. He squirted between cars. A Muni bus swerved precariously.

"Fucking asshole!" the driver yelled at him, and suggested an alternate destination. Mullin bounded heavily across the tracks, relieved no trolleys were near, and into the traffic. A brown truck screeched to a halt. The driver shouted an epithet understandable in any language. Ahead, the bus belched smoke and gave an uphill lurch like a fat guy's first try out of the chair. Mullin ran faster, arms waving. He clambered onto the bus and rooted through his pockets shooting change across the floor. Thank God, he'd decided not to do the hit. If he had it wouldn't be dimes rolling under seats, it'd be bullets.

He got off at Pacific and walked three blocks.

The Groom house was on the bay side of the street, with a view to kill for. From habit, he stood across the street to get his bearings.

The Groom garage door opened. A shiny expensive black car oozed out. Once he'd have known if it was a Mercedes, a Jaguar, a Maserati. Now they all looked the same, archeological artifacts of a long dead life. Now, the only way he'd be connected to one of them would be in a hit-and-run. Just the idea of being compressed behind the wheel, squeezed in by the closing door, turned his stomach sour. He shook off the thought. But there would be other ways to enjoy Mr. Groom's gratitude.

He shook off that thought, too. In less than five hours someone else would be after Maddis Groom, and *him*, and the only reward he'd get would be eternal.

He waved his arms as Maddis Groom backed out across traffic. Straight at him. He threw up his hands in warning. The car kept at him. He leapt to right. The bumper skimmed his jacket. His arm was still raised. Groom waved absently.

Mullin started after the car, half-running, half-staggering. A car pulled up next to him. A cab, he thought in the hopeful instant before he turned his head. On a scale of ten the cab would have been a ten. "One," he muttered under his breath as he took in the black and white.

"You looking for trouble, buddy?"

Mullin forced a sticky smile. "No sir, officer." I don't have to *look*.

❖

He was panting by the time he got to a phone at Van Ness Avenue. The chill wind iced his face. A big reward, that's what Groom better come up with. Huge. The man could have killed him! And him still trying to help out. He spotted a pay phone, dialed Groom's cell phone and stuck his head into the nook to mute the roar of traffic.

"Yes?"

"Mr. Groom, I called you this morning. I said I was calling about the news photo."

"You hung up."

"You left me on hold."

"Mr. er — I am a busy man. I'm already late for a lunch. I don't have time to discuss risotto."

"This won't take long. I just want you to know that I was hired —"

"Hang on, I've got a call through."

❖

"News photo!" He would have shouted, if his time hadn't run out. When he dialed back he couldn't get through. He looked at his watch: 12:30. He couldn't hang around the phone here all afternoon, watching the fog grow thicker, the wind whip faster, the chilly sands of his life run out.

Guaymas, he thought. Maybe Groom was flying out this afternoon. Then they'd both be saved, for a while. "A miracle," his sainted mother would say. He looked down and saw another miracle: a phone book, still hanging under the phone nook. It was a moment before Mullin realized that in his miraculous awe he'd looked up Guaymas, rather than an airline.

But Guaymas was there. A restaurant!

Groom wasn't skipping the country. The man was just going to lunch. At Guaymas. In Tiburon.

Tiburon! The suburbs!

Tiburon. There was a bay between San Francisco and Tiburon. Did buses run there? Did they arrive the same day? The whole thing was impossible. Maybe he could call back the connected tough, tell him . . .

The ferry, he'd forgotten the ferry. Through the fog, he spotted a cab across the street. A nun was getting in. He shoved her out of the way. "Ferry, and step on it!" he said.

The driver grinned, shot forward, whizzed right, flew left, slammed to a halt at a stop sign and shot forward again. Mullin's fingers overshot his forehead and shoulders as he tried to make the sign of the cross. *Won't help*, he muttered to himself, *not after the nun*. When the cab hung a U across four lanes and screeched to a stop an inch behind a cement truck, Mullin's feet were wedged against the front seat, his hands clinging to window and seat, his eyes stuck shut. He flipped the cabbie a ten.

"Hey! Is that all! For a Grand Prix ride . . ."

But Mullin was out of the cab and trying to get through the crowd in front of the ticket hut.

"Cheapskate!"

Mullin ignored the cabbie. He had bigger problems than pique. He'd forgotten it was summer — an easy thing to do on a typical cold, foggy July San Francisco day. But the tourists hadn't. Pairs of pale, shivering legs stuck out of Bermuda shorts, two in front of two, sometimes two beside two, in a line half a block long — enough to fill the ferry six times.

Mullin raced to the front, pulled an extra twenty out of his wallet. His hand was extended, palm still closed when he eyed the tourists more carefully. Leather jackets, gold jewelry. A twenty wasn't going to buy their place in line.

He stepped in front of the woman. "Excuse me, Ma'am. I'm sorry. Please excuse me. My wife — I just got to the call. Hospital. I have to get home." He sounded upset, desperate. He *was* upset, desperate.

"Of course, of course. Go right ahead," the man said.

"Poor man," his wife added.

Mullin flushed, thrust the twenty at the ticket seller and grabbed the ticket. As he stood waiting for the change he could see the tourist couple exchanging glances. He grabbed the bills, stuffed them into his pocket and edged back when the man spoke. "Look, we've got friends picking us up in Tiburon. We can take you to the hospital."

"No, no." The panic in Mullin's voice was very effective. "I can manage."

"It'll be no problem," the wife insisted.

"No, really. I'll call a cab from the boat."

"We insist. *Anything* we can do."

Corner Maddis Groom in the restaurant and make him listen to me, can you do that? "Sarcasm never helps, Cornelius," his sainted mother had said. "Use your brain to think, Cornelius." He pulled himself together and adopted his most solemn expression. "Thank you. You're too kind. Now you won't think the worse of me if I take the time on the boat to prepare myself for the ordeal — alone? I'll just ride on the upper deck."

They understood, of course. They were so sorry. They pulled their jackets tighter around them and shivered in the summer fog.

Mullin was sorry, too. If he'd used his brain to think, he would have sent them to the top level and stayed on the bottom himself where he could make a quick exit. Now he'd have to figure out how to scoot around them.

But he'd have the twenty minutes on the ferry to do that. Twenty minutes to figure his approach to Maddis Groom in the restaurant. How to get to him, cut him loose of whoever he was meeting? Mullin wasn't so shabby as to be denied service, but no one would mistake him for Groom's peer. He looked, he had to admit, like a bill collector, a skip tracer, an aging ex-hitman who got his sartorial taste when he was hanging around with hoods back east.

So how to make sure he got Groom's full attention — enough so he'd take measures — but not so much that his lunch friends would remember Mullin in the restaurant, in case he failed to convince Groom, and *He* sent in the messy guy to do him? And do Mullin.

Mullin shivered in the wintery gust. In his mind his sainted mother whispered, "Spot your opportunity, Cornelius. Find the ray of sun in the clouds."

Mullin stood, his back toward the tourist couple, his face drawn down in worry, watching the ferry angle into the slip. The last San Francisco-bound passengers were barely off when he hurried on and bounded for the stairs.

Even in port the wind whipped his hair. The tourists would think he was crazy to be up here. No one but a loon would choose to face the icy fog when they could be in the warm saloon having a glass of Chardonnay.

Surely, no one.

But there were footsteps on the stairs.

The boat lurched away from the dock.

Mullin turned and stared into the face of the first good fortune of his day. Emerging at the top of the stairs was Maddis Groom.

It was all Mullin could do to keep from racing over yelling "Eureka!" Maybe his mother did have an In with the saints. Twenty minutes alone with Groom! Surreptitiously he eyed the mark. The man's news photo was a miracle in itself. The real Groom was not impressively barrel-chested, he was more like a barrel on sticks. Groom veered to the far side of the boat, and rested his gut on the side rail.

Mullin waited till the ferry was out of port. Alcatraz was a foggy blur on the left, Angel Island ahead on the right, Tiburon straight on. He strolled across the deck and stood beside Groom, as if both of them were fascinated by the water passing along side of the boat. "Mr. Groom."

Groom glared. "Who are you?"

"I called you twice today, said it was about the news photo."

"Oh, the *news photo*." Groom was fingering something in his breast pocket.

Automatically Mullin moved into defense mode. He shot a glance around. No cover. And himself totally unarmed. Maybe *He* had heard about Mullin. Maybe *He*'d hired Groom to . . .

"I'm a busy man," Groom said, not even looking toward Mullin. "It's almost one o'clock. If I don't reach him by one, my lawyer's going to be gone for the weekend." His hand came out of his pocket. In it was a cell phone.

Mullin sighed deeply. It was a moment before he refocused on the real threat. He grabbed Groom's arm. "Groom," he shouted over the wind, "I've been hired —"

"You've been *fired*? Then why are you hounding me about the newspaper?" He punched in a phone number.

"I've been hired — h-i-r-e-d — hired, employed, commissioned," he screamed, "to kill—"

"I know you're grilling me!" Groom's ear was to the phone.

Mullin took a deep breath, thought of his sainted mother, and waited to see that ray of light so well hidden behind the clouds.

Groom shouted into the phone, "Yes, it's about the divorce."

The clouds opened, sunshine shot down on a grateful Mrs. Groom.

Mullin lifted up her husband's stick-like legs and tossed him into the bay.

A German magazine commissioned this story, with the stated instructions that it had to be just 600 words, and the implicit requirement that it translate easily. Writing short, I discovered, is trickier than writing long, but it was fun to see if I could get a whole story in so few words. (What you've just read is 52 words.)

ALL THINGS COME TO HE WHO WAITS

Snyder slammed down the phone, stalked back to the dining table and dropped into his chair. "What makes these salesmen think interrupting a man's dinner will encourage him to buy burglar alarms he doesn't need?" he grumbled. "What I *need* is a peaceful meal!"

"They call now because they know they'll find people at home." The instant the words left her mouth, Mrs. Snyder was sorry.

But Snyder wasn't listening. "I'm at home, all right," he shouted, "but not likely to buy from those pests. What kind of idiots are they?"

"They're working for minimum wage, Uncle. It's a wretched job!" His nephew Karl's face was red. She could see what effort it had cost the thoughtful young visitor to oppose his blustering uncle.

"Let 'em get worthwhile jobs! Lazy pests! You could do the same, boy, instead of wasting your time teaching school — poetry yet! Pull your own weight." Snyder glanced around at the signs of his wealth that were only a bit beyond the standards of good taste. "I got what I have by spotting opportunity, taking chances, not by waiting for opportunity to knock, like you, Karl," he added, sarcastically.

Mrs. Snyder looked at neither her husband, wolfing down his over-large portion of prime rib, nor Karl, picking thoughtfully at the meat as if he knew he would never be able to afford more than hamburger, never possess the key to a house this size. "All things come to he who waits," she said to comfort Karl. But he glared at her with the same show of disgust as did Mr. Snyder.

❖

Wednesday night it was salmon, imported from Nova Scotia, that was interrupted by the phone. "Burglar alarms!" Snyder slammed down the phone and smacked back in his seat, his face crimson. " 'I don't want your alarm', I told the young idiot. 'I don't need it.' "

"They'll give up trying, dear," she said. "You know all things come to he who waits."

Snyder growled a reply she chose not to translate into words.

❖

Thursday's Beef Wellington was rare, but not so red as Snyder's face when he smashed his fists on the table and sat so hard in his chair it bounced. "What is this, national alarm-sales week? Safest-Bet is the third company to call me. They're so sure their alarm is better than their competitors 'they'll replace anything I've got — at cost.' Humph!"

Mrs. Snyder put down her fork. Long ago she'd learned to read Snyder's mind. It was a drab and simple volume. "Do they think you'd permit anyone — even a security firm — in your home to see your art and silver and china? Do they assume you'd trust strangers to set up an alarm system that they'd know how to beat?"

Snyder plowed ahead as if she hadn't spoken, "Told 'em I wouldn't deal with them. I didn't get where I am worrying about strangers."

"Or anyone else, dear."

But he was chewing too loud to hear her.

❖

She sat in a restaurant with Snyder Friday night, imagining the phone at home ringing endlessly. She knew all things come to he who waits, but it was Karl who incorporated Snyder's rule for success: spotting opportunity.

❖

Saturday Snyder's hamburger was piping hot. He lifted it from the plastic kitchen plate — the china, along with the silver, art and cash was gone after the burglary.

Mrs. Snyder smiled. "Quiet, isn't it dear, with no phone interrupting dinner?" She was too wise to add: you see, all things do come to he who waits. Snyder would never understand that. Nor would he realize that she was merely waiting to spot the opportunity to join Karl and the Snyder fortune.

The idea for gimmick in this story — a gift of sorts — was one I'd held for a few years, but couldn't find the story to surround it. Then, having forgotten it, I had the urge to write a story that focused entirely on the characters of four women friends. But, of course, those women had to do something. That's where the gift comes in.

BAD REVIEW

The darker the clouds, the more silvery the lining, or at least so writers believe. Every situation has the potential to drop the story of a lifetime into your waiting computer. That is such a tenet of the craft that we never discussed it. And when we should have focused clearly, when Kay Washburn suggested her pact, she dazzled us with its boldness, and blinded us with her logic. Kay never left a loose end.

I've asked myself whether she had a window to the future, perhaps a leaded-glass affair that let in colors but blurred crisp outlines of events to come. Or was the pact merely a more macabre than normal whim of hers? None of us voiced those speculations. The question everyone has asked over and over, that I've searched my mind about every day for the past two years is this: What possessed Louisa, Cyn and me, ostensibly three normal middle-aged women, to join in Kay's pact?

I've come up with plenty of explanations, some with more of a ring of truth than others. But whatever our underlying motivation, the fact is that we all did agreed on the plan. That was twenty years ago when we none of us could have imagined that we'd be famous, rich, or dead, much less that conditions of the pact would come to pass. Admittedly, Kay had unveiled it after several bottles of Chardonnay at a Monday afternoon lunch. But we were used to the Chardonnay, too. It was as much a ritual as having the lunch on a Monday to celebrate the writer's freedom from the 9 to 5. What stunned us as much as the pact itself was Kay suggesting aloud that one of us might actually become a literary light. (Then, affording dental insurance seemed an unattainable goal.)

We rolled the idea of renown-and-riches around as deliciously as we might a black olive before biting into the meat. And being writers we soon narrowed the speculation to a more professional theme — if one of us became really famous, what wonderful book idea would trickle down to the rest? Of course we all had different ideas of what that best-seller would be: *Expose of Famous Writer? Self-aggrandizing Autobiography* (ghost-written, of course)? *Her and Me?*

Had we been willing to speculate on who might hit number one on the bestseller list, we wouldn't have guessed Kay. My choice would have been Louisa.

Louisa's novels deal with the loving befuddlement between mothers and daughters. There's a kindness to Louisa's perceptions. It's as if her own body — which now looks like throw pillows sticking to a surprisingly strong frame — took literary form.   Like her fictional mothers, she gives and takes, settles and resettles, she reshapes herself, and then just at the point when it appears she'll lose any semblance of herself she stands firm, strong, unyielding, and able to support everyone else.

People tend to underestimate Louisa, to see the pillows and forget the steel frame. I remember the first time I really talked to her about Kay. Louisa was sitting on an old floral couch in her living room, by no means a spectacular room but certainly better than where she's living now. Then her dark brown hair — parted in the middle, held back by clips, flopping in loose waves over her shoulders — was just beginning to gray. She never fingered that hair or played with it as so many women do; she wasn't that self-conscious. That day she sat, feet drawn up under her, drinking not tea as I might have expected but espresso she'd made with a machine she'd brought back from Grenoble well before gourmet coffees became a fad. A huge vase of gladiolus, purple hydrangea flowers (the gauzy ones, not the pompons) and Queen Anne's lace stood on the hearth, almost overpowering the small room. Lifting the espresso cup for a sip, she moved as if both the temperature and humidity were near one hundred, though, in fact it was cool that spring. But she kept her gaze on me as if my ruminations were ice cubes.

"It seems like nothing ever bothers Kay," I began. "I can't recall anything she couldn't handle with that half-smile of hers and an offhand comment that most often leaves us laughing. Does anything frighten her?"

"Do you mean does Kay confide in me about her fears? No, Vivian, not Kay. The Cabots may talk only to the Lodges, and the Lodges only to God. But I'm sure Kay Washburn wouldn't put herself at the mercy of any of the three."

I laughed, but her choice of phrase — put herself at the mercy — is one I haven't forgotten over the years. It didn't enlighten me about Kay, but it made me a lot less trusting of Louisa.

"It says something for Kay," Louisa went on that day, "that even with that brittle reserve she gives us something we wouldn't want to do without."

"Us and her readers," I said.

Louisa nodded, half-smiling, her eyes half-closed, as if she were sifting all this into herself. "Her readers and us." And in the corrected order of that phrase she summed up what mattered to Kay. Later, I decided that wasn't quite accurate. For Kay, it was her work that was important, and the fact that people read it allowed her to keep writing it. If I had said that to Louisa she would have taken another sip of espresso and said, "Well, we all feel that way about our writing." But Louisa, as perceptive as she is about characters and relationships, would have been wrong there. Louisa is committed to the people who people her fiction, those mothers and daughters of hers. At times I know she sees them as more real than we, her friends, are. But with Kay, her characters are just one part of the whole mystique of her books, and it's that mystique that grips her. What Kay truly loves is returning to the manuscript she's had in the works for years. She never talks about it. The rest of us question whether she will ever finish, or if she will polish and repolish it year after year till she's rubbed it entirely away.

Still, if I'd been asked to guess who would make it big, I wouldn't have chosen Kay. I never once pictured myself writing magazine articles entitled "A Trip Through Kay Washburn's Psyche," or "Travels with Kay," or penning a best-seller, "Kay Washburn's Fateful Pact."

Had I been forced to predict startling success, I would have picked Cyn Ciorrarula. Her heroines were great adventurers, braver than brave, cleverer than even their faithful readers expected, like high jumpers who clear the bar with so many inches to spare we're left wondering how we could possibly have assumed the challenge was worthy of them. Cyn created heroines with long sinewy muscles, control that allowed them to trot across broken rope bridges over Himalayan gulches, and coordination worthy of .400 hitters. They were the women we all wanted to be: women who took no shit.

Cyn wasn't young but she was still all angles, and too narrow for her height. It was as if she and Louisa had split two persons' physiques: Louisa'd gotten the softness, Cyn the hard. And she worked at staying in superb shape. It was her heroines' fault, she'd insisted laughing in that matter-of-fact way of hers — no edge of undelved fear like Kay had. "Each year it means one more hour in the gym just to keep close enough to imagine how they might feel. Some people write till they die. That won't be what stops me. There'll just come a point when I won't be out of the gym long enough."

I can still picture her lifting weights or running around a track. But it was a sad moment when I realized she'd never again lope easily along the pine-edged country road where I bicycled beside her a decade ago. I remember how the branches hung over the road, turning the macadam from shining denim blue to black, shifting the temperature ten degrees in a second. Cyn was panting softly with each breath and the wind rustled her short reddish-blond hair like it would a dog's. Sweat coated her tanned skin, her aquiline nose, and under the awning of the pines she was still steamy and glowing, while I, riding beside her, felt the residual chill even in the sun.

A couple of days before Kay had given us copies of her latest manuscript before she sent it off to her editor. As Cyn started down an incline I said, "What do you think possessed Kay to ask for our opinions of her book? It's not like she thinks that my travel articles are on a par with her novels."

"Or my adventures," Cyn said in that gravelly voice of hers. "I'm sure she thinks I write for over-aged adolescents."

"So why does she want our opinions?"

Cyn laughed. "Maybe she thinks we have the common touch."

"But 'art' is above the common touch. Why does she care?"

"Because," Cyn said, taking a longer breath as we started up the rise toward the lake where she would end the run, dive in, and swim to the raft. I'll bet she misses that now. I'll bet she's thought of that irony every day for the past two years — if she hadn't kept in such good shape, she could still be swimming in that lake. "Because," she repeated then, "Kay is fanatic about tying up every loose end. She probably wouldn't make a change based on your opinion, but she'd want to be prepared for that criticism. She wouldn't take the chance of your saying it when it was too late for her to do anything about it."

It occurred to me then that Cyn was not the simple, straightforward, best-way-to-the-goal woman I had assumed. And later when Kay announced that fateful pact, I'll bet Cyn was less shocked than I was.

If the spotlight had shone on Cyn I wouldn't have been surprised. But I doubt any of them ever considered me a possibility for fame. I certainly didn't, which was just as well. You don't become a celebrity writing travel books. Not unless you elect to go places where your roommates have more legs than you do, and the humans' vision of you is in several pieces and ready for the rotisserie. Not for me. I had endured a sepulchralish half-hour in a mud bath wondering just who had been in there before me and how much of their skin was still here touching mine; I'd spent a week in a Thai nunnery where instead of blessings I'd gotten diarrhea, fleas, and ringworm. The sufferings of a travel writer are legion. Indications of sympathy, respect, and adulation are not. I don't go out of my way for adventure like Cyn. My idea of risk is trying kiwi syrup in my mai tai. Bicycling along that country road beside Cyn was as bare bones as I hoped to get.

My dream of fame was that it would befall Cyn, and I would describe the journey through her life to its happy conclusion. For me it would be the chance to translate the micro-novels that make up travel writing to full-blown form, the chance for respect and maybe a soupcon of adulation. My vision ended with me accepting praise and glory in a penthouse suite atop the Four Seasons Hotel!

But if either Cyn or I had had real visions of hitting it big, I can't imagine we'd have come up with the idea of the pact like Kay did.

And Kay was the least likely of any of us to really "make it." She wasn't tough like Cyn, or earthy like Louisa, and she certainly didn't have the unpleasantly-garnered ability to adjust to the unpalatable situations that I had acquired eating raw worms that didn't quite pass for squid at one hotel on the Pacific.

Kay was a tiny, dark woman with sharp features and a patrician nose down which she observed the world. Only occasionally did I look at her and focus on her pale hazel eyes which seemed to lurk in the sockets and shift back and forth nervously. Then she reminded me of a chipmunk peering out of its hole into a world of predators, always poised to make a dash to the next safe spot. Kay's novels were seemingly without form, books that demanded all your concentration and still left you feeling like you might be asked to repeat the grade, books that left you laughing so hard you wondered what kind of mind created them. And when you thought about them afterward you realized that, in fact, there was a form supporting the flights of fancy and fear much like the steel bars under the pillows that made up Louisa. When you turned the last page every question was answered, every thread tied up.

If it couldn't have been me who stepped into the spotlight, in one way I'm glad it was Kay. I wouldn't have wanted to live with the thought of Kay, with her biting humor, writing a tell-all about me.

Still, even knowing that side of her, I wouldn't have wanted to do without her at lunch. She was too entertaining. She'd sit there on the deck, silent for long periods, then slice in one soft comment that would ricochet for the next five minutes. Kay was like her books in that sense; they, too, had a final twist, an irony that left you laughing, or gasping, or both.

Besides, Kay's houses, particularly the last one at the top of the mountain, were too magnificent to be missed. And, the unfortunate pact was, in fact, fair and right, and uniquely suited to our foursome.

That's what makes the events of her death so ironic.

We were sitting on her deck that afternoon. This was years before she had the sauna put in and the deck enlarged and edged with lacy trees that filtered the sunlight. Years before the light of fame shone on her and she moved to the top of the mountain. This deck was a few ramshackle square yards of redwood, the table one of those old metal ones with the hole for the beach umbrella. A clear bowl held the remains of shrimp salad, and the knobby end of a baguette lay next to a shapeless mound of butter on a gold-rimmed saucer Kay'd gotten as a gift at her first wedding. Both bottles of Chardonnay stood in the middle of the table, one empty, the other with its wine line hidden behind the label. Kay sat across from me, the shade from the umbrella thrusting half her face into relief, sharpening her cheekbones, darkening the sloughs in the sides of her nose. As she spoke I had the sense that I was seeing her flipping ahead to her last chapter. "Ladies," she said, lifting the glass she'd just refilled. "I propose a pact. A modified tontine. You recall the tontines." She'd paused here and waited for Louisa to fulfill her responsibility and ask for the working definition. Secure in the cocoon of love and warmth she'd woven around her, Louisa had no qualms about admitting she was hazy on dictionary skills.

"In a tontine the members bequeath their worldly goods to the last surviving member."

"So that would mean one of us would inherit enough to enable her to continue living indoors?" Cyn laughed. Of course, that was before Kay's film deal and the hilltop villa.

"But what about our children?"

"*Your* children, Louisa," Kay reminded her. "We haven't all planned to bequeath to them. As for husbands, Cyn will outlive Jeffrey and anyone she chooses to take on after that."

"So much for my prospects," I muttered, but Kay was too engrossed in her presentation to be distracted.

"What I'm suggesting is not a tontine but the reverse of it."

"An enitnot?" I'm still embarrassed to have said that, as I was then when I saw Kay's nostrils draw inward.

"Despite that," she persevered, "I consider you three my dearest friends and the only people I truly trust."

I was both taken aback and flattered by that designation. For an instant Louisa's face revealed pity, and Cyn's showed nothing so much as a lack of surprise.

Acknowledging none of our reactions, Kay went on. "My suggestion is that you become my literary conservators."

"*If* you die before we do, and Kay . . ."

"I know, Louisa, you wouldn't want to think that. But that's not exactly what I mean." Kay plucked the butter knife from the yellow mound and tapped her delicate forefinger against it. "We've all seen women who've lived too long, who are formless shades held up by too-bright rouge, too-yellow hair, who look with watery eyes through holes edged thickly in black." I remember thinking then that her words didn't sound natural but as if she were reading them off an invisible computer screen, one on which she'd been writing and rewriting. "They've become parodies of themselves, crones they once would have laughed at." The butter knife slipped out of her hand and clanked against the metal table. Kay looked down, surprised. It was clear she'd forgotten she was holding it. Picking up her napkin, she wiped the yellow smudge off the table, then put the knife in the salad bowl so carefully it made no sound.

There were no other sounds — no birds, no traffic noises, no hum of distant conversations. It was as if the moment and we in it were frozen, no longer alive. At the time I thought it was in reaction to the painted women clutching their decaying pasts.

Kay waited a moment to let the tension ease. "Dreadful as it is for those women, they at least are just making spectacles of themselves to their family and friends, the people — as you say, Louisa — who love them." She paused and looked at each one of us. Her face was dead-white, and it was the first time I noticed wrinkles crowding in on her eyes. "Think what they would do if they wrote books. They could turn out ninety thousand words that would stamp their memories in purple, or whatever color humiliation and ridicule wear. They would mock themselves all across the country, day after day, year after year, as long as libraries last." She swallowed, and then had to swallow again before she could go on. "And all that because no one cared enough to stop them."

She drained her wineglass slowly, letting her eyelids close as she drank. No mascara, no shrieking aquamarine eye shadow. I glanced at Cyn in time to see her shiver in the sun. Louisa, sitting on a soft deck chair with her feet under her, totally in shade, moved her hands as if to draw an imagined shawl tighter around her. The first afternoon breeze blew across my back; or maybe I've just painted that onto my memory of the scene.

When Kay opened her eyes she looked at each one of us and said in that crisp, so logical voice of hers, "What I propose is an agreement that if any of us should be in that position the others, her dearest friends, the people she trusts the most, would save her."

"Critique the manuscript? We already do that." Louisa rubbed her fingers over an African leather bracelet her second daughter had sent her from wherever it was that that one lived. "If you mean we should tell her the manuscript is a stinker, that's tough, but, well, okay. It's one of those things that has to be done."

"But what if she doesn't believe you?" I asked. "What if she decides *you're* the one who's lost her judgment?"

"We're talking group decision, right?" Cyn was sitting up so straight, thighs so tensed that it was fifty-fifty whether she was touching the chair at all. She hated limits and discussions of limits. And criticism.

Kay leaned forward, her face now totally in the shade. Maybe it was that darkness, or maybe I'm painting over the memory, but her pale eyes seemed to be drawn back more than usual, as if she'd seen the snout of a predator halfway down her hole. "Let's say it's my novel. You three read it. It's trash. Vivian says, 'Gee, if Kay weren't so out of it she'd be humiliated to have anyone read this.' Cyn agrees, 'Suppose someone were willing to publish it. Unlikely, but still . . .' And, Louisa, you say in that sad way you have, 'Well, we did tell her.' You all agree, 'But poor Kay, she can barely remember what she says from one minute to the next; she's dribbling her food down her cleavage. She's past the point of accepting sense. And you know her work is the only thing that matters to her — ' "

Louisa gasped, then forced a shrug. As much as she would like to have believed Kay valued friendship — *our* friendship — more than painting a masterpiece with words, even she didn't delude herself enough to protest.

"So?" Cyn or I asked.

"So what I'm asking is that before I commit to a mistake that I — the me you now know and love — should have been sorry for, that would scar my name through eternity, or however long they might mention me in parodies of literature, you stop me. Permanently."

Again the world seemed silent. I remember thinking that I was stunned, not so much that Kay would ask us to decide if she needed to be killed, much less to commit murder, but that she would even consider having us pass that kind of judgment on her work. It drove home to me how essential her work was to Kay — more essential than herself.

It was a ridiculous scene — four law-abiding middle-aged women sitting at a table discussing the fine points of a pact to kill one, or more, of us. Sometimes I can hardly believe we went on with the discussion. How many times have I replayed that scene with a different end, a sensible, happy end?

But at the time, with the sun and the wine, and the repartee, Kay's pact didn't seem too odd to consider. Just a little literary insurance policy.

Before any of us could speak, Kay reached into the straw bag she always carried, pulled out a green velvet box, and laid it on the table. The velvet was a dark green, the color you might find in an English gentleman's library. It looked wildly out of place on the white metal deck table. Kay caught her closely clipped thumbnail under one of the edges and opened the lid.

I don't know what I expected, a poison pen? A switchblade knife? Certainly not baby spoons. Four silver baby spoons lay in a row, their handles widening from the neck up so that near the top there was room for one letter to be monogrammed. L K C V (Louisa, Kay, Cyn, Vivian). Cyn laughed. It was the type of elaborate, prickly joke that was not out of character for Kay.

Kay picked up the spoon marked K and laid it down apart from the others. "It's clear there is no other way to stop me. I've lost my marbles. My elevator no longer goes to the top floor."

"You're paying sixty cents on the dollar," Cyn said, in that gravelly voice. "Your thermometer stops short of boil."

Unconsciously, Louisa sank back away from them and her brow tightened. She looked at neither Kay nor Cyn, but her expression was what one of her fictional mothers would have had hearing the exploits of an immature offspring. Then, as if to reaffirm the rules of behavior, she proffered the wine bottle around, and ended up filling only her own glass.

Kay stared at her and then Cyn and me, much as she might control a trio of dogs. When we were still, she said, "If, in fact, I become hopeless, I am asking you, my friends, to kill me." Seemingly, as an afterthought, she added, "I assume you would want me to do the same for you."

This was the penultimate Kay, the master of tying up all the ends.

It took another bottle of wine before we all — albeit uncomfortably — agreed to the pact. Death or doddering humiliation? If they were the only two options then what were friends for? Besides, we weren't talking about murdering a friend just because she was senile, she had to be so out of it she'd lost her judgment, yet organized enough to write a one-hundred-thousand-word book.

I had misgivings, to put it mildly, but under the circumstances, it was hard to make a case for producing drivel. And after Kay's total commitment, how embarrassing would it have been to proclaim myself happy as a clam to publish anything that would allow me to spend my declining years on the veranda of the Raffles Hotel in Singapore or a suite at the Top of the Mark in San Francisco, or even some fine nursing home that caters to your every —

ever vaguer — whim. Besides, if I started to mix up the Top of the Mark with Motel 6 my friends wouldn't have to kill me to keep me out of print.

"So the question becomes how and who?" Kay went on. "It's one thing to do your friend a favor, it's another to fry for it." We'd all laughed then. Clearly, Kay intended to leave no thread hanging. I remember smiling to myself, thinking how ridiculous to imagine that Kay would ever need someone else to make her decisions. I wondered which of us she was really eyeing as the likely incompetent. But I couldn't imagine her deciding a diminution of anyone's work but her own would really matter much.

Louisa drained her wine glass. Cyn perched on her chair, arms clasped around knees like a kid. I leaned back in the half-shade. Life was beginning to take on that open-ended feeling that an afternoon of sun and wine brings. The pact began to look like a diverting puzzle.

"So we have a little ceremony," Kay continued. "We've always liked ceremonies. By this time the recipient — shall we go on saying it is I? — knows she has created dreck."

"You mean she knows her *friends* think she's created it," Cyn reminded her.

"Right. At that point I'll know you all scorn my *grand oeuvre*. You'll all have discussed it with me, doubtless at much greater length than I'll want. I'll be appalled. But in the end I'll trust you. If I trust you with this pact, I'll certainly trust you to show literary judgment. So I'll come to lunch, and when we've finished the last shrimp in the salad, polished off the heel of the french bread, when we're sitting here drinking wine just as we are now, one of you — say, you, Vivian — will take out the box. You'll open it. Inside all three of your spoons will be lying just as they are now, bowl down, monogram down. But mine will be reversed, bowl up, monogram showing. I'll look. I won't believe it." Kay pantomimed her expected horror, eyes and mouth snapping open, hands flying up. But no one laughed. "Then I remove one of your spoons — it doesn't matter which one — I mix the others, and put them back, bowl down, monogram hidden. One of those three, of course, is mine. I hand the box to each of you in turn and you pick one, keeping the monogram hidden." She paused till Cyn, Louisa, and I nodded in acknowledgment. "The one who gets my spoon kills me."

It was a moment before Louisa said, "But why the elaborate ceremony?"

"Because, my friend, this way none of you knows who the killer will be. If there's an investigation, the innocent two can't rat on the guilty."

Cyn glared. "Thanks a lot."

Kay laughed and I and then Louisa, and finally even Cyn couldn't help but laugh, too. Ratting was one of the cardinal sins in Cyn's characters' creeds of life. A rat never makes it to the top of Everest. No gold ring for the rat.

There was more discussion, of course. What if the appointed victim was in her right mind but the rest of us went crazy? Odds of that were small. It was worth the risk, Kay insisted. What if the killer tried to carry out her sworn duty, and failed? We talked What-if's the rest of the afternoon. And in the next week we must have made sixty phone calls among the four of us. We ended up having dinner the following Monday and it was there that we did finally agree. Now, of course, our handling of the whole thing seems ridiculously cavalier, but at that time death was an unlikely possibility and the idea that anyone would be clamoring to publish an opus of ours that even we found wanting was much less conceivable.

But, in fact, three of Kay's last four books topped the best seller lists. Critics raved. (And none of these even was her oft-returned-to so-well-polished manuscript still in her drawer.) The books went into fourth and fifth printings. They've been translated into French, Spanish, German, Japanese, Norwegian, and languages spoken in places that weren't countries a few years ago. Kay was on "Oprah" twice.

Kay had changed by then. Her eyes had sunk farther into the sockets and she'd come to look more like a cornered possum. Those hollows in her cheeks had sagged, the sharp edges of her face dulled, and her observations had changed from rapier blades to gnarled kitchen knives that rasped rather than cut.

She'd moved away from interruption and people, to a house atop a mountain — not a hill but a full-size mountain. The view was great. The privacy was unparalleled, because Kay bought the entire mountain. An unpaved winding one-lane road led up to the gate. But the road washed out with the first heavy rain of winter, leaving her with a whole lot more privacy than I would have found appealing. Even now — when I find myself living with women I would never have chosen as housemates, women who are rarely quiet, and never interesting — Kay's four-month regimen of breaking her fast with dry cereal and powdered milk, closing the day with canned tuna dinners, and no company to look forward to but her own doesn't sound good. But — Cyn, Louisa, and I laughed at the time — surely there she'd finally finish the great manuscript.

The only way up Kay's mountain in the winter was a steep, wet, treacherously slippery, two-mile climb worthy of a Sherpa. Not a prospect to attract visitors, even friends as close as we were. But as Kay said, we cherish our rituals. It was this climb that Cyn made every winter to prove to herself she was still in shape and to experience something of what her latest heroine, an Everest conqueror, might.

Laughingly, Cyn commented that *My Ascent to Kay Washburn's* was as close as she was going to come to the great book dropping in her lap.

Not to be left out of this ritual, Louisa and I created a ceremony to herald Cyn's departure. Louisa made a casserole of Kay's favorites: smoked salmon with fresh vegetables Kay hadn't tasted in weeks. She packed it in Cyn's backpack, along with chocolate bars to keep Cyn going on her climb. At the top, Kay was waiting with hot bath for Cyn, hot oven for the casserole, and plenty of brandy for after dinner. What this meant was that Cyn's descent the next day was frequently more harrowing than her climb. But at the bottom, I completed the ceremony with more brandy and a massage technique I'd learned in Bali.

The trek before last, Cyn said Kay seemed distracted, forgetful, her words out of focus. For the first time Cyn had gone to bed, not exhilarated from the climb, the dinner, and the repartee, but exhausted from her vain effort to get a clear picture of what Kay was saying.

Even so, when Kay sent us that last manuscript we were shocked. After we'd all read it, it was two days before Cyn finally said in uncharacteristic understatement, "It's not top drawer." Another day and half and a bottle of wine passed, and I admitted, "It's not even in the dresser."

Then the question of censorship arose. Who were we to pass judgment on Kay's work? If Kay liked it, maybe her readers would, maybe . . . If this was the great manuscript, all those years of polishing had rubbed it down to dross. It was not merely a bad book. It was a bad book, written in a pompous and blowzy style. In it her characters ridiculed all her previous work. And worse yet, ours. There was no chance it would slip quickly into the ditch of well-deserved oblivion. By then a grocery list with Kay's name on it would have been literary news. The world would have gobbled it down. And then spit it back up. Kay's worst nightmare. And, in this case, ours.

The manuscript, alas, fit perfectly into Kay's pact.

We stopped talking about the merits of the book and focused on the pact. The three of us hashed over our decision, trying to find an escape clause that we knew didn't exist. Kay never left loose ends. But still we had to try. You don't decide to commit your first murder, to kill one of your best friends, who disagrees with your decision, when you are not going to inherit her newfound wealth, or even have access to the amenities it provided — not without a lot of thought. When Kay died we would lose not only her and her wonderful house to lunch in, but the lunches left to the survivors were hardly a cheerful prospect, to say nothing of the considerable tension we'd feel every time we finished a manuscript.

We suggested to Kay we quash the pact, but Kay insisted it was still valid. There was no give in her position, no wit in her arguments. Kay was impatient. She snapped at Cyn when she disagreed, at me when I criticized her pact. It was Louisa, who'd been the most reluctant about the agreement all along, who finally said to Cyn and me, "If Kay can't stand criticism of this little ritual of hers, how will she ever live though the reviews she'll get for his book? She'll kill herself. And that will start another round of gossip. In the end her work will be overshadowed by her bizarre death, speculation about it. And she'll be as dead as if we'd gone ahead with the pact and killed her ourselves."

There was no other choice but to kill her.

It pains me to recall Kay's reaction when I presented her the green velvet box. I don't know whether it was merely shock, or disbelief that it should be she who ended up on the receiving end of her own pact. She must have had suspicions, after all the discussion and reconsideration of the pact. But, clearly, it had not occurred to her that we found her book so awful we were invoking the pact. But once she did realize that, she pulled herself together and for the first time that day looked like the Kay of old. She didn't defend her book, much less suggest discarding it or even rewriting it. If there's one thing I'm certain of, it's that if Kay Washburn couldn't write her kind of novel she had nothing to live for.

We drank champagne that day. Kay must have downed a bottle by herself before she opened the green velvet case. Still, her hands shook as she removed one engraved spoon and laid the others bowl-down for us to choose. Purposely, I didn't look at Cyn or Louisa when we drew spoons. I forced myself not to sigh when I checked mine and realized it was not the one with the K, that I would not be Kay's killer.

The next day I considered my options and chose the most cowardly course. I booked a flight to Thailand, and spent the following month in that appallingly flea-ridden nunnery. Tempting ringworm, I walked barefoot under the gaze of the Mother Superior, spent days scrubbing outhouses, nights sleeping on a hard pallet. Never once was I free of bugs, busy work, or penitents. After a week I stopped mourning Kay; after two weeks I gave up worrying about Cyn or Louisa. After a month I just wished whichever of them had gotten the damned spoon would get on with her job and let me get out of here. (And, being a writer, I have to admit the thought did occur to me that there wasn't even a chance of writing any kind of article on this place, unless I was doing it for *Microbiology Monthly*.) But the Mother Superior would provide me an unshakable alibi. It wasn't till I got word of Kay's obituary that I flew home.

Needless to say, my trip didn't ingratiate me with Cyn and Louisa. And when the police realized that Kay had been poisoned by eating a casserole made of salmon, corn, potatoes, and enough *amanita viroza siami* mushrooms to kill a football team, things began to look bad for Louisa.

Amanita viroza, or destroying angel mushrooms, were the method one of those literary daughters of hers had used to dispatch her overbearing mother.

The police surrounded Louisa like blowflies on a corpse. She was terrified. And I was terrified for her. (Especially after my own show of cowardice.) But not so terrified as I soon would be when those same police discovered that the only place *amanita viroza siami* grow is in Thailand.

Blowflies are quite willing to move onto fresher meat. And it was all I could do to convince the police that my old car was hardly in any shape to make it up Kay's hillside in February. Nor, for that matter, was I.

It took them another week to discover Cyn's ritual climb to Kay's retreat, and to posit my giving the mushrooms to Louisa, Louisa adding the salmon, corn, potatoes to the ritual casserole and packing them in Cyn's backpack, and Cyn mountaineering up with her deadly load.

It did stretch credulity to imagine Kay sitting down with one of her murderesses to eat a dish she had delivered. But, of course, I couldn't tell the detective that — not without exposing the pact and making the three of us look a helluva lot more suspicious than we already did.

As it turned out more suspicious would not have been possible. I proved I was out of the country, Cyn swore she hadn't made the trek up the mountain in a year, and Louisa insisted she didn't make the casserole, adding rather charmingly, I thought, that she would be humiliated to cook with canned corn. It took a jury less than an hour to find us guilty of murder and conspiracy to commit same. The judge had no hesitation about incarcerating us for an unpleasant number of years.

I've been here for two already. Louisa and Cyn are at other ladies' establishments, so, presumably, we won't conspire again. I supposed this place isn't bad as prisons go. Physically, it's better than the nunnery in Thailand — no fleas, or outhouses. But every day for the first year I swore I would put up with a camel-load of fleas to get revenge on Cyn or Louisa.

I spent that year alternately trying to figure out which of them was the culprit, and silently berating her selfishness. Could Cyn or Louisa have expropriated some of my Thai mushrooms? Of course. Could Cyn have cooked the casserole? No chance. Cyn's culinary skills peaked at the can opener. Could Louisa have driven the casserole up the mountain before the snow? No way. And more to the point, Kay would never have eaten it.

The pact was supposed to be foolproof. Kay was a master at tying up loose ends.

Kay had told us that she'd given a lot of thought to the mechanics of our agreement to protect the innocent from endangering the guilty. But, in fact, it was the guilty who'd done in the innocent.

It took me almost the entire next year to realize the truth, the miserable, stinging truth of the only one who could have killed Kay.

We'd all thought of writing *Me and Kay Washburn's Murder*. I'd envisioned it as the travelogue up to Kay's body. Cyn, I'm sure, had imagined it as the trek to same. And Louisa, a sort of Last Supper, with corpse and recipes.

Louisa would never have gone to print with corn from a can.

I'd like to think it was because Kay changed her mind and saw the wisdom of our decision. But my suspicion is that what she saw was the inevitability of the pact she had instituted. She knew one of us would kill her, so she took the mushrooms, opened cans of salmon and corn, cubed the potatoes she had up there with her, cooked the casserole, and she ate it. And as she lay there dying she must have been smiling at the literary irony of it all. I'd like to think that. But the truth is that from the beginning she planned her death and our conspiracy in it. How do I know? Kay's great manuscript, the one she kept polishing all those years, was just published. It is stunning. The characters are, if not flattering, definitely Louisa, Cyn, and I to a T. And none of us will have to scramble to sell our version of *Me and Kay Washburn's Death Pact*, because Kay's brilliantly written book is the final word on it.

For this one, I took a collection of my own faults, distributed them between the characters, and postulated results.

A BURNING ISSUE

I am not thorough.

I don't explore every minute detail, every aspect and angle of a subject. Only fanatics do that. But there is a basic amount of preparation required of any adult who seeks to live in relative comfort, without being pummeled by recurrent blows of humiliation. And that preparation is what I fail to do.

It is not that I am unaware of this fault. *Au contraire.* Rarely does a day pass without it being thrust to my attention. There are the small annoyances: grocery lists I tell myself I needn't write down; recipes I skim only to discover, as my guest sits angrily getting looped in the living room, that the last words are: "Bake in 350 degree oven for 90 minutes."

There was the time when, as a surprise for Andrew, I painted the house. Anyone, I told myself, can paint a house. I did, after all, have two weeks, and it's not a mansion. This time I did not neglect the instructions on the paint can. I read them. What I did not do was consider if any preparation was necessary.

"Everybody knows you need to scrape off the old paint first," Andrew told me later. Everybody? I had the second coat halfway on before I realized that the house looked like a mint-green moonscape. But all was not lost. The day I finished, it poured. As Andrew observed. "You don't use water-based paint outside."

I could go on — but you get the picture. I've often puzzled as to what causes this failing of mine. Is it laziness? Not entirely. A short attention span? Perhaps. "You don't prepare thoroughly," Andrew has told me again and again. "Why can't you force yourself?"

I don't know. I start to read directions, plodding through word by word, letting each phrase sink into my mind, like a galaxy being swallowed by a black hole. But after two or three paragraphs I'm mouthing hollow words and thinking of Nepal, or field goals, or whatever. And I'm assuring myself that I already know enough so that this brief review will stimulate my memory and bring all the details within easy calling range.

In fairness to Andrew, he has accepted my failing. And well he should, since my decision to marry him was one of its more devastating examples.

I met him while planning a series of man-in-the-street interviews in Duluth. Easy, I thought. People love to hold forth on their opinions. (Not standing on a Duluth street corner in February, they don't.) Among the shivering, pasty males of Minnesota's northernmost major city, Andrew Greer beamed like a beacon of health. Lightly tanned, lightly muscled, with bright blue eyes that promised unending depths, he could discuss the Packers *and* Virginia Woolf; he could find a Japanese restaurant open at midnight; he could maneuver his Porsche through the toboggan run of Duluth streets at sixty miles an hour and then talk his way out of the ticket he deserved. And, most important, my failing, which had enraged so many others, amused him.

And so six weeks later (what could I possibly discover in a year that I hadn't found out already?) I married him.

We spent a year in Duluth, bought a Belgian sheepdog to lie around the hearth and protect us. (Belgian sheepdogs are always on the move, I read later as Smokey relentlessly paced the apartment.) I left the interviewing job and had a brief stint as an administrative assistant, and an even briefer one as a new-accounts person in a now defunct bank. In January Andrew came home aglow. He was being transferred to Atlanta.

I packed our furniture (which is now somewhere near Seattle, I imagine — there was some paragraph about labeling in the moving contract) and we headed south.

It was in Atlanta that I painted the house. And it was in Atlanta that I discovered what I had overlooked in Andrew. For all his interest in literature and sports and his acumen in business, he had one passion that I had ignored. The evidence had always been there. I should have seen it. Another person would have.

Above all else, Andrew loved sunbathing. Not going to the lake, not swimming, not water skiing — sunbathing. He loved the activity (or lack thereof) of sitting in the sun with an aluminum reflector beneath his chin.

Each day he rushed home at lunchtime for half an hour's exposure. He oiled his body with his own specially-created castor oil blend, moved the reflector into place, and settled back — as Smokey paced from the living room to Andrew and back again.

The weekends were worse — he had all day. He lay there, not reading, not listening to music, begrudging conversation, as if moving his mouth to talk would blotch his tan.

I thought it would pass. I thought he would reach a desirable shade of brown and stop. I thought the threat of skin cancer would deter him. (Castor oil blocks the ultraviolet rays, he told me.) I coaxed, I nagged, I watched as the body that had once been the toast — no pun intended — of Duluth was repeatedly coated with castor oil and cooked till it resembled a rare steak left on the counter overnight. On the infrequent occasions he left the house before dark, people stared. But Andrew was oblivious.

Vainly, I tempted him with Braves tickets, symphony seats, the complete works of Virginia Woolf.

In March the days were lengthening. Andrew's firm moved him "out of the public eye." I suggested a psychiatrist, but the few Andrew called saw patients only during the daytime.

By April his firm encouraged him to work at home. Delighted, he bent over his desk from sunset till midnight and stumbled exhausted into bed. By nine each morning he was in the sun. The only time he spoke to me was when it rained.

In desperation, I invited a psychiatrist to dinner for an informal go at Andrew. (That was the two-hour late meal and the looped guest I mentioned earlier.)

Finally I suggested divorce. But when I went to file, my lawyer insisted I read the Georgia statues, this time carefully. It is *not* a community property state — far from it. And as Andrew pointed out, I was unlikely to be able to support myself.

So the only way left was to kill him. After all, it would matter little to him. If he'd led a good enough life, he would pass on to a place closer to the sun. If not, he could hold his reflector near the fire.

For once I researched painstakingly, browsing through the poisonous-substance books in the public library, checking and rechecking. I found that phenol and its derivatives cause sweating, thirst, cyanosis (a blue coloring of the skin that would hardly be visible on Andrew's well-tanned hide), rapid breathing, coma, and death. A fatal dose was two grams. Mixed thickly with Andrew's castor oil blend, I could use five times that and be assured he would rub it over his body in hourly ministrations before the symptoms were serious enough to interfere with his regimen. If he got his usual nine a.m. start Saturday morning, he would be red over brown over blue — and very dead by sundown.

I hesitated. I'm really not a killer at heart. I hated to think of him in pain. But given his habit, Andrew was slowly killing himself now.

I poured the phenol into Andrew's castor oil blend, patted Smokey as he paced by, tossed the used phenol container into the trunk of the car, and went off for a long drive.

I don't know where I went. (I thought I knew where I was going — I thought I wouldn't need a map.) Doubtless I was still in the city limits as Andrew applied the first lethal coating and lifted his reflector into place.

It was warm for April, ninety degrees by noon. I rolled down the window and kept driving. If I'd thought to check, I wouldn't have run out of gas. If I'd thought to bring my AAA card, I wouldn't have had to hitch a ride to the nearest hamlet.

The sun was low on the horizon but it was still well over a hundred degrees when I pulled up in front of the house. Andrew's contorted body would be sprawled beside his deck chair. I hoped Smokey hadn't made too much fuss. Cautiously, I opened the door. Warily, I walked through the living room.

I heard a sound in the study and moved toward it.

Andrew sat at his desk.

He looked awful, but no more so than usual.

I ran back to the car and grabbed the phenol container out of the trunk. It was too hot to hold. I dropped it, picked up an oily rag, and tried again.

Slowly I read the instructions and the warning: "If applied to skin can cause sweating, thirst, cyanosis, rapid breathing, coma and death." I read on. "Treatment: Remove by washing skin with water. To dissolve phenol or retard absorption, mix with castor oil."

I slumped against the car. The sun beat down. *Why wasn't I more thorough?*

Glaring at the phenol container, I read the last line on the label: "Caution: Phenol is explosive when exposed to heat or oxidizing agents."

I dropped the oily rag. But, of course, it was too late.

JILL SMITH STORIES

Following here are the Jill Smith stories, though not all the stories I've set in Berkeley. I've put these in chronological order and you can see that Berkeley plays a greater role as time passes. By Berkeley, I mean less the geographical city than the Berkeley aura. I love Berkeley and its essential respect for the integrity of the individual. But like most Berkeleyans I admit that the outgrowths of that respect lead to a number of bizarre situations, about which I, as a writer, am delighted. "Hit-and-Run" is more of a police story, but "only in Berkeley" applies to the rest.

Jill Smith started out as a patrol officer at the time Berkeley Police Department patrol officers handled a case from beginning to end and used the specialized details for expert consultation. When BPD changed to the more standard arrangement and Homicide Detail handled homicides, Jill Smith was assigned to Homicide as a detective. But she has always been "more Berkeley than cop," "the authority" in the city that most resents authority. It was a matter of time before she got herself bounced back to patrol.

As for her relationship with Vice and Substance Abuse Detective Seth Howard, it escalated from friendship to her moving into the house he loved and rented.

I think that's everything you need to know for these stories.

This is the first Jill Smith story, done when I was writing and Jill was behaving "by the book." It's only at the very end, that you get a glimmer of what she will become. You'll note the difference when you read the remaining stories. (And, not only has Jill Smith changed since I wrote this story, so has Berkeley and this neighborhood.)

HIT-AND-RUN

It was four-fifteen Saturday afternoon — a football Saturday at the University of California. For the moment there was nothing in the streets leading from Memorial Stadium but rain. Sensible Berkeleyans were home, students and alumni were huddled in the stands under sheets of clear plastic, like pieces of expensive lawn furniture, as the Cal Bears and their opponents marched toward the final gun. Then the seventy-five thousand six hundred sixty-two fans would charge gleefully or trudge morosely to their cars and create a near-gridlock all over the city of Berkeley. Then, only a fool, or a tourist, would consider driving across town. Then, even in a black-and-white — with pulsers on, and the siren blaring — I wouldn't be able to get to the station.

The conference beat officer Connie Pereira and I had attended — *Indications of the Pattern Behavior of the Cyclical Killer in California* — had let out at three-thirty. We'd figured we just had time to turn in the black-and-white, pick up our own cars, and get home. On the way home, I planned to stop for a pizza. That would be pushing it, but, once I got the pizza in my car, I would be going against traffic. Now, I figured, I could make good time because University Avenue would still be empty.

When the squeal came, I knew I had figured wrong. It was a hit-and-run. I hadn't handled one of those since long before I'd been assigned to Homicide. But this part of University Avenue was Pereira's beat. I looked at her questioningly; she wasn't on beat now; she could let the squeal go. But she was already reaching for the mike.

I switched on the pulser lights and the siren, and stepped on the gas. The street was deserted. The incident was two blocks ahead, below San Pablo Avenue, on University. There wasn't a car, truck or bicycle in sight. As I crossed the intersection, I could see a man lying on his back in the street, his herringbone suit already matted with blood. Bent over him was a blond man in a white shirt and jeans.

Leaving Pereira waiting for the dispatcher's reply, I got out of the car and ran toward the two men. The blond man was breathing heavily but regularly, rhythmically pressing on the injured man's chest and blowing into his mouth. He was getting no response. I had seen enough bodies, both dead and dying, in my four years on the force to suspect that this one was on the way out. I doubted the C.P.R. was doing any good. But, once started, it couldn't be stopped until the medics arrived. And despite the lack of reaction, the blond looked like he knew what he was doing.

From across the sidewalk, the pungent smell of brown curry floated from a small, dingy storefront called the Benares Cafe, mixing with the sharp odor of the victim's urine. I turned away, took a last breath of fresh air, and knelt down by the injured man.

The blond leaned over the victim's mouth, blew breath in, then lifted back up.

"Did you see the car that hit him?" I asked.

He was pressing on the victim's chest. He waited till he forced air into his mouth again and came up. "A glimpse."

"Where were you then?"

Again he waited, timing his reply with his rising. "Walking on University, a block down." He blew into the mouth again. "He didn't stop. Barely slowed down."

"What kind of car?" I asked, timing my questions to is rhythm.

"Big. Silver, with a big, shiny grill."

"What make?"

"Don't know."

"Can you describe the driver?"

"No."

"Man or woman?"

"Don't know."

"Did you see any passengers?"

"No."

"Is there anything else you can tell me about the car?"

He went through the entire cycle of breathing and pressing before he said, "No."

"Thanks."

Now I looked more closely at the victim. I could see the short, gray-streaked brown hair, and the still-dark mustache. I could see the thick eyebrows, and the eyes so filled with blood that it might not have been possible to detect eye color if I hadn't already known it. I took a long look to make sure. But there was no question. Under the blood were the dark brown eyes of Graham Latham. Graham Latham? What was he doing here, on foot?

Behind me, the door of the black-and-white opened, letting out a burst of staccato calls from the dispatcher, then slammed shut. "Ambulance and back-up on the way, Jill," Pereira said as she came up beside me. "It wasn't easy getting anyone off Traffic on a football day."

I stood up and moved away from the body with relief. The blond man continued his work. In spite of the rain I could see the sweat coming through his shirt.

I relayed his account of the crime, such as it was, to Pereira, then asked her, "Have you ever heard of Graham Latham?"

"Nope. Should I?"

"Maybe not. It's just ironic. When I was first on beat, I handled a hit-and-run. Only that time Latham was the driving. The victim, Katherine Hillman, was left just like he is. She lived — until last week, anyway. I saw her name in the obits. She was one of the guinea pigs they were trying a new electronic pain device on — a last resort for people with chronic untreatable pain."

Pereira nodded.

"I remember her at the trial," I said. "The pain wasn't so bad then. She cold still shift around in her wheelchair and get some relief, and she had a boyfriend who helped her. But at the end it must have been bad." I looked over at the body in the street. "From the looks of Graham Latham, he'll be lucky if he can sit up in a wheelchair like she could."

"Be a hard choice," Pereira said, turning back to the black-and-white. She took the red blinkers out of the trunk, then hurried back along the empty street to put them in place.

Despite the cold rain, the sidewalks here weren't entirely empty. On the corner across University, I could see a pair of long pale female legs, shivering under stockings and black satin shorts that almost covered the curve of her buttocks — almost but not quite. Above those shorts, a thick red jacket suggested that, from the waist up, it was winter. The wearer — young, very blonde, with wings of multicolored eye make-up visible from across the street — stood partially concealed behind the building, looking toward Latham's body as if trying to decide whether it could be scooped up, and the cops cleared off, before the free-spending alumni drove down University Avenue.

On the sidewalk in front of the Benares Cafe, one of Berkeley's street people — a man with long, tangled, rain-soaked hair that rested on a threadbare poncho, the outermost of three or four ragged layers of clothing — clutched a brown paper bag. Behind him, a tiny woman in a *sari* peered through the cafe window. In a doorway, a man and a woman leaned against a wall, seemingly oblivious to the activity in the street.

Between the Benares Cafe and the occupied doorway was a storefront with boxes piled in the windows and the name "Harris" faded on the sign above. There was no indication of what Harris offered to the public. Across the street a moon-and-pop store occupied the corner. Next to it was the Evangelical People's Church — a storefront no larger than the mom-and-pop. Here in Berkeley, there had been more gurus over the years than in most states of India, but splinter Christian groups were rare; Berkeleyans liked their religion a bit more exotic. The rest of the block was taken up by a ramshackle hotel.

I looked back at Graham Latham, still lying unmoving in his herringbone suit. It was a good suit. Latham was an architect in San Francisco, a partner in a firm that had done a stylish low-income housing project of the city. He lived high in the hills above Berkeley. The brown Mercedes parked at the curb had to be his. Graham Latham wasn't a man who should be found on the same black as the brown-bag clutcher behind him.

I walked toward the street person. I was surprised he'd stuck around. He wasn't one who would view the police as protectors.

I identified myself and took his name — John Eskins. "Tell me what you saw of the accident."

"Nothing."

"You were here when we arrived." I let the accusation hang.

"Khan, across the street" — he pointed to the store — "he saw it. He called you guys. Didn't have to; he just did. He said to tell you."

"Okay, but you stick around."

He shrugged.

I glanced toward Pereira. She nodded. In the distance the shriek of the ambulance siren cut through the air. On the ground the blond man was still working on Latham. His sleeves had bunched at the armpits revealing part of a tattoo — "ay" over a heart. In the rain, it looked as if the red of the letters would drip into the heart.

The ambulance screeched to a stop. Two medics jumped out.

The first came up behind the blond man. Putting a hand on his arm, he said, "Okay. We'll take over now."

The blond man didn't break his rhythm.

"It's okay," the medic said, louder. "You can stop now. You're covered."

Still he counted and pressed on Latham's chest, counted and breathed into Latham's unresponsive mouth.

The medic grabbed both arms and yanked him up. Before the blond was standing upright, the medic was in his place.

"He'll die! Don't let him die! He can't die!" The man struggled to free himself. His hair flapped against his eyebrows; his shirt was soaked. There was blood — Latham's blood — on his face. The rain washed it down, leaving orange lines on his cheeks. "He can't die. It's not fair. You've got to save him!"

"He's getting the best care around," Pereira said.

The blond man leaned toward the action, but the medic pulled him back. Behind us cars, limited now to one lane, drove slowly, their engines straining in first gear, headlights brightening the back of the ambulance like colorless blinkers. The rain dripped down my hair, under the collar of my jacket, collecting there in a soggy pool.

Turning to me, Pereira shrugged. I nodded. We'd both seen Good Samaritans like him, people who get so involved they can't let go.

I turned toward the store across the street. "Witness called from there. You want me to check it out?"

She nodded. It was her beat, her case. I was just doing her a favor.

I walked across University. The story was typical — a small display of apples, bananas, onions, potatoes, two wrinkled green peppers in front, and the rest of the space taken with rows of cans and boxes, a surprising number of them red, clamoring for the shoppers' notice and failing in their sameness. The shelves climbed high. There were packages of Bisquick, curry, and Garam Masala that the woman in the Benares Cafe wouldn't have been able to reach. In the back was a cooler for milk and cheese, and behind the counter by the door, the one-man bottles of vodka and bourbon — and a small dark man, presumably Khan.

"I'm Detective Smith," I said, extending my shield. "You called us about the accident?"

"Yes," he said. "I am Farib Khan. I am owning this store. This is why I cannot leave to come to you, you see." He gestured at the empty premises.

I nodded. "But you saw the accident?"

"Yes, yes." He wagged his head side to side in that disconcerting Indian indication of the affirmative. "Mr. Latham —"

"You know him?"

"He is being my customer for a year now. Six days a week."

"Monday through Saturday?"

"Yes, yes. He is stopping on his drive from San Francisco."

"Does he work on Saturdays?" It wasn't the schedule I would have expected of a well-off architect.

"He teaches a class. After his class, he is eating lunch and driving home, you see. And stopping here."

I thought of Graham Latham in his expensive suit, driving his Mercedes. I recalled why he had hit a woman four years ago. It wasn't for curry powder that Graham Latham would be patronizing this ill-stocked store. "Did he buy liquor every day?"

"Yes, yes." Turning behind him, he took a pint bottle of vodka from the shelf. "He is buying this."

So Graham Latham hadn't changed. I didn't know why I would have assumed otherwise. "Did he open it before he left?"

"He is not a bum, not like those who come here not to buy, but to watch, to steal. Mr. Latham is a gentleman. For him, I am putting the bottle in a bag, to take home."

"Then you watched him leave? You saw the accident?"

Again the wagging of the head. "I am seeing, but it is no accident. Mr. Latham, he walks across the street, toward his big car. He is not a healthy man." Khan glanced significantly at the bottle. "So I watch. I am fearing the fall in the street, yes? But he walks straight. Then a car turns the corner, comes at him. Mr. Latham jumps back. He is fast then, you see. The car turns, comes at him. He cannot escape. He is hit. The car speeds off."

"You mean the driver was trying to hit Latham?"

"Yes, yes."

Involuntarily I glanced back to the street. Latham's body was gone now. The witnesses, John Eskins and the C.P.R. man, were standing with Pereira. A back-up unit had arrived. One of the men was checking the brown Mercedes.

Turning back to Khan, I said, "What did the car look like?"

He shrugged. "Old, middle-sized."

"Can you be more specific?"

He half-closed his eyes, trying. Finally, he said, "The day is gray, raining. The car is not new, not one I see in the ads. It is light-colored. Gray? Blue?"

"What about the driver?"

Again, he shrugged.

"Man or woman?"

It was a moment before he said, "All I am seeing is red — a sweater, yes? A jacket?"

It took only a few more questions to discover that I had learned everything Farib Khan knew. By the time I crossed the street to the scene, Pereira had finished with the witnesses, and one of the back-up men was questioning the couple learning in the doorway. The witnesses had seen nothing. John Eskins had been in the back of the store at the moment Latham had been hit, and the woman in the Benares Cafe — Pomilla Patel — hadn't seen anything until she heard the car hit him. And the man who stopped to give C.P.R — Randall Sellinek — hadn't even seen the vehicle drive off. Or so they said.

They stood, a little apart from each other, as if each found the remaining two unsuitable company. Certainly they were three who would never come together in any other circumstances. John Eskins clutched his brown bag, jerking his eyes warily. Pomilla Patel glanced at him in disgust, as if he alone were responsible for the decay of the neighborhood. And Randall Sellinek just stood, letting the cold rain fall on his shirt and run down his bare arms.

I took Pereira aside and relayed what Khan had told me.

She grabbed one back-up man, telling him to call in for more help. "If it's a possible homicide we'll have to scour the area. We'll need to question everyone on this block and the ones on either side. We'll need someone to check the cars and the garbage. Get as many men as you can."

He raised an eyebrow. We all knew how many that would be.

To me, Pereira said, "You want to take Eskins or Sellinek down to the station for statements?"

I hesitated. "No . . . Suppose we let them leave and keep an eye on them. We have the manpower."

"Are you serious, Jill? It's hardly regulation."

"I'll take responsibility."

Still, she looked uncomfortable. But she'd assisted on too many of my cases over the years to doubt me completely. "Well, okay. It's on your head." She moved toward the witnesses. "That's all, folks. Thanks for your cooperation."

Eskins seemed stunned, but not about to question his good fortune. He moved west, walking quickly, but unsteadily, toward the seedy dwellings near the bay. I shook my head. Pereira nodded to one of the back-up men, and he turned to follow Eskins.

Sellinek gave a final look at the scene of his futile effort and began walking east, toward San Pablo Avenue and the better neighborhoods beyond. He didn't seem surprised like Eskins, but then he hadn't had the same type of contact with us. I watched him cross the street, then followed. The blocks were short. He came to San Pablo Avenue, waited for the light, then crossed.

I had to run to make the light.

On the far side of University Avenue the traffic was picking up. Horns were beeping. The football game was over. The first of the revelers had made it this far. I glanced back the several blocks to the scene, wondering if the hooker had decided to wait us out. But I was too far away to tell.

Sellinek crossed another street, then another. The rain beat down on his white shirt. His blond hair clung to his head. He walked on, never turning to look back.

I let him go five blocks, just to be sure, then caught up with him. "Mr. Sellinek. You remember me, one of the police officers. I'll need to ask you a few more questions."

"Me? Listen, I just stopped to help that man. I didn't want him to die. I wanted him to live."

"I believe you. You knocked yourself out trying to save him. But that still leaves the question of why? Why were you in this neighborhood at all?"

"Just passing through."

"On foot?"

"Yeah, on foot."

"In the rain, wearing just a shirt?"

"So?"

"Tell me again why you decided to give him C.P.R."

"I saw the car hit him. It was new and silver. It had a big, shiny grill. Why are you standing here badgering me? Why aren't you out looking for that car?"

"Because it doesn't exist."

"I *saw* it."

"When?"

"When it hit him."

"But you didn't notice passengers. You couldn't describe the driver."

"The car was too far away. I was back at the corner, behind it. I told you that."

"You didn't look at it when it passed you?"

"No, I was caught up in my own thoughts. I wasn't going to cross the street. There was no reason to look at the traffic. Then the car hit him. He was dying when I got to him — I couldn't let him die."

"I believe that. You didn't intend for him to have something as easy as death."

"What?"

"There wasn't any silver car or shiny grill, Mr. Sellinek." He started to protest, but I held up a hand. "You said you were behind the car and didn't notice it until it hit Latham. You couldn't possibly have seen what kind of grill it had. *You're* the one who ran Latham down."

He didn't say anything. He just stood, letting the rain drip down his face.

"We'll check the area," I said. "We'll find the car you used — maybe not your own car, maybe hot-wired, but there'll be prints. You couldn't have had time to clean them all off. We'll find your red sweater too. When you planned to run Latham down, you never thought you'd have to stop and try to save his life, did you? And once you realized you had to go back to him, you took the sweater off because you were afraid someone might have seen it. Isn't that the way it happened, Mr. Sellinek?"

He still didn't say anything.

I looked at the tattoo on his arm. All of it was visible now — the full name above the heart. I said, "Kay. You were Kay Hillman's boyfriend, weren't you? That's why you ran Latham down — because she died last week and you wanted revenge."

His whole body began to shake. "Latham was drunk when he hit Kay. But he got a smart lawyer; he lied in court; he got off with a suspended sentence. What he did to Kay . . . it was just an inconvenience to him. It didn't even change his habits. He still drank when he was driving. He still stopped six days a week at the same store to pick up liquor. Sooner or later he would have run down someone else. It was just a matter of time.

"I wanted revenge, sure. But it wasn't because Kay died. It was for those four years she *lived* after he hit her. She couldn't sit without pain; she couldn't lie down. The pills didn't help. Nothing did. The pain just got worse, month after month." He closed his eyes, squeezing back tears. "I didn't want Latham to die. I wanted him to suffer like Kay did."

Now it was my turn not to say anything.

Sellinek swallowed heavily. "It's not fair," he said. "None of it is fair."

He was right. None of it was fair at all.

Herman Ott is, in his way, a personification of the spirit of the sixties Berkeley as it hung on decade after decade. I love him as a character. But I'm glad he doesn't live next door. He, like Berkeley, may be casual about Christmas, but never about politics.

Jill Smith is 'the authority' in the city that most resents authority. She, herself, bridles against it. And when it comes to Berkeley versus police she is pulled both ways. So her bond with Herman Ott goes deeper than merely needing a source of information.

When Charlotte MacLeod asked for a story for her Christmas anthology, I was, well, 'challenged.' Christmas, particularly in the 1980's was not the kind of event in Berkeley that it was back east. It was rare to see lights outside houses; many California transplants didn't have family here to gather; and a movie and dinner at a Chinese restaurant was not an abnormal way to spend the day.

But for Jill Smith, I wanted not merely a 'not abnormal' day; I wanted her to have the very worst.

There is no murder or even dead body in this story; only a potential death of the spirit.

OTT ON A LIMB

Telegraph Avenue may be the spiritual repository of Berkeley radicalism but during the Christmas holidays it goes whole hog capitalist. The sidewalks are crowded with street artists and their displays of tie-dyed long johns, stained glass panels, and crystals of every hue for every ache, pain, or psychic need. Turbaned men offer hand massage, foot massage, or tarot readings, $8 each. A violinist plays Mendelssohn. String bands strum blue grass. You can sip a strawberry-mango smoothie or eat a falafel sandwich as you peruse card tables of used socialist books, hand-tooled belts, Peruvian sweaters, embroidered Cambodian jackets, feather earrings, beaded earrings, earrings with dangling rubber frogs. Artists display watercolors, gardeners hawk potted pine, palm, and persimmon. And there are the ever-popular T-shirts that extol the peculiarities of the city — "Berkeley, A Radical Solution," "Berserkley" (a perennial favorite), and "People's Park Lives" commemorating the city's biggest anti-government demonstration when then Governor Ronald Reagan (*not* a perennial favorite) called in the National Guard.

When dusk fades to night the street artists pack up their display cases, fold their card tables and leave the Avenue as deserted as a dry water hole. And yet the aura remains and makes the darkness darker, the emptiness blacker. On Christmas Eve, Telegraph Avenue seems like the last place on earth.

It was the last place I wanted to be. I had passed up five invitations in favor of the one Seth Howard had whispered: "Homicide Detective Jill Smith is invited to a night of champagne, Howard and . . ."

Now, at eight-thirty Christmas Eve, Howard would be sprawled in front of his fireplace with the champagne. *I* was headed through the litter of pizza plates and smoothie cups on Telegraph Avenue to the office of the Herman Ott Detective Agency.

As a nocturnal companion Howard was a "10"; Herman Ott would be a minus 6. As a nocturnal habitat Ott's office slid below the scale.

I could have done the prudent thing and avoided Ott, but he'd tracked me down at eight p.m. just as I was heading out of the station, pondering if sausage rolls and chocolate macaroon ice cream would go with champagne. Herman Ott had said the only thing that could have diverted me from both Howard and ice cream. He said, "I need a favor."

Herman Ott asking a favor from the cops was like Fidel Castro proposing to Princess Margaret.

But Princess Margaret would not have chucked the Royal Ball and hopped the next plane to Havana.

I, on the other hand, told Howard I'd be late, and hot-footed it for Telegraph.

Ott had established his reputation on the Avenue by never voting for anyone more conservative than a Peace and Freedom party candidate, never cooperating with the D.A., and never, never giving information to an officer of the Berkeley Police Department — unless it was unavoidable, innocuous, and he got something in return. Usually that something was money from the discretionary fund, and usually the detective he got it from was me. When I did squeeze a piece information out of him, it was a something I could get nowhere else. At least two murderers were behind bars because of Herman Ott (a fact that neither of us would ever admit). I couldn't afford to ignore his request.

And besides, I was too curious.

And I owed him two hundred dollars. It was part of Ott's code never to spend the money on himself. It was an even bigger part to make sure he got it.

Two months earlier I'd leaned on Ott till he came close to snapping. He'd bent that rigid code of his, and given me the key fact that linked Angus Simpson, a slippery weasel with friends on the Avenue to a felony assault wrap. Simpson was, for the moment, out on bail; Ott's info would send him back to Atascadero. In an unguarded moment Ott had announced that Angus Simpson had just one redeeming quality: he was even more adamant that Ott in his refusal to talk to the police.

There was no way I was going to get Simpson without Ott's help. Ott knew it and I knew it. I'd promised Ott two hundred dollars from the discretionary fund. I suspected he'd planned to give it away before Christmas to salve his conscience. But it still hadn't come through. And now, on Christmas Eve, I knew that the ball would drop in Times Square before he saw that money.

I hurried past the pizza shop. It was closed, but the smell of garlic and tomatoes still filled the empty street and made me think of Howard downing the sausage and champagne. The door to Ott's building had been left open again. No surprise. Between the World Wars, Ott's building had been a snazzy address for advertising agencies, dental offices, and groups of C.P.A.'s. In the following decades it had gone seedy. By the seventies there were few other commercial ventures, some of which the guys in Vice and Substance Abuse busted, some Forgery-Fraud merely watched. But the old building had taken a good turn in the eighties.

I, too, took a turn now, from the landing of the double staircase to the left. The hallway formed a square around the stairs. On the outside of the hall were two-room "offices," on the inside the old fashioned bathrooms with the toilet in one room and the sink in another. In the seventies the halls had reeked of marijuana and urine, and stepping over a crumpled body had not been a startling experience. Now what I had to watch out for was tricycles and toy trucks careening around corners, small legs pedaling like mad on the straightaways. The offices had been taken over by refugee families, and the hallway had become the Indianapolis of the under five set. The odor of marijuana had been replaced by the smell of coconut or peanut sauce, or curry.

But tonight the hall was empty. Through the open doors in the "offices" I could see children seated close together on old sofas, as if posing for sepia- tone family portraits. Christmas music mixed with the smell of coconut satay. And small faces eyed cardboard fireplaces with Woolworth's stockings.

My knuckles barely brushed the opaque glass on Herman Ott's door before it opened. Standing by the door, Herman Ott was short enough for me to have a distressingly good view of his those limp blond strands that composed his thinning plumage. His rounding stomach perched over thighs so thin that his pant legs fluttered like turkey wattles. His clothes were exclusively from the Goodwill, the politically correct couturier of the sixties, and exclusively yellow (or as close to yellow as he could find). I never saw the man without wondering if he knew how much he resembled a canary.

At first I had assumed his sartorial statement was an elaborate joke. But it wasn't. His manner of dress was not a joke; nothing he said was in jest. Because Herman Ott had no sense of humor whatever. None. He never saw the humor in any situation (an accomplishment of no mean proportions for a man with an office on Telegraph Avenue). And, of course, he hated being laughed at himself.

Which made his dress all the funnier. And had tested my self-control more than once.

"No need to scowl, Ott. You invited me," I said, walking into his small, tidy office. Never had I seen a file drawer left open here, or papers strewn on his desk. The only thing that looked out of place here was Herman Ott.

With the same appalled fascination that keeps one from graciously looking away from a wart on the nose of a friend, I glanced into Ott's other room. A jumble of blankets and pillows decorated a decrepit armchair (Salvation Army circa '66). Blankets, clothes, and newspapers cascaded to the floor. It looked like the bottom of the canary's cage. Many times I'd wondered what a psychiatrist would make of Ott's two rooms. Which was the spiritual home of the real Ott?

Now Ott perched on the edge of his mustard-colored leather desk chair and said, "I've got a deal for you, Smith."

"I'm a homicide Detective, Ott. I don't do deals."

Unlike some, Ott, of course, didn't laugh. "You owe me, Smith."

I settled on the corner of his desk. "Ott, you know our files are closed. There's nothing I can run for you."

He shrugged, lifting his narrow, sloping shoulders to almost normal height. "I don't need anything from *the police*. I need it from you, just you."

I looked down at Ott. Frayed cuffs hung over pudgy hands which caressed an empty coffee cup. A forefinger traced the lip. An appalling thought crossed my mind.

I could have sworn I saw the shadow of a grin on Ott's pallid face. But it was probably just gas.

"I want you to spend the night here." He paused so long that my whole life could have passed before my eyes. "Alone."

"What is this, Ott, a test of my 'manhood'?"

Ott shifted in his chair. He glanced behind me, those pale brown deep-set eyes straining not for a view of an intruder sneaking in the office door, but for someone — anyone — more desirable than me to deal with. But that was something Santa wasn't bringing him. Ott sighed; his narrow shoulders dropped so low that it looked like he had no shoulders at all. "Smith, someone's been breaking into my office at night."

"So, have a couple of cappuccinos and keep watch."

"Don't you think I've tried watching!" He pushed himself up and walked quickly to one of the file cabinets, taking short rapid steps so that his weight was never wholly on one foot. It was a careful, balancing walk, the walk of a high wire artist, or a bird on a phone line — or a detective whose bedroom floor is perpetually covered with sheets, blankets, and newspapers. Ott could probably ford the slipperiest stream in the state with the daily training he got here. He rested an ecru sleeve against the file drawer handle. "If I'm here, Smith, nothing happens. Even when I've been asleep, nothing's happened. I've tried sitting here in the dark all night; I've driven around town till I was dead sure no one was following me and then looped back and came up the fire escape at two a.m. Nothing."

"Well, why don't you have a friend stand guard? You've got to have closer friends than me. Me, a cop," I couldn't resist adding.

Ott apparently couldn't resist glancing in the direction of the Avenue. It was a small slip, and one that someone unfamiliar with the community of Avenue regulars Ott counted as his friends and clients would not have noted. It reminded me that no secret stayed secret down there. Ott crossed his arms over his chest. "You owe me, Smith."

I plopped down in his client's chair, leaned back and said, "What is it, Ott, that's so secret you can't trust your friends to find out? So secret you have to turn to an Officer of the Peace?"

Ott glared.

Usually it was me trying to wheedle something out of him. God, it was wonderful to have the trumps for a change. Trying to restrain myself from becoming too obnoxious, I said, "What is your thief taking?"

"Nothing."

"Nothing! Is this a joke! Candid Camera for Cops?"

Ott shook his head. The limp blond strands trailed the movement like a fringe from a particularly decrepit ball gown. If Ott was setting up a practical joke he was doing one helluva job. But, of course, he wasn't. To create a joke, Ott would have needed an instruction manual. "He takes nothing. He leaves something each time — an envelope, wrapped in Christmas paper."

"Containing what?"

"I can't say."

I laughed. "Ott, this is a delicacy I hadn't expected of you. Are these gifts of too personal a nature to be discussed in mixed company?"

Ott's scowl deepened. Nothing ruffled his feathers like being laughed at.

I felt like I was pulling out those feathers one by one. But I couldn't help myself. There is something so irresistible about teasing the humorless. It's like giggling at a funeral: you know it isn't right, but once you start it's almost impossible to stop. I stood up and braced my hands on his desk. "Ott, you call me away from my plans on Christmas Eve. You ask me to spend the night in your office, which doesn't even have a bathroom. I'm not going to play blind here."

Ott turned and took five short, rapid steps to the window. Looking out at the six feet of nothingness between him and the next building, he said, "It *is* personal."

I started toward the door. "Merry Christmas, Ott!"

He spun around. "Okay, Smith. Wait. It's about my ex-wife."

"Ex-wife!" There were things I had considered Ott having, many of them contagious, but a wife was definitely not one of them. "You were married!"

He hunched forward. His head lowered and tilted toward his right shoulder. I had the distinct feeling he was about to tuck it under his wing and pretend I had disappeared. "Long time ago," he muttered.

"Go on."

"I was in college."

"Ott, you were in college for the better part of a decade."

His shoulders drew closer. "It was nineteen sixty-nine. We met in the People's Park March." That was the biggest of the anti-war era marches in Berkeley, when tens of thousands of students and residents protested the University of California's plan to turn that block of green by the Avenue into a parking lot. "We got married six weeks later. In Reno," he added as if that made his accommodation to law acceptable.

"What was your wife's name?"

"What difference does it make?"

"Ott!"

"Saffron."

Saffron! With an Olympian effort, I swallowed the urge to laugh, or say I could certainly see what had attracted him. To say that must have been a match made in the lemon-yellow clouds of heaven. To contain myself, I had to picture Ott in the full-blown rage of being laughed at. I had to remind myself how much I needed him. I had to stare hard past Herman Ott to the window. Opening on a narrow alley three stories up, it wouldn't have been an easy one to clean, and before tonight Ott had never made an effort. But now the window was spotless. "What happened to Saffron?"

Ott began to pace, five little steps from the window to the file cabinet, turn, return. "Divorced. By the end of the year."

I nodded. I had been through my own divorce. No matter what the circumstances, it's never a pleasant experience. Still, it hardly explained Ott's mysterious deliveries. Or his clean window. "So what's in these packages?"

"Messages" — he stopped in front of the file cabinet — "with letters clipped from the newspapers, just like on television," he added in a tone of disgust.

"Messages, saying?"

Ott hesitated, then pulled open his desk drawer and extricated an envelope, a plain white envelope with no return address, and an Oakland postmark. He didn't bother to hold it by the edges. I didn't offer to get the I.D. tech to dust for prints. I opened it and unfolded the plain sheet of cheap paper. On it, newsprint words said, "1971 Saffron Sacramento. 1989? Have a Merry Christmas."

"After the divorce, she moved to Sacramento," Ott explained.

There were two more messages, both originally wrapped as Christmas presents. The first said, "$200 a month. Have a Merry Christmas."

"Ransom?" I asked. "Do you think Saffron's been kidnaped?"

Ott shook his head so abruptly and definitely that I couldn't doubt his reaction, or at least his belief in it. "I got a Christmas card from her last week. She's been living in D.C. since '81. She's done real well for herself. The card said she'd gotten another job there with the Interior Department. It was one of those mimeographed Christmas letters. It's not like she writes me personally."

I couldn't resist asking, "Do you send her a Christmas card?"

Ott looked at me as if I'd lost my mind. The reaction was deserved. I almost got the giggles picturing one of those red and gold cards embossed with "Holiday Greetings from the Herman Ott Detective Agency."

"Then if the two hundred dollars isn't a demand for ransom for her, what's it for?"

"Not ransom. I called her; she's fine. She doesn't know anything about this."

"You sure?"

"Oh yeah. She's making fifty thousand a year. What could she want from me? Besides she's not the devious type. That's half of the reason we got divorced." Ott almost smiled. "You know how it is, Smith, if they're not always on the lookout for an ulterior motive, they're just not very interesting."

I laughed uncomfortably. I knew exactly how it was. I wanted to ask Ott what the other reason was for his divorce, but I doubted I could push him any farther than I already had. Instead, I said, "Okay, if not ransom then just what does two hundred dollars a month mean?"

Ott studied his shoes, tan sneakers, the old type made when sneakers were still three bucks at Woolworth's. They must have been Salvation Army specials, too. He mumbled something.

I moved around the desk closer to him. "What?"

"Alimony," he muttered to the shoes.

I leaned closer.

"Two hundred a month for two years," he told his shoes. "Figured she needed it. Wrong! By her second year in Sacramento, she was making more than I was. But I didn't know that."

Before I could stop myself, I shook my head. It was hard to say which amazed me more, Ott opting for legal marriage in the days when mere monogamy was considered selling out, or Ott paying alimony at a time when most child-free women would have been affronted by the offer. And yet there was Ott's code. It was like Ott to do the decent thing when he felt he should, in this case the more than decent thing.

I looked back at the envelope on my lap. If Ott's first two messages might have been considered innocuous, the third certainly could not. Cut from a movie ad for "The Night of the Living Dead," it had the word "Life" stapled over "Night." "The Life of the Living Dead. Have a Merry Christmas." I looked questioningly at Ott. He shook his head. But there was none of the definiteness that had underlined his previous denials. Ott knew something. What I knew was that I wasn't about to get that something out of him. But I might get another piece of information in its stead. "What does this message-leaver want from you?"

"Silence."

"About?"

But Ott didn't answer. Instead he said, "You've seen what I've seen. There's been nothing else. Someone's out to ruin me."

"How?"

"By ruining my reputation."

I felt a cold wave of fear. With Ott's clientele his position was always precarious; his reputation was what kept him in business. And made him useful to me. And, well, I had to admit — to myself, never to anyone else, least of all Herman Ott — I did have a certain grudging fondness for the guy, like you do for the ugliest puppy in the litter, particularly if you know you won't have to take him home.

Another chill shook me. What could this last threat be? What would be a greater blow than merely passing the word along the Avenue that Ott had ratted to the cops? My dealings with Ott were all within the law, but publicity about them wouldn't do much good for either of us. It would hold the department up to question (the city of Berkeley expects a particularly high standard from its police), grease the already shaky ground on which Ott stood with his clientele (though Ott's client pool had few other choices), and within the police department, it would make me the receptacle of every complaint every inspector, detective, or patrol officer had about Herman Ott. Which meant that I could plan on fielding five to ten calls a day for the rest of my career or Ott's, whichever lasted longer.

I walked to the clean window and stared out. If I looked sharply to the right, I could make out a glimmer of light from Telegraph, and the one cafe open Christmas Eve. Despite my considerable hesitations about the whole set-up (I could deal with those later) I said, "So what do you want from me, here, alone, all night? I'm not about to compromise a department case or find myself in one of those headlines that begin: Off-Duty Cop . . ."

"I just want you to stay here till the drop comes. 'Have a Merry Christmas': the last drop will be tonight. I'll be across the street in the cafe. When the package comes through the door, don't do anything but turn on the light. I'll be watching. There's only one way out of this building. The fire escape's been sealed for months."

"You can expect the building inspector Monday for that one."

"Fine with me. So is that a yes?"

I glanced at my watch. It was just after nine o'clock. I could be sitting next to Ott's mail slot till dawn, and dawn comes late in December. I walked slowly into the bedroom, glancing at bookcases that must have held every radical publication ever printed, through the cascades of blankets, taking quick, little steps like Ott's. By the window (not cleaned) was a hotplate. Next to it was an empty pan, a can of coffee, two boxes of tea, and a jar of honey that was so thick and grainy that it might have been abandoned by the office's original tenant between the Great Wars. There might have been milk in Ott's fridge, but I doubted it. On the floor was a bottle of water, there presumably to save Ott from scurrying across the hall to the bathroom every time he wanted to make tea. I poured some in the pan and turned on the hot plate. Then I picked up a stained and chipped mug and walked back across the threshold into the orderly world of Ott's office. Ott was still sitting behind his desk. It was like him to put out his offer, then just sit and wait. "Ott," I said, "I know you're not telling me everything. I'm willing to accept that. But you have to assure me that whatever I don't know is not going to screw me. If it does I'll call in every favor from every cop I've ever met, and I'll get you."

Ott's face relaxed. He looked as if I'd opened the door of the cage. "You got my word, Smith. And you'll be off the hook for the two hundred you owe me."

"Okay. I just hope this is a Christmas Eve, not a Christmas morning Santa."

"It will be."

Holding out Ott's cup, I said, "Here, wash this before you leave. I'm going to make tea, and I don't want to face gastrointestinal collapse before Santa comes."

Ott glowered. He really did hate it when I laughed at him. Even in the form of his mug.

In five minutes I poured the boiling water over a tea bag, and watched Ott turn out the lights and depart. I let the tea steep for another five minutes — it could be a long night and I wanted the tea strong.

Counting on Ott's Santa's perseverance and ingenuity, I taped the mail slot shut. Then I made one phone call, settled next to the door, on the cold wooden floor.

At nine-thirty the heat went off. Somewhere in Washington, D.C. was a woman who had changed her name back from Saffron to Helen or Barbara. While I was here shivering in Ott's unheated office (and Howard was downing the champagne and sausage without me), she was asleep in a big bed, under a thick down comforter, dreaming of her fifty thousand dollar a year paycheck.

I leaned back against the wall, sipping my cold tea. From the hallway the only sounds were the dim rumble of televisions.

I've done my share of stakeouts, I know the games to keep boredom at bay. I can name all fifty states, alphabetically and geographically starting from Maine or Hawaii. I can name all the capitals without even the temptation to think of Louisville instead of Frankfort, or Portland instead of Salem (or Augusta, for that matter).

The games had become too easy. But that didn't matter tonight. Ott had provided me with his own game.

I thought about the first two of those three messages again: 1971 Saffron Sacramento, $200 a month. Ott had divorced Saffron by the end of 1970. By l971 she had moved to Sacramento and hadn't needed his two hundred dollars. And the third message that threatened Ott with a living death. It didn't take a detective to guess what would be death in life for him. For Ott his reputation was life. So whatever the Santa knew was enough to destroy it.

Half an hour later my tea cup was empty, and I regretted having poured that eight ounces of liquid from it into me. Stakeouts were so much easier for men. But during that hour in the dark, I had had time to guess the contents of the final message, as, clearly, Ott already had. For anyone who knew the Telegraph scene and Ott's place in it, that message was contained in the other three. What I figured was the fourth message, the one that Ott would rather die than have circulated along the Avenue, would say that Ott had paid Saffron forty-eight hundred dollars in alimony, and it would announce exactly where Saffron had channeled that money, Ott's money.

It was just ten when I heard the footsteps tap in the hallway. I stood up and moved beside the door, and shifted my revolver to my left hand. The steps stopped outside. Knees cracked. Santa was bending down. The mail slot flap pushed against the tape. I could picture him stopping, staring confused at the unbudging mail slot, then angrily trying again, which he did.

The door was locked, but the dead bolt was off. The lock would take no more than a credit card. Which was what it sounded like he was using.

Holding my breath, I waited.

The door opened slowly.

Still, I waited, till a hand, bearing a small package crossed the doorsill. The hand was twenty or so inches off the floor. Santa was still bending to put the package on the floor.

I grabbed the hand, yanked it back and up behind him, sending him forward, head down, into the corner of Ott's desk.

I flicked on the light. "Freeze!" I yelled. "Police!"

He groaned. He was Angus Simpson, the con Ott had fingered for me. I wasn't surprised. He was about to have his bail revoked. And since Simpson was even more rigid about stonewalling the police than Ott himself, he was about to spend some more silent time in stir. He would never even admit what he was holding over Ott.

"Spread your arms wide. Spread 'em! Now! And the legs. Move!" A package, wrapped in red Christmas paper slipped out of his hand. I kicked it behind me.

I didn't pocket the package until the back-up arrived. Ott was not going to be pleased I'd called to alert the beat officers. At this moment Ott would be in the cage of one of the patrol cars, no doubt squawking up a storm. It was for his own good, but I'd never get him to believe that. Were it up to Herman Ott, I could expect a load of coal in my stocking.

But Ott of all people would understand that I, too, had my code. And he would have to be satisfied with my Christmas present to him: no one would see this last package and no one on the Avenue would ever know the threat of the Life of the Living Dead, the revelation that would make him the laughingstock of the Avenue. The message said, "Sacramento 1971, Saffron received $2400 from Herman Ott and donated it to the Ronald Reagan for Governor campaign."

This was inspired by — but you can just imagine!

POSTAGE DUE

Berkeley is not like other towns.

We are proud of that. Other towns are proud of that.

The citizens of Berkeley pride themselves on being on the cutting edge. Historically their communal sharp teeth have bitten into segregation (the first major city to voluntarily integrate its schools), verbal restraint (the Free Speech Movement, the mother of all protests), viewing restraint (the Tree Ordinance, intended to resolve conflicts between citizens who have trees and their neighbors who *used* to have views) and lack of restraint (the Nudity Ordinance, no rash uncoverings — or, depending on their locations, uncovering rashes).

Berkeleyans thrive on controversy. All issues, all institutions have potential for the Berkeley bite. Over the years it has pleased Berkeleyans to chew lovingly and long on the failings of their city, their state, their nation . . . and their post office.

Perhaps, if the Berkeley postmaster here hadn't been on leave, and if the temporary postmaster, John Malvern, had not insisted on making one — and only one — change in the operation of Berkeley Post Offices . . . Perhaps things would have worked out differently.

Malvern did it quite innocently, he told me later. It just seemed a common sense move. He was sitting at dinner in the house he had rented in city of Pleasant Hill, an inch to the right of Berkeley on the map, considerably more than an inch in life (the Pleasant Hill Post Office is not cater-cornered from a park formerly named for a Dutch anarchist group), and complained to his wife that he had seen a Berkeley postal customer spill her caffe latte on the post office floor. "Why do you let them bring drinks into the post office?" the wife had asked. "Stores don't allow food and drink."

And so John Malvern had posted *No Food or Drink* notices on the post office doors.

In Berkeley, you don't make bureaucratic decisions without consulting the citizens you've decided for — or against. And you certainly don't separate a Berkeleyan from his latte. But John Malvern didn't realize that. Not then, anyway.

❖

The "situation" began normally enough at 4:54 a.m. the morning after the *No Food or Drink* signs went up.

"Control? This is Adam 38," the patrol officer said into his radio mike.

"Go ahead, Adam 38."

"I've got a citizen's report of a possible two oh seven in the main post office."

"Did the reporting party see the possible kidnap victim?"

"R.p. says she saw a man dragging something that could have been a person inside the post office."

"Did she describe the 'victim'?"

"Negative."

"The responsible?"

"W M, short dark hair, average height, thin, no hat, dark jacket. No descript for the pants."

"Did the r.p. see a weapon?"

"She thinks so, but she can't be sure. I'm going to do an exterior check."

"Copy, Adam 38. With Adam 31 to cover."

"Adam 31, here. Copy."

"Ten-four."

The wind, thick with the damp of the Pacific Ocean and San Francisco Bay, whistled down the open arcade of the Beaux Arts main post office, strumming off the rough edges of the stucco, humming over the terra cotta, whipping through the eleven arched bays of the portico. *Sunny* California it was not, not in January. And not at five in the morning.

By the time Adam 38 pulled his patrol car into the *10 Minutes At All Times* zone in front of the post office, three other patrol cars had notified Control they were in the area and were heading to the scene. Adam 38 eased out, noting to himself that five a.m. was about the only time to find a parking spot here, ten minutes or otherwise.

The building was a rectangle, the long side facing him. Cement steps ran the length of the portico. He was almost to them when he spotted the barricade inside the glass door and the sign outside it:

NO VEXATION WITHOUT LIQUIFICATION

Pasted to it was an empty paper cup from *Peet's Coffee and Tea*. Beside that, in small letters, was written "I've got a hostage."

❖

The police dispatcher flipped through her private numbers directory, one of the many volumes Control kept for emergency contacts. She dialed the postmaster's home number, listened to the phone ring three times before the answering machine picked up and announced the supervisor would be gone for ten weeks, consulting in the third world. "Maybe he'll pick up some tips," Control muttered, then dialed the number to which the message referred her: John Malvern's, the acting postmaster.

"An intruder in the Main Post Office?" Malvern said sleepily. "Can't you handle that? You're the police! I've got a big day coming up."

"We thought you'd want to know," Control said with the exquisite politeness of one whose calls are recorded and can be subpoenaed into court. "There is a strong likelihood of a hostage situation. We'll need keys and a layout of the building for the Tac Team."

Malvern sighed mightily. "Very well. Let's see, I have to shower and dress and get something to eat and warm up the car."

"This is an emergency, Mr. Malvern."

"Emergencies are for the ill-prepared." He sighed irritably. "Very well, I will be in Berkeley in forty minutes."

❖

Control hadn't called me yet, but at five-thirty I was awake. Awake and freezing. It was freezing in bed, and freezing outside. Freezing is something we don't get much of in Berkeley. Here, it has snowed once in the last quarter century — and then the snow didn't stick. But when the wind blows in off the Pacific, batting the fronds of palm trees, creaking the eucalyptus, any warmth generated during the day departs, leaving 120,000 people in ill-insulated dwellings and grumpy moods. No mood was grumpier than mine; no house draftier than the shambling brown shingle where Howard and I lived. Inside here it might have been a few degrees above 32, heated by the intensity of my complaint when the furnace belched its last.

"Look at it like camping," Howard had said.

I recalled why it is people don't camp in the middle of the winter. We had spent one Christmas in Yosemite where we came to realize the ultimate gift would have been a motel room. Now I nudged Howard with the icy lump at the far end of my leg.

"Gerumph?" He turned over, pulling all three blankets and the comforter with him. I followed, trying to press as much of myself against him as possible. But he might have been comfortable enough to sleep. Warm, he wasn't. And I was still shaking. I could have gone downstairs and turned on the oven. I could have gone farther — to a motel. But after hours of waking from dreams of ice plant, ice hockey, Iceland, and icebergs, I wanted more than mere warmth. I wanted recompense. Well, revenge. I poked both berg-like feet in the small of Howard's back and pulled away the blankets.

It was a petty thing to do.   I know this because the Powers-That-Be punished me. At quarter to six, my beeper went off. I scrambled out of the cold bed, onto the colder floor, ran to the icy bathroom to wash in frigid water, climbed into frost-nipped clothes and prepared to race to the station to find out why they needed the Primary Negotiator of the Hostage Negotiation Team.

Howard glanced up at me and went back to sleep.

Sun doesn't rise in California; the fog merely thins and the dark fades. And when — and if — the sun appears it's full blown, like Athena from the head of Zeus. A sort of Olympian Excedrin Moment.

The sky was still charcoal gray as I wedged my old Volkswagen bug between two pick-ups and ran the remaining block and a half to the station, up the curving stairs and into the main meeting room where the hostage negotiation team was gathering. If a motel room could have passed for a gift from Heaven, this scene would have been an ante room in Hell. The tac team guys in their black duds and half combed hair looked downright satanic, and we in the negotiating segment of the team, still waiting for the first burst of caffeine to hit, could have been mistaken for the newly dead. By the door Inspector Doyle, the team field commander and my regular duty boss in homicide detail, looked liked he'd just passed over after a long, painful, and debilitating illness. But Doyle always looked like that. In the middle of the room all the tables were pushed together forming a twelve foot square covered with charts, papers, clipboards, coffee cups and enough doughnuts to supply every office meeting in the Bay Area. There were sugars, glazeds, maples, cruellers, old-fashioneds, chocolate old-fashioneds. But not one jelly.

I like all doughnuts; they form the crux of my diet. But a luscious, gooey jelly is to an ordinary doughnut as a dinner at Chez Panisse is to one at Chez San Quentin.

Still too sleep-dazed to hide my disappointment, I groaned.

Before I could speak, Inspector Doyle, handed me a napkin-wrapped mound, with a tell-tale red glob at the end.

I saluted him with the jelly doughnut. And he, whose finicky stomach had balked at sugar for the last year, held up his well-lightened coffee in return. I took a big, luscious — and careful — bite. With jelly doughnuts, the heedless eater courts disaster. "Thanks. This is high level thoughtful, particularly for quarter to six in the morning."

"Just good management practice on my part. You're going to need every bit of sugar you can muster today."

"So," I said with a new level of awareness, "what've we got?"

"Probable hostage-taker holed up in the post office. Don't know how many hostages. Don't know who he is or what he wants."

I nodded.

"We've notified the feds; they'll be here in an hour or so."

"Eager to tell us how to run our operations," I put in.

Diplomatically, Doyle didn't comment. But he had seen enough of his orders overruled, enough credit snatched, enough ill-will left for him to deal with from previous joint endeavors over the years to be even less pleased about the prospect of the feds striding in than I was. "In the meantime," he said, "I've closed off the streets around the p.o."

"And the high school?" The high school complex was directly across Milvia Street, though the actual classrooms were at the far end of the school complex.

"Heling," Doyle called. "Get ahold of the principal. Tell her to close the school."

"Right."

I swallowed another bite of the doughnut. "So, it looks like I'm going to start negotiating with zip."

"Not quite. There's the note."

"Note?"

"Note, Berkeley style." He pointed to the 2' by 3' sheet of oak tag.

NO VEXATION WITHOUT LIQUIFICATION
I've got a hostage

I shook my head. "If I'm on target about this, I'm going to need a dozen jellies to get me through."

He nodded.

"Looks like the handiwork of Willard Wright."

Willard Wright had been a Berkeley fixture when I was still a high school student in New Jersey. By some he was called an activist, by others a pain in the ass. Wright was aptly named; he'd had made it his life work to see that things were done right. No confrontation, from the Free Speech protests of the sixties, to the People's Park demonstrations of the seventies, eighties, and nineties, escaped the watchful eye, pen, mouth, and legal connections of Willard Wright. No business was too well-operated to evade advice from Willard. No public transport was too fast, too safe, too graciously run to avoid his public letters of remonstrance.   No police action was too well-orchestrated, too quick or too compassionate to dodge his label of "Keystone." Rarely did the local newspaper hit the street without a missive from WW. "The Keystone Kops Strike Again," was his favorite opener.

But it wasn't just us Willard chewed up. His taste was catholic. He could see every side — and find fault with them all. When the city and merchants proposed a plan to revitalize the shopping strip of Telegraph Avenue, Willard was first to grumble about the umbrellas proposed for the blocked-off street (potential sails in the sunset, he'd called them), the street people who might take up residence under them, and the beat officers who would spend every windy sunset and a good bit of the taxpayers' money guarding and chasing those umbrellas.

Willard was nothing if not evenhanded. He whined about everyone, and he irritated everyone. He had once complained that the patrol car I was driving was dirty. And worst of all, from the viewpoint of us, his subjects, he might be niggling, frequently focusing on an issue so petty, so extraneous no one had allotted time from the main problem to worry about it, but there was almost always a word of truth in his screed.

He would have been dismissed as a pest, had he not also been the founder and tireless supporter of the Berkeley City Fair, an annual June event that benefitted many of the city charities. This event had garnered him the support of influential political forces in the city, and, frankly, made him all the harder to deal with about everything else.

Power and the certainty of rightfulness are an appalling combination.

For a man who prided himself on spotting inefficiency, when Willard settled his gaze on the Berkeley Post Office, he must have felt like the first gold rusher at Sutter's Creek. Gold as far as the eye could see.

"Inspector." Heling handed him a sheet of paper.

Doyle read it and stood, his head rotating very slowly back and forth. "Christ, Smith, the man's a genius." As operations commander, Inspector Doyle had never completed a hostage negotiation situation without a full Wrightian review — or roast — in the local paper.

"Willard, you mean?"

"Oh yeah."

"More of a genius than just to choose the post office?"

"Oh yeah. Sitting in the post office is like drinking room temperature coffee. Barricading himself in the main post office is lukewarm. But, this, Smith, this is hot from the stove." He didn't wait for any word of encouragement. "Seems we already had a call for security at the main post office for ten this morning. Seems the acting postmaster has scheduled a news conference then. He's going to announce this city's implementation of the new Postal Service logo on all the trucks and envelopes and whatever. The seven million dollar change of logo."

"If I know Willard Wright that won't be all the postmaster will be discussing."

"If he gets to speak at all."

"How is the postmaster taking all this?"

"He's not. He hasn't arrived."

"Shouldn't he have been here half an hour ago?"

"Smith," Inspector Doyle said, returning to shaking his head, "this is the post office we're dealing with."

♣

The sky had lightened to a battleship gray; fog hung thick and close, like a battleship must appear to a mackerel. Even though it was not long after six a.m., the line of cars slowing at the detour was ten long now as Berkeleyans headed toward Oakland or San Francisco for jobs that started at eight. Men in watch caps and layers of gray-brown unwashed coats gathered up their blankets and rags from the blue-tiled walls in Provo Park, and looked suspiciously at the van Doyle had sent to drive them to one of the churches that provided a hot breakfast.

"Better breakfast than we got," one of the patrol officers grumbled.

"We're not doing it for nutritional enhancement," I said. Doyle's goal was to clear the area. But as I reached the corner across from the post office, I could see that was a losing effort. Half of Berkeley is addicted to police scanners. Nothing we do is a secret. Already a crowd pressed at the barricades. I hated to think how big that crowd would grow once the sun came out. Down here near restaurants, bus stops, the rapid transit station, and parking lots, it was a gawker's paradise. By the time of the ten a.m. press conference there wouldn't be room in front of the post office for reporters or camera operators, or — at this rate — the postmaster himself. The lure of free publicity would draw every protester in town. If I couldn't get Willard Wright out of the post office quick, we'd have a circus here.

I stepped over the yellow tape, walked into the operations van across the street from the post office and called Doyle. "Has the postmaster arrived yet?"

"Nope," he said and hung up.

I looked across the street at the post office. Willard Wright had been known to complain about public waste of electricity, but that issue wasn't on his mind now. Lights shown from both floors of the post office, flowing out through the arches, between the pillars, through the decorative grating that formed a fence between them. The light was so bright I could see the sculpture medallion at the left end of the portico.

For a moment I stood gathering in my concentration, seeing afresh the pillars and cornices, the decorative tiles beneath the red tile roof. I raced up here two or three times a week to toss in a letter, wait in line to mail a package; I never stopped to note what a lovely building it was.

"He's in the postmaster's office in the corner, Smith," the guy in the van said as he handed me the phone. I took it outside where I could see the postmaster's windows. The wind was still icy, but it kept the crowd too chilled to make much noise. I dialed the postmaster's number.

Willard picked it up on the third ring. He didn't sound breathless as if he'd run for it; more like he was doing other things and answering a call from the police negotiator was not at the top of his list of pressing activities.

"Willard, this is Detective Smith. We need to make arrangements to get you out of there safely."

"You're the Primary Negotiator, huh?" Of course he would know our lingo.

"Right. It's you and me. So, Willard, who else is in there with you?" Intentionally, *with*, rather than *subjugated, threatened, endangered, under your power.* "How many of you are there?"

He laughed. "Is that a metaphysical question?"

"This is serious." I really do hate playing the straight woman. "How many people are inside the post office?"

"Not as many as there'd be in line at the window when it opened." He laughed again. "Not that that limits it much, does it? Could be twenty of us in here, all waiting for one clerk to sell us stamps because the other windows are closed."

I couldn't argue with that. Who could? The lines in post offices in Berkeley were so long that one branch had put couches in their waiting room! And once people got accustomed to them, the postal authorities removed them. I tried another tack. "The best way for you to come out —"

"I'm not coming out."

"Then send out your hostages and we can start talking."

"My hostage? Can't do that either."

My *hostage.* So, no more than one hostage. It's standard operating procedure for a hostage-taker to inflate his numbers; but unheard of for him to minimize them. You don't commit a high profile crime like this and then opt for modesty. With an unknown perp I'd have still been skeptical, but Willard Wright wasn't likely to be fuzzy about the number of his hostages. "So, Willard, who is your hostage?"

"Want to know about my hostage, huh? Not just any old hostage, one the citizens of Berkeley would really miss."

Would, not *will*. A good sign. "Let me speak to him."

Willard laughed. "Not so fast. Let's see a little good faith first."

Who was he holding in there? A night janitor already in the post office when he broke in? Did the post office *have* a night janitor? The postmaster could tell me, *if* he ever got here.

Another perp I would have pressed, but with Willard, as much of a pro in adversarial situations as I was, that would be a waste of time and a foolhardy expenditure of what personal credit I had with him. "So what can we do for you, Willard?"

"First clear off the cops and open the street."

I laughed. "Willard, be serious. I can't let civilians wander up to drop their letters in the box. You could have an M-16 in there."

He made a sound somewhere between a snort of laughter and a grunt of disgust. "I'm insulted that you'd think that. Surely you know my reputation better than that. I wouldn't harm the people in the street. It's them I'm protecting."

"Protecting from who?"

"From *whom*."

Sheesh!

"They'll be thanking me."

"Who*m*?"

"Anyone who's waited for a letter to make its way through the Berkeley Post Office."

❖

"Willard is going to get a lot of sympathy. The post office is not people's most esteemed institution," I said to Inspector Doyle, in the understatement of the day.

"Yeah, Smith. My mother in New York writes to my brother in Marin County and me. Sends the letters on the same day. By the time I'm opening mine, he's already got an answer back to New York. Don't think I don't hear about that. 'Don't understand about Jimmy,' she says. 'He can run an entire police investigation, but he can't answer one letter from his mother. Now, my son, Tony in San Rafael . . .' "

"So, sir, you're willing to clear the street? We can tell him we'll keep the side entrance to the YMCA open, and then use it for surveillance."

I expected Inspector Doyle to sound abashed about his uncharacteristic outburst, but he didn't. "Tell you, Smith, if the post office wasn't such a marvelous old building, I'd be tempted to wait Willard out. We'd just seal off the building. Customers would never know the difference. They'd just assume the lines were a little slower than normal."

❧

"Willard, Jill Smith here. I've got the street cleared — my part of the bargain. Yours was to let me speak to your hos — your *companion* in there."

"Go ahead."

"This is Detective Smith. Give me your name." I could hear breathing on Willard's end of the phone line. I smiled.

No one spoke.

I stopped smiling. "Hello?" I said to the hostage.

No reply.

"Willard! We made a bargain. A fair, just bargain. Surely you of all people will do the right thing."

"And I have. I said I'd let you speak to the hostage. Neither one of us mentioned an answer."

"Willard, don't play semantic games."

"Smith, I am doing what I agreed to. It's you who wants to change the rules because *you* weren't paying attention."

I could have slammed him head first in the mail box — happily. It was, I reminded myself, not an unusual feeling in hostage negotiating, and a distinctly normal one in dealings with Willard Wright. He had, in fact, been the recipient of several 240s (assault) and one 217 (240 with intent to murder), and by the end of the investigation into them I had asked the D.A. if there was a legal category of justifiable assault.

"In the meantime, I'll make you another deal, Smith. Pay close enough attention now. I'll swap you two for two. You with me?"

I had to swallow before I could be sure my voice wouldn't betray me. It was going to take more than a jelly doughnut to get me through this. "Go ahead."

"I'll give you the identity of the hostage, and I'll tell you what my weaponry is."

"In return for?"

"The postmaster. Give him to me."

"Willard, you're an intelligent man. You know we can't give you a hostage." The idea of letting the postmaster handle this situation had a lot of appeal. *If* the postmaster ever got here.

"Regulations, huh? Just like the post office."

"Common sense. This is Berkeley. We've got moral, ethical, and political disputes all over town. If we delivered people to settle scores we wouldn't have a police department, we'd be running a taxi service."

"Touche! Much as I hate to inconvenience you . . . Get him down here." He hung up.

The command center moved from the station to the YMCA lobby across the street from the post office and right behind the communications van. I walked in and found myself facing Inspector Doyle, and next to him a man whose expensive suit was creased at both elbows, whose expensive shirt was open at the collar, leaving his silk tie hanging limp and to one side. His pale skin shone with sweat, he hadn't been pulling out his well-cut and sprayed hair but clumps of it stuck up in unseemly directions, and he clutched a half-crumpled map in his hand.

"Get lost, did you, Mr. Malvern?" Inspector Doyle asked with a straight face. "We thought you would take six-eighty to eighty, get off at University Avenue and be right here."

"You didn't tell me about *nine*-eighty! I thought I was going to spend the rest of my life lost in Oakland." He glared from Doyle to his map and back.

I looked at Doyle and he at me. Neither of us said a word. Doyle, I knew, was thinking about the circuitous path of those letters from his mother.

"The criminal hung up on *her*," Malvern glared from me to Inspector Doyle. "I demand you treat this case as a priority. Show him you're serious," he said, wagging a finger at Doyle. "You do the negotiating."

Inspector Doyle is hardly a feminist. But he's not fond of outsiders telling him how to run his operations, either. He waited a beat. "When you deliver mail from New York on time, Mr. Malvern, then you can run the police department."

Malvern turned as red as the jelly in my doughnut. "Well, I demand to see everything that goes on in these negotiations."

"There's a perfect vantage point right here in the Y, Mr. Malvern," I said, smiling with the full pleasantness of insincerity at his pudgy form. "You can keep an eye on the post office from the fitness center right here in the Y. Willard can see in the window there, so you'll have to pass as one of the center members. All you have to do is climb on the exercycles and make sure you keep the pedals going."

❖

As Malvern clambered aboard his stationary cycle, Inspector Doyle and I exchanged knowing looks. "Maybe," I said grinning, "we should hold off till the Feds get here and watch them battle it out between Malvern and Willard." But as soon as I said it, I knew that was the last thing I wanted. The Feds would no more understand Berkeley than Malvern did. And, I realized, despite his many, many, extremely irritating qualities I didn't want to see Willard Wright become the focus of a federal attack brought on by misunderstanding, the Feds' intransigence, or Willard's infuriatingly quixotic behavior. I didn't want to see Willard dead.

I dialed Willard and let the phone ring. No answer. I switched lines and dialed the main number. No answer. Then I dialed the philatelic office and let that ring. By the time I got to the sixth line and called back the postmaster's number, six phones were ringing in the post office. I might want to save Willard, but he sure wasn't opening up a way for me to do it.

He picked it up on the twelfth ring. "You're making me mad."

"Likewise, Willard. Do you want to showboat, or you want to deal realistically? You let me see and talk to the person with you, and tell me your weaponry in return for . . .?" I held my breath, wondering what Willard would come up with next. The postal service underwriting his beloved City Fair? Malvern giving him keys to all the postal trucks in town? A million dollars in postcard stamps?

"A scone and a caffe latte — a doppio alto low fat latte."

"Chocolate or cinnamon?" I asked.

If Willard caught my sarcasm, he chose to ignore it. "Chocolate. From Peet's, of course."

"Of course." No situation was too extreme to deny a true Berkeleyan his cherished brew.

"And the scone — a blueberry corn scone from the Walnut Square Bakery."

"The bakers have been up for hours, but Peet's isn't open yet. We'll have to get the owner up."

"It's worth it."

"He'll be pleased to hear that," I said, failing to keep the sarcasm from my voice. "Now have the person with you answer my questions."

"When I get the latte."

I took a breath. "Willard. You're on federal property. The F.B.I. is on its way.   They're not going to waste time with you and your breakfast preferences. You better deal with me while you've got the chance."

"How do I know I'll get the scone and the latte?"

"You've got my word, *if* you co-operate about your companion." God, it was hard not to use the term hostage.

"Okay, okay. You want the hostage, you're looking at it."

♣

"He's holding . . . the post office . . . hostage?" John Malvern said. His expensive jacket was off; his new shirt was sodden with exercycle-induced sweat, and his face was the color of a Christmas stamp. Clearly, it had been many years since John Malvern had walked a postal route. "If that building blows . . . the *main* post office . . . replacing all the records and documentation will be a nightmare."

"And people will lose their mail," I said.

"Yeah. That, too." Glancing through the glass doors toward the post office he added, "And the stamps, thousands of dollars of stamps. They'll go up in the explosion. It'd be an accounting disaster!"

"Willard will negotiate."

"I'm the postmaster; I can't bargain with a criminal." He shot a glance at the counter before leaning an soggily-clad arm on it. "He's bluffing."

"Don't count on it."

"If I give in to one of you Berkeley crazies, I might as well run the post office for free."

♣

The area around the post office was blocked off. Busy any time of day with Berkeleyans coming to the library, the YMCA, the post office, Armstrong College, or the Deja Vu Metaphysical store; where even a ten minute parking spot was like finding a green curb of gold, the block was now startling in its emptiness. Once the sun cut through the fog the main post office would shine the golden yellow of the California missions. But now all that was visible from the street was the post-dawn muted light pouring out through the postal wall of mullioned windows. And opposite it, inside the YMCA facing the window, were four patrol officers pedaling briskly and one postmaster puffing like he had the Everest route.

In the distance I could hear brakes screeching as early rush hour drivers, no doubt clutching travel mugs of French Roast they hoped would wake them up before they got to work, checked out the scene. I could see a T.V. crew at the barricade. And just behind the barricade, I spotted half a dozen students walking into the high school!

From the communications van I called Doyle, a few yards away inside the Y, and reported that.

"Yeah, Smith," he said. "They couldn't cancel school. Too late, they said. No way to get the word out. Be more dangerous to have kids get here and then turn them loose in the street. So, they'll just close the campus and keep the kids inside the buildings or the courtyard all day."

"Weren't they considering closing the campus full time anyway? Wasn't that already a hot issue at the high school?"

Doyle paused. I could picture him shrugging his loose sloped shoulders. "Not our problem."

"Words a cop loves to hear." I clicked off and turned my attention back across the street to Willard Wright. This time he picked up on the second ring.

♣

"Here's your scone and your latte, Willard."

"What took so long? Did you have them mailed here?"

"Willard!"

"Okay, okay. Put the box in front of the right side door — the departure door."

"You want me to walk out over in front of the windows when I don't know what kind of weapon you have? You think I'm crazy?"

"We have a bargain. You promised food."

"You promised a name and weaponry. I'm not taking the chance of being blown sky high."

"Smith, I told you the street wasn't in danger. Can't you interpolate?"

"Not and chance my life. You want the food, you tell me what you've got in there."

He hesitated so long I thought he'd wandered off. Finally, he said, "Okay. I've got bombs. Not big enough to endanger the street, but hefty enough to turn this building into rubble."

Bombs. Small, numerous bombs. Would Willard blow the building down around him? I doubted it. But then yesterday I wouldn't have said Willard would barricade himself inside the post office. When the Feds got here they wouldn't view Willard as a local eccentric who might have a home made bomb or two which could conceivably go off if things got very extreme. To them he'd be a lunatic bomber with a sizeable rap sheet.

I gave the sack of food to one of the tac team guys and watched as he got an extender tray and maneuvered it till the box was in front of the post office door.

As soon as the box hit the mat, the door opened automatically, and a shepherd's crook scooped it inside.

My phone rang. It was Willard. "Now bring me the postmaster."

"No! Willard, the F.B.I. is going to be here any minute. You deal with *me* now. Or you deal with them. That's your choice. The F.B.I. is not tolerant of bombers, Willard."

For a moment there was silence from his end of the line. Then chewing. The man was eating his breakfast! "Willard, you've gone to an enormous amount of trouble to put yourself in trouble. You could end up dead! Now what is your real gripe?"

"I should be in Acapulco."

"I'll second that."

"And you know why I'm not in Acapulco?"

"No."

"Because of the inefficiency of the Berkeley Post Office, that's why! Because the notice of the first prize that I won, an all-expense-paid week in sunny Acapulco, had to be acknowledged by the end of the year. The notice, Smith, didn't hit my mailbox till the third of January! Now some guy from Willow Spring, North Carolina is sunning his butt on the beach in Mexico."

"Willard —"

"And, how did the post office offer to recompense me, you're asking?"

"Well —"

"The postmaster told me there was nothing he could do. But if it made me feel better — he actually said that: *if it made me feel better* — I could write a letter!"

I restrained comment.

"He can't be bothered to make the post office more efficient. He can't make sure they have books of stamps to sell. Or that letters are delivered on time. But forbid coffee in the postal lobbies, that he can do!"

I started to speak, but Willard was not to be denied.

"No food or drink in the post office! I've been in lines so long I've called out for pizza. It got there before I got to the window!"

"Willard, just what is it you want?"

"I want the postmaster to take responsibility."

"You want the postmaster to allow coffee?"

"I want my week in Acapulco."

I was just thinking things couldn't get worse when I spotted a beige car speeding through the barricade and screeching to a halt. Two brown-suited men leapt out and ran into the YMCA. Feds.

♣

I looked down the street to the barricades. The television vans from more stations than I had realized existed crowded behind them. Print reporters and photographers hung over the wooden horses. The sky was a pale gray now, the wind almost still. It was going to be a good day, a perfect day for hanging out in the park, watching the show at the post office. Already the crowd had seduced work-bound drivers out of their cars, morning cyclists off their bikes, and joggers to jog in place, and enticed hundreds of high school students out to see government in action. A man who could have been Neptune carrying a loaf of french bread harangued the crowd from a park bench. A trio of shivering nudists was handing out flyers. Once the sun came out and news of the stand-off hit the airwaves, all three rings of the circus would be going.

I grabbed Malvern, pulled him into the communications van and called Willard. "Willard, the F.B.I.'s here. This is your absolute last chance. I've got John Malvern from the post office. Now let's negotiate." I switched on the phone speaker so Malvern could hear.

"I want Malvern to take responsibility. He can pay for my week in Mexico."

I glanced at Malvern.

He looked like I'd suggested a return to the penny post card. "I can't do that. The United States Postal Service doesn't send criminals on vacation!"

"Only packages, eh, Malvern?" Willard called. "And the bulk mail — you must send that to Club Antarctica before you get it to Berkeley!"

Malvern glared at the mike. "Listen you —"

"Gentlemen, be reasonable!"

"Sure, Jill," Willard insisted. "That's what *they* always say. 'Don't rest your packages on the post office display cases!' they say. Why, not, huh? So we can develop muscles holding our boxes for half an hour?"

Malvern scowled.

"I'll tell you why — so we could see those enamel pins and sweatshirts and T-shirts with the pictures on stamps on them — the ones no one ever bought."

For the first time Malvern looked abashed.

An enormous noise went up outside, so loud it stung my ears and defied naming. The van shook. Malvern hit the floor. I braced myself, then moved to the window and looked out.

In the street between the Y and the post office nothing had changed.

Then sirens wailed, loudspeakers barked, and the source of the noise —

a crowd that by now must have comprised every high school student in the city — gave roar and began chanting "No Closed Campus! No Closed Campus!"

"Was it a bomb?" Malvern, still down on the van floor, asked.

"Flash and Sound device? A stun canister? Some illegal fireworks left over from last July Fourth, maybe." To Willard, still on the phone, I said, "I'll get back to you." I hung up and turned to Malvern. "The longer this goes on the worse it will get. By the hour of your press conference, we'll have every demonstrator in town here, all vying for air time. The press will be eating it up. Between the demonstrators, the crazies, and Willard and the threat of blowing up the post office, there'll be a circus that will have the Ringlings drooling out here. And you, Mr. Malvern, will be the chief clown."

Malvern paled.

"But," I went on, "if we work fast we can pull off a deal here that will benefit everyone."

He looked about as trusting as if I'd asked to send my letter postage due.

"Have a few of those T-shirts and sweatshirts left, do you? Enough to dress the poor of Berkeley? Offer them to Willard in lieu of his week in Mexico. There's no way he can turn that down, not and maintain his counter-culture credentials. He'll look good; you'll look good."

"No. The United States Postal Service does not barter."

"Just what are you going to do with tons of rejected sweats? The Postal Service should be pleased to be rid of them."

"That's an internal decision."

I could have smothered Malvern with his own excess sweatshirts. Or crammed one down his throat. I felt like . . . like Willard. "Willard Wright is about to make an internal post office decision." I took a breath. "Look, Mr. Malvern, I know accommodation is not the way of the Postal Service. You could, after all, make do with your old logo and use the seven million dollars to put more staff at the stamp windows —"

"No, we cou —"

"But this time you don't have a choice. You're not a monopoly here. Willard Wright can take your offer or he can turn it down. And if he turns it down, he may not blow up the post office, but you can be sure this situation will blow sky high. Willard Wright will be a hero not only in Berkeley, but nationwide. Willard Wright imitators will turn up in post offices from Portland to Pensacola. And you, Mr. Malvern, will be responsible. Unless you find a way out right now."

It was another five minutes before I was able to say, "Willard, I've got you a deal. Worth a whole lot more than a week in central America. Warm sweatshirts for every needy person in town."

Willard Wright, the adversarial pro, was stunned. Gamely, he tried a save: "If the post office wants to support the poor, why don't they take the money they're spending on the Olympics and give it to the homeless. Or direct some of that new logo money locally to something like the Council for Economic Fairness. They could underwrite their booth in the City Fair next summer." His voice trailed off. He knew I had him. He had won: a moral victory, but no week in Acapulco. It was only a moment before he said, "Okay, but I want to talk to the head of the Council for Economic Fairness. Get him down here."

I called Doyle.

❖

The good news was that the chief councillor was easy to find. He was already in the crowd behind the barricades. The bad news was he strode into the van, picked up the phone to Willard, and said, "Hell, no! Don't you be stigmatizing the poor with those sweatshirts! Poor got enough problems without pasting the post office on their chests!" With that, he strode back out behind the lines.

❖

"Don't blame them," Willard said with obvious glee. "No sensible American would advertise the post office! Serves them right for wasting money on a fool idea like that — and then wanting to raise rates."

I didn't look at Malvern. I was sure he'd mutter something about different sources of revenue, or such.

"They're sponsoring the Olympics, and changing their logo — as if money were no object. As if advertising made a difference. What are we going to do if we don't like their service, send letters across town UPS? What are —"

Inspector Doyle walked in, followed by the two feds. Before they could take over, I said, "I think we've got a deal."

Malvern stared.

I put my hand over the mike before Willard could shriek. "Mr. Malvern, the Postal Service supports good causes like the Olympics, right?"

"Of course," he said, pushing himself up. "We pride ourselves on that kind of commitment."

"And you would be glad to represent the Postal Service at a booth in this summer's city fair?"

Malvern glanced at the Feds; the Feds glanced at their watches, crossed their arms and glared expectantly at Malvern. Hesitantly, Malvern said, "I would be happy to do something suitable for one of my rank. Not some crazy Berkeley thing; some traditional charitable endeavor."

I let my hand ease off the mike. "A booth like the Lion's Club does?"

Malvern had qualms, I could tell. But there was nothing tangible for him to hook them to. "Well, yes, that would be suitable."

"And you'll announce that at this morning's press conference?"

"I see no need to rush —"

"I'm sure *you* don't," Willard muttered, for once too softly for Malvern to hear.

Muffling the receiver, I said to Malvern, "You won't have to announce it as a compromise. It can just be a good will gesture from the post office."

"Very well. As long as this guy, Wright, won't have anything to do with that booth."

"That okay with you, Willard?"

"What choice do I have?"

The press conference went off beautifully. Malvern made his public commitment to the Fair. The city was happy, the postal officials were happy.

Willard went to jail, of course. But jail was not unfamiliar territory. For him, an old lefty, stripes were stripes of honor.

And while he's had to wait six months for a report on the city fair and John Malvern in the booth like the ones the Lions Club traditionally hosts, those months have been warmed with anticipation.

Eager to put the whole unpleasant morning with Willard behind him, John Malvern didn't worry about the fair. He didn't bother to contact the Lions. And so it wasn't until he arrived at the fair booth this July day that he had his first inkling of the traditional Lions dunking booth.

There's a lot John Malvern doesn't know about Berkeley. One thing is that some days in July can be as cold as January. But he has come to realize that as he's been sitting on the platform waiting for each ball to hit the mark, ring the bell, and drop him into the tank of chilly water.

There are a lot of Berkeleyans willing — anxious — to contribute to this charity. The line of them John Malvern sees is as long as in any of his post offices.

And since the agreement is that he must stay till the line is gone, he'll have the same opportunity to learn patience that the post office provides the rest of us.

When Carolyn Hart requested a Valentine's Day story for Crimes of the Heart *I thought of 'a little service' I had offered a Berkeley friend the year before — offered, but never carried out.*

A CONTEST FIT FOR A QUEEN

You can always sunbathe in Berkeley on Washington's Birthday, they say. Maybe so. But it was already Valentine's Day and it had been raining since New Year's. I was willing to believe we'd be able to bathe in another week, but odds were it'd be with a cake of *Ivory*.

Tonight, the thermometer was not ten degrees above freezing (polar by our standards). The rain pounded on the portal like a door-to-door salesman. It was a night made for staying home.

Or it would have been if one of the other tenants in Howard's house hadn't booked the living room for his club meeting. A meeting of the South Campus Respect for Reptiles Committee.

"Do they bring the esteemed with them, Howard?"

"Don't ask. But if you're going through the living room keep your shoes on." Howard shook his head. Clearly, this was a topic he didn't dare dip into. The corners of his mouth twitched. He wanted to dip. His mouth opened and shut again. He was dying to dip.

I grinned.

He gave up. "It's an emergency meeting for the Reptilians, Jill. Their status in the animal rights union has been challenged. By the Save the Goldfish Committee."

It took me a moment to recall just what it was snakes ate. "May the better vertebrate win." And thinking of the fish, I added, "I suppose it's too late to make a dinner reservation."

But even before I finished the sentence, I knew the answer. You'll never starve in Berkeley. Even on Valentine's Day there is always a restaurant with an empty table for two. But while Howard insists I am his number one love, number two (this house in which he dwells as Chief tenant and lusts to own) is close behind, and he would never abandon its nurturing nooks and cave-like crannies to the Reptilians.

"Better than that!" he said, running his hand around my back, under my arm till his fingers caressed the side of my breast. "I've got an evening so romantic, a night so exotic, so continental it should have subtitles. The lover's answer," he said pulling me closer, "to one stop shopping."

"Ah ha. Dinner in bed, you mean."

"And with a new tradition I think you're going to like."

❖

The California King-sized bed was covered with a spotted Madras spread (we'd done dinners here before), and dotted with white cardboard cartons (Styrofoam is outlawed in Berkeley), and plastic plates from freezer dinners. Howard had bought the bed for its mission style headboard with the four inch wide runner at the top — the perfect size for coffee mugs and wine glasses. (By now we had a number of spotted pillow cases.)

"Happy Valentine's Day," Howard said uncorking the chardonnay. (White goes better with the pillow cases.)

"And to you," I said, saluting him with a spring roll.

From downstairs came a muffled shout. I bit into the spring roll.

He said, "Valentine's Day is a traditional sort of holiday —"

"I thought it had been created by the card companies —"

"So I propose a tradition of our own. A tradition suitable for two esteemed police detectives, like us."

"Here on the bed?"

He leaned forward, puckered his lips, opened his mouth, sucked in the rest of my spring roll. When he'd swallowed, he said, "Valentine's Day collars. Other traditions come later. What's your most memorable Valentine's collar?"

I laughed. Only Howard would come up with a tradition celebrating the best Valentine's Day arrests. I could have negotiated a prize, but as everyone in coupledom knows, no object is to be as cherished as the hard-won right to lord it over. The Collar Queen, I liked the prospect of that. "In Homicide or patrol?"

"Either one. In your entire time on the force." Howard reached for another spring roll.

I could see the lay of the land here. "Oh no! You first."

"Don't you have a collar?"

"Yeah, I've got one, from when I was on patrol. But I'm no fool, Howard, and if I let you sit and listen for twenty minutes, by the time I finish talking there won't be any food left. You start."

From downstairs came a loud hiss. I preferred to think of it as a delegate's indication of dissent. As opposed to his subject's hiss of disgruntlement.

Rain splatted against the window and the wind scraped the glass with a branch of the jacaranda tree. But in here, enclosed by the warm green walls and the crisp white moldings, with the smells of Asian spices mingling with the aroma of wine, the whir of the space heater, it was turning out to be an okay Valentine's. Howard shepherded half the rice onto his plate, added a heaping scoop of vegetable satay, four chicken brochettes, and wad of eggplant with black beans. He crossed his long legs, propped his plate on one knee and began. "This is from patrol, too. I'd already been working detective detail but I'd rotated back onto patrol for a while. The call was a D.B.F., a natural death of an L.O.L. The L.O.L. was in her seventies, but she looked to have been old for that age, not one of the Gray Panthers who'd stomp a mugger into the ground and walk off shaking the dust from her Birkenstocks; no, she was an L.O.L."

I nodded, leaning against the headboard, balancing my satay on my thigh as I reached for my wine glass.

"She lived in a four-room cottage, west of San Pablo. Hurricane fencing around the perimeter, big dog in the yard. House a square, four identical-size rooms."

"Like a sandwich you cut into quarters?"

"Right. Neighbors heard the dog barking and got concerned that he hadn't been out in that yard all day. Valentine, that was the dog's name, because he had a white heart on his rump."

I smiled. That bit of whimsy made me like the old lady. I could tell it grabbed Howard, too. "How did she die?"

"Heart attack, I think. Certainly, natural cause. And fast, I think. The TV was still on. She was sitting in front of it on one of those maroon flowered antique sofas with the buttons covered in the same material, and all of it looking too hard to sit on. Makes you understand the energy of the Victorian age."

"Had to keep moving, huh?"

"Oh no!" One of the reptilians shouted downstairs. I glanced at the foot of the door. There wasn't a quarter of an inch between it and the jamb.

Picking up his pace and volume, Howard said, "Not much in her living room — the sofa, one chair, two end tables, a bookcase, a couple pictures on the wall, but no photos or knickknacks strewn around like you find with most L.O.L.'s."

"Maybe she didn't have anyone."

"No relatives, right. Nothing unnecessary in the kitchen or the bedroom. Looked like she lived frugally, but not desperately so like a lot of people on social security. She was tidy, and she knew what she liked, that Victorian stuff.

If someone had told me it was *eighteen* ninety-four instead of nineteen ninety-four in her house, there wouldn't have been much to contradict it. Even her books tended to be things like Jane Austen."

I finished my satay and glanced at the carton. Despite his monologue, Howard had managed to down his portion and was eyeing the same carton. I served. "So that's it? *That's* your most interesting case?"

"Wait. I haven't gotten to the interesting part: the fourth room. You've got these three austere, Victorian-lady rooms, then the fourth. It was crammed, floor to ceiling, with the oddest collection of stuff I've come across. Golf clubs, electric trains, stamp collection, a set of something like twenty-seven drill bits, leather suitcases, a black plastic stool in which the middle of the cushion comes out, the scroungiest looking stuffed pheasant — thing was missing an eye and all its tail feathers — with a Valentine's heart on a ribbon around its neck."

"Must have been easy to shoot."

Ignoring that, Howard went on. "Place was so full you couldn't even see the windows."

"Her late husband's things?"

"Nope, maiden lady. Neighbors said they'd never seen a male visitor. Besides, some of the stuff was almost new, a lot never used. It wasn't like mementos from the love of her life who died in nineteen forty-nine or fifty-two."

I put down my second spring roll. "It's all guy stuff, except the stool and that's just weird. Things like the drill bits; you'll find women who've got them, but —"

"Yeah, you can picture the owner: one of those guys who *thinks* he's going to be a handyman and his wife or kids give him the complete deluxe home handyman's set. And in this case I'd bet my last spring roll those bits had never been out of the box."

"Over by the door," a reptilian shouted downstairs.

Howard tensed, ready to charge downstairs and defend his second love from invasion.

I put a hand on his arm. "Berkeley, the city of diversity, should create a snake run, like the dog park. It'd only take a narrow piece of land. Owners'd put their cobras and pythons on little alligator leashes to exercise them. And the best part for the sedentary snake lover, is they wouldn't even have to be in good shape for the walk. Not like our burglar who had to hoist a massage chair, a backbend bench the size of a sofa, and enough photography equipment to furnish a studio."

"Jill, how'd you —"

I put up a hand to quiet him. The thought was tiptoeing across the back of my head, just out of reach. Something about his story . . . Somethi — "The fucking pheasant!"

"What?"

"That's what his wife called it." I put down my glass. "Howard, I remember that pheasant. I took the call on the burglary it came from. On Linden Terrace. It was just an ordinary case; I wouldn't remember it at all — it must have been six or seven years ago — but the guy insisted on describing his missing pheasant. Seems it was the first thing he ever shot, and in honor of that he gave it to his wife for Valentine's Day back when they were engaged."

"She married him anyway, huh?" He dumped the satay on his rice.

"For better or worse. He even showed me a picture of it, with the red ribbon and the heart. A velvet heart with lace around it like you'd find on a box of candy."

"Probably where it came from. Guy probably gobbled the chocolates while he was waiting for the pheasant to fly." For Howard, the department's Sting King, an uneven match like rifle vs. wing is certainly not sport.

It had been years since that burglary. "I suppose there was no reason to confiscate pheasant and company from the old lady's house."

"Hardly. It'd've filled half the evidence room. But the pheasant, I think the neighbor took it, strange as it is to think there could be two human beings who'd want it." Howard fingered the last spring roll and grinned. "So my L.O.L., Rosamin Minton, was an L.O.F."

"Little Old Fence?"

"A fence with the worst taste in town. Or a fence who'd moved the electronics and jewelry but couldn't get rid of the rest of the junk." Howard took a bite of satay and nodded. "Still, not a bad Valentine's entry. Not so easy to top. So, Jill, what's your Valentine collar?"

I took a swallow of wine, leaned back against the headboard, adjusted the pillow — that little ledge is great for cups and glasses, but it does nothing for my neck. I picked up my wine glass, looked Howard in the eye and grinned back at him. "You could have won by a mile, Howard. But not now. Your entry was good, a real competitive racer of a case. I was in bad shape . . . until . . . you reminded me." I lifted my wine glass in salute. I don't often win these contests with Howard — nobody does — but when I do I make the most of it. The robes of the Collar Queen were going to hang quite nicely off my shoulders. "The pheasant burglary took place, Howard, on Valentine's

Day!"

Howard gave me a tentative salute. He could see he was being edged out, but he wasn't throwing in the towel yet.

"Howard, the R.P., what was his name? — I remember thinking it was a funny name for a reporting party — Robert Parton, that's it — he was just outraged that his bird —"

"Flew the coop on Valentine's?"

"Right. His wife did point out that it was on the mantel where he put it for the occasion. A thief could hardly miss it. Then Parton complained about the loss of a stained glass lamp he'd made himself —"

"Lamp with a band of chartreuse hearts at the edge of the shade?"

"Could there be two?" I grinned wider. The lamp had propelled me to neck-and-neck with Howard. "And Parton was really pissed that the thief had used a couple of his old jackets to wrap the things in. His wife kept reminding him that the stereo and the TV were still there and they were worth plenty more than a bag of used clothes, a lamp, and a moldy bird. But Parton wasn't buying that. He ranted at her, at me, and even at the Chihuahua, for God's sake. Like it should have stood off the thief, single paw-edly!"

"That's it? Your whole Valentine offering? You lose! The answer's obvious. The wife did it?"

"Au contraire, my dear Howard. Mrs. Parton was out with the doctor at the time of the burglary. And she's hardly the type to hire a few unemployed mafiosi. And more to the point, there were two other burglaries that Valentine's night. And the next year another three with the same m.o. And three the following year, when we were half-expecting them and still couldn't prevent them. Drove us crazy. And then they stopped."

"And never started again?" He meant did the thief get pulled in for something else, or merely move out of town.

"Nope, nothing more. Burglary Detail was keeping an eye out. Simpson there really went over those cases, but he couldn't find a link. The Bensquis were in their twenties, the Partons near forty, the Yamamotos in their late sixties. Victims were a bakery chef, an engineer, three artists, one nurse, one doctor, an airline pilot, a copy editor, a short haul-truck driver. There was no connection through their jobs, religious groups, hobbies, clubs, zilch. They were all in different parts of the city. Some victims had standing Valentine's plans, some went out to dinner on the spur of the moment, one couple just went out for a walk, and bingo! their darkroom was cleaned out! No prints, no suspicious characters, no vans or trucks loitering out front. Stuff never turned up in pawn shops, flea markets, or any of the normal places. Not lead one. And Parton, the doctor . . . well, if he made that number of follow-up calls to any patient, they'd die of shock." I leaned back, took a long swallow of wine and said, "It was a very frustrating case — nine disparate couples, burgled of stuff of no particular value, and it all ends up with one little old lady who kept it sealed away from her in a back room! But, Howard, reward comes to the worthy. And thanks to your accidental discovery, you have given me an assist to winning the First Annual Valentine's Day Collar Contest. Pay homage to the Collar Queen!"

"No you don't! This is a *collar* contest. There was no collar in your case. You, Jill, got nada!"

"Outside! Look outside!" Downstairs doors banged. Howard hesitated, clearly torn between defending his house or his contest.

"It sounds good," I said. "But I'm not using the bathroom till you make sure everyone's accounted for."

Howard headed downstairs and I cleared off the bed the remnants of the first course, preparatory to the more traditional Valentine's Day tradition.

Tomorrow, I'd track down the department's files on the burglaries. No way was Howard going to win!

❖

What I did not track down the next morning — Monday — was Simpson of Burglary Detail. While Howard and I had been setting our bet, Simpson had been flying off to the Bahamas.

What was waiting for me in the station was a batch of In-custodys held over the weekend. When you bungle your burgling Friday night, the city gives you free lodging all weekend. By Monday morning you are a sorry, and surly soul. I didn't finish running the checks on the In-custodys before Detective's Morning Meeting, and afterwards ended up transporting one of the surly and sorry to San Mateo County an hour away. In the afternoon I had a court appearance on an old 217 (assault with intent to murder) and I didn't get around to the late Rosamin Minton's neighbor till after 5 o'clock.

The Minton house was just as Howard described it: a square clapboard box behind a hurricane fence, in a neighborhood where shabby didn't stand out. Two scraggly trees now stood watch over the walkway, obviously the work of a newer, if not more horticulturally-talented tenant. The present neighbor, the nephew of the pheasant-taker, hadn't known Rosamin Minton. He handed over the contraband bird without question. If he could have asked for a sworn statement that I'd tell no one it had nested in his house, he would have. Clearly, he was too embarrassed to ask why, after all these years, it was needed by the officialdom of his city.

I picked up the thing gingerly. Taxidermy, apparently, is not forever. The bird was not just eyeless and sans tail feathers, there were bare spots on its back, and it looked like it had used one wing to fight off its assailant. Even the lace and velvet heart looked like it had been slobbered over.

❖

Robert Parton stared at the deceased bird with an expression of horror that matched my own. "It's been chewed! How could anyone —"

"No accounting for taste, Mr. Parton."

He brushed its moldy feathers. "Still, you found it! After all these years! Monica, it's still got the heart I got for you."

Monica Parton looked even more appalled. A woman of some discretion, I felt.

Only the Chihuahua found merit in the miserable memento. He was running from one side of the spacious living room to the other, bouncing and lowing like he'd treed the foul himself.

"Where did you find it?" Parton asked.

"The other side of Berkeley."

"Did you get my lamp? Stained glass; took me six months to make. And my jackets?"

"Robert," Monica said, "the Salvation Army wouldn't even want those clothes. Be glad you've got your bird."

Before they could continue the sartorial debate, I opened my pad and read off a list of the other Valentine's Day victims. "Do you recognize any of these names?"

"No," Robert said, still holding the pheasant overhead, away from his other admirer.

"Mrs. Parton?"

She looked thoughtful, as if giving the list more consideration than had her booty-enthralled husband. But in the end she shook her head.

"Dr. Parton, I know how concerned you were about this burglary. In the five years since then have you come across anything connected to it? Any motive?"

Both shook their heads. And as I left he was beaming at the bird and she was still shaking her head.

❖

It was the next day before I had time to go over the old Valentine burglary files thoroughly enough to make a list of the losses. The stool with the hole belonged to Jason Peabody.

The Peabody house was one of those two bedroom stucco jobs with one room over the garage. I'd been in enough of them to know that the living room would be too small for an eight-by-ten rug. The whole Peabody house could have fitted in the Parton's living room. It was just before noon when I rang the Peabody bell. And a minute or two after when the door opened.

"Mrs. Peabody? I'm Detective Smith." I held out my shield.

"Yes?" She had that you've-found-me-out look we see so often that we mistake it for a greeting. "Sorry it took me so long. I needed to put Spot in the back room. Come on in."

A leather couch, matching overstuffed chair, and a coffee table made for a normal-sized room pretty much filled the space. The television sat atop the built-in bookcase, blocking the window. The dining room, too, was a space that could not accommodate one more fork or candlestick, much less a chair. I almost felt guilty as I said, "I have good news. We've found the black plastic stool that was taken in your burglary, the one with the cushion that pulls out to create a hole in the middle."

"Jason's toilet seat chair." If she was pleased she was hiding it well.

"Your husband is incapacitated?"

She laughed uncomfortably. "No. No. When you take the center out, the chair looks like a toilet seat, a padded black plastic toilet seat."

"But it's not?"

"Oh, no. I should make you guess what it's for." She almost smiled before she recalled who she was speaking to. I've seen that reaction often enough, too. "Jason kept the stool right there." She pointed to the side of the fireplace, next to the bookcase with the television on it.

The stool was eighteen inches square. With it in place, the Peabodys would have had to inch between it and the coffee table. "What is it?"

"A headstand stool."

Even in Berkeley . . .

"You know, for people who want to do headstands, but don't want all their weight on their heads." She was eyeing my reaction, almost smiling. "They stick their heads through the hole, like they're ready to flush them." She swallowed a laugh. "Then they hang onto the legs and kick up. Jason's tall and thin. He always looked kind of like a fern in the wind with his feet waving back and forth by the mantel as he tried to keep his balance." Now she was laughing. "And the TV; it's a miracle it survived."

On duty, we are not encouraged to join in an R.P.s merriment, lest they later forget, or regret theirs and become outraged about ours. With some difficulty, I waited for her to stop and said, "One of the other items you lost was a backbend bench."

She glanced at the tiny room. "Oh, gees, you didn't find that, too, did you?"

I was going to give her the standard "Not yet, but we're still looking" but clearly that was not what she wanted to hear. "No."

She brightened. "Nor the massage chair, or the statue of Shiva?"

"Not yet." I would have noticed a leather recliner and a three foot tall image of an Indian god of destruction.

"Well, officer, thanks for all your effort. Who would have thought you'd still be working this case after all these years. We appreciate it. But we'll certainly understand if Jason's stuff doesn't turn up. To tell you the truth, he's gone on to other interests. I doubt he'd attempt a headstand now, even if he had the stool."

"And you'd be hard pressed to make room for the massage chair, or even the Shiva."

It was a moment before she smiled, shrugged and agreed. But that moment said it all.

The next three victims, or wives of the bereft of golf clubs, ratty chairs, garden equipment, books of stamps barely used, aged racing bicycles, aged skis, enough exercise equipment to fill the YMCA, had clearly been warned. Their performances were not worthy of Berkeley Rep., but they'd have made the cut in many little theaters. They were delighted at our discovery, they assured me. Their husbands would be thrilled. They thanked me, thanked the burglary detail, the Berkeley Police Department, and the entire Berkeley criminal community that hadn't gotten around to fencing their conjugal wares.

I didn't believe a word of it.

Esme Olsen, a sturdy gray-haired woman nearer to seventy than sixty, looked as if my knock had jerked her out of another dimension. I found her in her basement folding gold foil carefully along the edges of a piece of teal glass cut in the shape of a tulip leaf. The sketch of the stained glass panel she was working on was pinned to the wall above the glass cutter and extra foil rolls at the far end of the work bench. Irregularly shaped pieces of glass — red, yellow, green, and three shades of purple — filled the rest of the bench and larger sheets stood in specially made cases behind her. On the top of the cabinet was a photo — probably fifteen years old — of her and a white-haired man as happy-go-lucky as she was intense.

It was almost a formality when I asked, "How would you feel if I told you we're on the trail of your husband's tools: the drill bits, the straight saw, the jig saw, the shag-toothed saws, the clamps, the hammers and all?"

"Oh, my God! You're not bringing that junk back here?" No Berkeley Rep. role for her! And from the horror that lined her face as she looked around her stained glass studio, I could picture the room in its previous incarnation.

"Your husband didn't do much work in this shop, did he?" It was a hunch, but a solid one.

"Work? No. Oh, he had intentions. He'd get on a kick about building bookcases. At one time we had six of them upstairs, more cases than books, I told him. Fortunately they came apart before he could find things to fill them with. Then he thought he'd build a gazebo. He had wood stacked in the yard for a year, and kindling enough down here to cook the entire house. Then there was the hope chest, or more accurately hope*less* chest. For a while he bought used tables and chairs and thought he was going to refinish them. See, he liked the *idea* of woodworking better than the precision of it."

Some police officers never get suspects so naively open with the police. But I've dealt with enough artists in Berkeley to know that the shift from their total absorption in the visual takes a while, and as they cross the bridge from right brain to left brain good sense can stumble over the railing. "So you gave yourself a Valentine's Day gift. You arranged for his stuff to be 'stolen.' "

She didn't answer. She'd zoomed to the other end of the bridge. And what she found there horrified her. I wouldn't have been surprised if this was the first time it truly struck her that she'd committed a crime.

The eight co-conspirators had warned each other; why hadn't they told Esme Olsen? It made me a whole lot less sympathetic to them. I wanted to reassure Esme Olsen, but I couldn't do that until she answered the questions everyone who'd worked the case had. How did the nine conspirators know each other? We'd been over every possible connection between them. Where did they come meet to conspire? Did they get together for afternoon tea and complaints, or drive to bars to map out their burglaries? And Rosamin Minton, how did she come to have the loot stashed at her house? "The police department takes a very dim view of false reporting."

She took a step back and actually looked even smaller than she was. "I didn't mean to get the police involved, honestly, Officer. I thought Harry would have left dealing with the police to me. I thought I'd just *tell* him I reported his stuff missing."

"Give me the names of the other women you planned this with."

She took another step back.

"Ms. Olsen, you have broken the law. The police department has spent tens of hours investigating. We've had patrol officers, sergeants, and inspectors on this case. This is a serious matter. The names . . . ?"

She looked tinier, paler, older than at any moment since I arrived. In a small voice, she said, "I don't know."

"You planned an elaborate heist that took place over several years, Valentine's Day after Valentine's Day, and you're telling me you don't know the names of your co-conspirators?"

"Yes." For an instant I thought she was going to explain that. Then she shut her mouth tight, like a little kid who'd rather be sent to her room than rat on her friends.

Friends who didn't deserve her sacrifice. "I'm afraid I'm going to have to take you to the station."

Her face scrunched in panic, but her question was not what I would have expected. "How long will that take?"

"Till your lawyer bails you out, Mrs. Olsen."

Her face fell. She really did look horrified. I wondered how long she had been hidden away down here away from the realities of society.

"I've got to be back by quarter to four," she insisted plaintively. "I've got an appointment at the vet at four."

I'd seen everything from Airedales to Chihuahuas today. I realized now that this was the first house I'd visited where if I hadn't been greeted by a dog. I hadn't even heard one barking in a back room. "I didn't see a dog?"

"When he's healthy he'd greet you at the gate. He's sick. On antibiotics. I'm keeping him in the back room. Oh, the vet says he'll be fine; and I believe him. I'm probably worrying for nothing, but my old dog died suddenly two years ago and I just don't want to take any chances now."

Now it all fell into place. I loved the idea of nine average Berkeley women who'd taken their spousal clutter into their own hands. A little service for each other. Personalized burglaries — we go to the address provided and steal only what you don't want. No wonder the televisions and compact disks, computers and the diamond rings had been untouched while the wily 'thieves' made off with aged hacksaws and head stand stools. Now I realized why her friends hadn't warned her. They hadn't seen her today. I smiled. "You weren't lying about not knowing their last names, were you?"

"Oh no. I wouldn't lie to the police."

"You all met at the dog run, right? And your dog was too sick to go out today."

She nodded.

"You could tell me the name of every one of their dogs, right, but you don't know their owner's names?" I knew enough about dog walking to understand that phenomena. By now, after years in the conspiracy, Esme Olsen might be able to call the humans by first name, but she wouldn't have a clue about last names. "You can skip the women, just tell me what the dogs were called."

She looked puzzled, but so relieved she didn't question my demand. "Let me see, Lucy is the black lab, and Sacha's the poodle. Then there's Emmet, the yellow lab pup, and Emily — she's mostly Tibetan terrier — and Hannah, the basset, and Sierra — he's a Chihuahua, and — wait a minute — oh, yes, MacTavish, the Scotty."

"And Val is your dog?"

She smiled before she realized she'd exposed her connection to Rosamin Minton.

Then she took me upstairs to see the whiskered brown mongrel with the white heart on his rump. He was a dog definitely on the mend.

"You went to a lot of trouble planning the burglaries. Why didn't you give the stuff to the Salvation Army?"

"Couldn't. That's where Harry shopped for the furniture to refinish. We never thought we'd be endangering Rosamin. She swore she didn't need that extra room. And she *did* need the twenty dollars a month we each gave her. And, Officer, it really did comfort her to know one of us would take Val when she died."

I smiled at her. We were still in the shadow of Valentine's Day, when acts of love are expected. And, I had to admit, there were a few items of Howard's for which I'd have hired Esme and Colleagues. For his tenant's snake I'd have given them a bonus. Besides, the city wouldn't want to look ridiculous in court.

There'd be some paperwork and formalities with this case later. And after that, I'd accept Howard's concession in the First Annual Collar Contest. But for now, I scratched Val gently behind one floppy ear, said, "Okay, Val, I'll leave you your mistress. Consider this your Valentine's gift," and smiled magnanimously.

Because, after all, magnanimity is a fitting quality for a Queen.

THE CELESTIAL DETECTIVE

Jill Smith and Kiernan O'Shaughnessy both appear in more than one story each, but of the characters who live solely in short stories, the celestial detective is the only one who detects more than once.

I played with the idea of using this character in a series of short stories that would become a novel. But that idea is better in fancy than fact because of logistic problems. As you'll see, each of these stories is a large frame enclosing a smaller picture, a story within a story. Each story must be able to stand alone. And yet the background of the celestial detective, life, death and unusual setting must be presented in each story. See how confusing it is? But you'll also see just how much fun it was to write these two.

When I was asked to contribute to an anthology of legal or courtroom mysteries, I was pleased, but also baffled. My knowledge of court was — thank goodness — very small, and compared to the lawyers writing stories for the anthology, it was likely to appear infinitesimal. So I decided to create my own court, in my own jurisdiction, with laws created by my own self. Taking the law into your own hands has always held a certain appeal. However, the California law I used is straight from the book.

THE COURT OF CELESTIAL APPEALS

Death is not all it's cracked up to be.

Heaven or Hell, or the forty days and nights traveling through the *Bardo* to the next incarnation? Limbo, Purgatory, or a return to the elements from which the body came? I wouldn't have bet my life on the location of my eternal domicile, but I assumed at least I would recognize the place when I got there.

But this? It's like waking up in another beige hotel room in another overcast city; you can't remember where you are or why you're there. For a moment you don't know who you are. I remember that feeling in . . . but the city's gone. Of course.

I'm gone.

I don't know who I am, or was. Or where I am. Or why I'm here. I just know I'm dead. And I've been summoned back to the Court of Final Appeals, for the third time. There's a lot of I don't know about this place, but I do know that in this court, the third time is not a charm.

The halls are all off-white here. They glow a little, but not as gaudily as the near-death books suggest — no blinding white light at the end of every corridor and — thank God — no powerful suction toward it. Moving down a corridor is hard enough as it is when you've got wings.

Actually, the wings were the first disappointment. To fly! I loved it. I raced down the hall, veering left, scraping the wall, correcting, over-correcting, ignoring the rasping pain on my wing edge, caught up in anticipation of that wonderful moment of take-off. But the snack machine room at the end of the corridor came first. I turned, banging a wing into the ambrosia dispenser, and raced full-out down the hall. No luck.

It wasn't till I saw the Sub-Authority that I accepted the humbling truth. In this place we only fly in the sense that penguins fly. Sort of a scurry and bounce. It's most appealing to those deceased meditationists who see it as levitating and take their new-found ability as a sign of enlightenment.

They're not in danger of arriving unprepared for a third Hearing in the Court of Final Appeals.

I should be spending my time researching my case, but . . . I play a little game. It involves twisting one of the Celestial Rules. The rules aren't shouted out over a loudspeaker like specials in the supermarket: 'Attention Dead Shoppers! Ultra Gold Halo Cleaner on aisle six! Snap it up while the supply lasts!' There are no proclamations, no notices posted. Here, things are just known. One of those 'things' is that you are forbidden to open the doors along the corridor. No reason for the 'Off Limits.' The Boss doesn't need to give out his rationale. And it seems superfluous to ask the punishment.

But few things are so seductive as a closed door. A closed *unlocked* door. There's a reason temptation has maintained its appeal all these centuries.

So I try a handle now and then. It's how I learned there are worse places to spend eternity than the white corridor.

In my first peek, I just about killed myself (or I would have if I hadn't already been dead) checking up and down the corridor for spies. Finally, not so much reassured as impatient, I inched open the door and found myself in a room that contained another world. Outdoors. San Francisco. And I was standing on the railing of the flyover that merges into the Bay Bridge. Traffic was backed up far as the eye could see (and one thing you get up here is 20 - 20). Rain bombarded the idling cars; the sky was five o'clock dark. A broken-down semi blocked the inner lane and traffic squeezed into the remaining lane. Half a mile back, cars from the on-ramp to the right had merged in, too. The surviving line of vehicles inched forward. A yellow Volkswagen bug puttered along in the lane, the driver's face rush-hour tight. A big blue Chevy pick-up raced along the shoulder. The driver should have merged into the VW's lane half a mile back. His lane had petered out. It was now-or-never for him. He slowed, veered closer to inching cars, eyeing each one predatorily until he spotted the little VW bug. He pounced left, barely missing the fragile bumper as the bug's brakes squealed. *Volkswagen Hell!* I thought. But just then, the Volkswagen driver hit his horn, an air horn loud enough to wake the . . . well . . . dead. And to terrify the pick-up driver. He swerved into the guard rail. Ah. *Volkswagen Heaven!*

The pick-up driver leapt from his wrinkled vehicle, turned to glare. And came face to race with a Highway Patrol officer. Not just Volkswagen Heaven but *Pick-up Hell!*

The pick-up driver could have pocketed his ticket and exited his Hell. He could have walked right out through the door with me. Instead, he leapt angrily into the driver's seat, screeched back, shifted into first, gunned the engine and found himself where he had started, a mile back on the entry ramp, and desperate to try to cut the line again, eternally.

I backed out into my hallway, shut the door and spun around with a second to spare before the Sub-Authority glided down the corridor. Had he spotted me? He didn't let on. But coincidences rarely occur up here.

I should have clutched my close call to my breast that day and never turned another doorknob. A wise person would have.

A wise person would be in Heaven.

Doors became my life, so to speak. I 'lived' to lurk, to sidle, to snoop. Held breath, panicked gasps became my norm of respiration. I tried every door on the corridor, on every corridor that crossed mine. I turned right and left, checking for spies till my wings were rubbed bare. The Sub-Authority never returned. I don't know when it struck me that the coast was always clear. I was the only real person on the corridor. It was then that I had the worst thought: that someone else might be sneaking open a door on a more rarified corridor, looking down and spotting me peering into forbidden rooms, eternally.

But now the call has come; they have pounced. The Boss frowns on dawdling when He's called you to court. If I thought there was any chance of escaping it, I would dawdle eternally. The Court of *Final* Appeals.

Like all the dead, I had had my day — *days* — in court when I arrived. The time of endless appeals is long gone up here. Once the Boss decides, who's to appeal to? That's one thing you know when you arrive. Not that it makes your initiation any easier.

Some of the newly dead — we call them *Cools* — have solid expectations of what this place should look like and how the Boss should handle things. Many expect to see their own face or similar ones on all around. They all expect the Boss to resemble themselves.

If they survived long enough to outlive friends and relatives, they expect the Dear Departed to be assembled and waiting anxiously. Not just rounded up, but on their best behavior, in many cases better behavior than they ever exhibited on earth. In the mind of the Cool the cousin he cheated, left destitute, and pushed into suicide, will not merely have forgiven him. That cousin will not have forgotten the event, but instead will see the Cool's motivation in a new light. He will, in fact, be eager to admit that he was wrong and it was the Cool who was the true victim. He'll be pushing in front of the Dear Departed to beat his breast and open his arms.

No other evidence need be shown to prove how quickly Cools forget life below. They expect the rest of those waiting relatives to be holding out hands toward them, comforting them after their traumatic experience, waiting anxiously their first words. They never picture cousins bored, uncles scarfing beers and dozing off in armchairs, and aunts too busy quarreling to be bothered with them.

But explicit as their expectations are, almost invariably the Cools' ideas of the Final Hearing are vague. They mutter about sheep and goats as if the Hearing — the only real thing among their fairy tale expectations — is all Brothers Grimm.

I don't know what I expected from my own Final Hearing, but what I found was certainly not it.

My first misapprehension was architectural. No way would I have guessed that the design of the Celestial Hearing Chamber would be based on the municipal court in Contra Costa County, California. Not even Superior Court! But there it was, a room paneled in middling wood, a judge's bench, and on the wall a gold disk about four feet across.

There is a bailiff — not in the ill-fitting tans of below, but in an off-white robe (straight out of the movies). "All rise," he calls. "The honorable Sub-Authority presiding." It's a bit of show, since no one but the Cool is in the room, and he's much too nervous to sit.

The bailiff reads the charges. He lists every trespass in deed, in word (and in words Cools assumed were whispered in confidence, not recorded for the ears of the heavenly host), and worst of all, the bailiff delineates, rather too lovingly, every transgression in thought. I mean, who would have thought . . .

The list goes on . . . and on . . . and on. It's the first time the Cool realizes what's meant by eternity. There may, in the fullness of time, be worse moments, and longer ones. I doubt it. Hours, days, aeons pass; his knees quiver like earthquakes, floods of sweat deluge his body, his eyes glaze over, and the synapses in his brain fire off in a war of their own. And when the list finally ends, and the Cool is reduced to a little formless blob of fear, the Sub-Authority looks him straight in the eye, pauses, and pronounces: "All is forgiven."

All is forgiven!

You would think the Cool would be ecstatic, right? Some are. Some inhale that forgiveness like oxygen into the lungs of the suffocating; they smile sheepishly, humbly, amazedly, clutch their clean slates to their breasts, and then, as if afraid the Sub-Authority might realize his mistake, they race through the great double doors that lead to — But, that *I* don't — cannot — know.

Some Cools accept the gift with grace. But not most. Most are, well, suspicious. To accept forgiveness for oneself is one thing, to sign on to clemency for *all* is another matter entirely. Just how all-encompassing was that divine pardon, they want to know. *I* wanted to know. Then their court-appointed lawyer asks for a continuance to the next day. The Sub-Authority granted *my* continuance, and my lawyer took me out in the hall, gave me a video tape of my transgressions and said: "Go over that tape and think about how lucky you are."

I did.

The next day I arrived back in court. The procedure was repeated. I knew I should have taken the offer — most people do by this stage, con men and crooks faster than the rest — they're used to playing the odds, and they know when those odds are not likely to improve. But I couldn't accept it. I don't know why. I wish I did. I would give a lot to know why. But, here, I have nothing to give.

My lawyer glared down the length of his nose at me, and asked for another continuance. The Sub-Authority's face pulled into a similarly un-angelic expression. But in the end he shrugged and granted the delay.

This time when my lawyer took me out into the hallway the very air was colder, thicker against my ribs. Each panicked breath smacked my ribs against the air; every beat of my heart hurt — phantom pain of phantom heart, but all too real panic. My lawyer's voice rasped my ears as he said, "You know what Three Strikes means?"

"When am I out?"

"Tomorrow, if you don't wise up and take the offer."

"And if I can't?"

He shook his head, smacked his wings tight against his scapulae, and glided away.

So I pace, up one corridor, down the next, hoping as I come to the intersections, that I'll turn the corner on my own problem and be whisked back to the final, triumphant hearing, and then on to . . . well, on to something so superbly wonderful it defies description.

Since then, I've opened a lot of closed doors, seen many things that shocked me, but none more than the scene inside the room marked 'Please Do Not Enter.'

I inched the door open and stood peering in on the Sub-Authority himself in his ostentatiously simple robe, thin lips pulled back in a scowl, glaring down his chiseled Puritan nose at a memo.

And facing him was the one Personage powerful enough to tell him No. All powerful. All knowing. All seeing.

Quickly, I slid behind the door.

It was then that I heard the Sub-Authority saying, "Can't stay here, Your Selfness."

It was *me* he was talking about.

"The corridor is for temporary stays, the occasional *one* night lodging for extremely indecisive and extremely *rare* souls."

I stuck my head beyond the door frame in time to see him shaking that memo impatiently.

I held my breath. Surely the Great Personage would come to my support. If this wasn't the time to demonstrate All Lovingness, what was?

But it was the Sub-Authority who spoke. "They all choose by the third hearing. The third hearing is *always* within a day of the second. This one" — I cringed — "has been stalling for longer than that already. This one is no closer to decision now than upon entry." His fingers tightened around the memo.

I strained to hear the reply. The Sub-Authority's jaw tightened; his fingers clenched into a fist. Dammit, if I could just get closer and *hear* . . . It was then I realized it wouldn't have mattered how close I was. I could have been standing between them. The voice of the Boss is never *heard*. He doesn't communicate in words.

"That one," the Sub-Authority countered, "has been spotted breaking the rules. What we've got here is a troublemaker. A troublemaker who cannot decide to go on and cannot keep the nose out of other penitents' business while here. Take that into account, Your Selfness. Make the judgment. Send that one down."

My whole soul went cold. I wanted to rush into the room, throw myself at the Authority's feet — if He had feet — and scream "I'll take the forgiveness. Please don't send me down. I'll forgive anyone — *all*."

But, even with the smell of brimstone rank in my nostrils, I couldn't. I just couldn't bring myself to. I folded my wings tight against my back and prepared for descent.

The Sub-Authority inhaled sharply and leaned forward, both hands shaking angrily. "But, Sir, we can't justify making an exception so unprecedented, not for this one."

My wings relaxed a scintilla.

"I know it's an important job," he admitted. "Admittedly this one has shown abnormal aptitude for the work. I suppose we *could* suspend the rules if the job is performed to satisfaction. But one failure and it's —" He glanced abruptly down, the hint of a smile on his face. In a moment the smile broadened.

And the door slammed shut.

I stood in the icy corridor. Damn, why couldn't I have accepted the forgiveness? Why? What could have been so terrible that I couldn't forgive it, even at the cost of my own eternal damnation? I strained, but not one image came to mind. Even under such extreme pressure I couldn't recall who I was, much less what had happened to me.

If I didn't figure out how to remember I was going to be in deep brimstone. But I had no idea how to go about it.

After that, the one thing you'd have expected of me was good behavior. You would assume I'd never have peered through another door. But, somehow the tenuousness of my position made me dart around more rashly than before. I felt like a gourmand sworn to start a diet in the morning, an alcoholic drinking his last bottle of scotch. It was that same day I came upon the pick-up driver on the Bay Bridge.

So, you see, I know how the Cools feel. Most of them go over and over that tape the first night, reliving some of the transgressing deeds they enjoyed entirely too much, shuddering at the anti-social thoughts that had sailed through their minds as if sent by a sociopath. By that second day they jump at the Hearing offer and nearly trip themselves running through the great double doors.

But the man at this trial . . .

I realized now I wasn't just *remembering* but was actually *at* a new trial. Time is funny here.

The defendant at today's trial was shaking his head, when his lawyer asked for not a continuance — under the rules he couldn't do that at that point — but a short recess.

Then he turned to me and said, "He can't make up his mind. He doesn't have a clue. He knows *how* he died, but he can't move on till he finds out *why* he died. You're the detective, you hunt that down."

"How am I going to —"

"My client doesn't have time for chatter. We're only recessed till after lunch. (The lawyer almost smiled. Up here we hardly 'do lunch.' There is no Food-For-The-Soul Cafe, no Veal Valhalla, no fresh greens from the

Garden of the Hesperides.) He's waiting for you in the hall."

What does a detective do? There had to be some job qualifications beside nosiness. Had I been a detective in life? I sure didn't picture myself as a pre-mortem gumshoe. How do you start an investigation, particularly when the subject is up here and the facts are down there? If I were such a natural detective I'd have been able to find out why I died myself instead of wandering around baffled up here.

A flash of anger shot through me. They expected me to find out how he died when *I* had died and no one had been assigned to do it for *me!* The hell to them! I'd refuse. A celestial sit-down strike. If they didn't like it they could —

An acrid whiff of brimstone cut through the bland air.

Then it occurred to me that I had a chance here. There was time on the off-white hallway to peek into rooms; why couldn't I make time in this investigation for my own search? Hundreds of thousands of people died every day; hundreds of thousands of trials go on simultaneously. As I headed out to this job the Sub-Authority would have plenty to worry about besides my time card. I'd just need to keep an eye out for my chance.

I walked slowly out the door and glanced at the defendant on the bench, sitting there within moments of the possibility of eternal damnation. He was a tidy, lightly-tanned Caucasian male of middle age, wearing an expensive blue pin-striped suit with lines so subtle I almost missed them, and a maroon silk handkerchief in his pocket. His hair was still dark, and despite his age no looseness of skin marred the firm, square line of his jaw. And his expression — had I considered the possibilities beforehand I might have expected fear or remorse — was one of outrage.

"You people have made a mistake!" he said by way of introduction.

"Wha —" I let out before I caught myself. *You people*, indeed. What did I look like, a sub Sub-Authority? I was offended. And shocked at how offended I was. I realized there was protective cover in this new role of mine.

I settled next to him on the wooden bench and restrained the urge to say: "A mistake? Ah, they all say that, Mr. Girard." Humor is so unappreciated in this place. There are times I think the real reason people are kept here at all is they are insufficiently venal to be sent below and too dull to be tolerated above. The Boss, after all, has to live up there. It's probably why he keeps the Sub-Authority down here.

I glanced over at Charles Girard, noting with some surprise how well he suited the name I hadn't known till a moment ago. "Mr. Girard, up here all things are possible. We can make whatever He wants. Mistakes is not one of those things."

He opened his mouth to protest. The words seemed to hover at the outlet of his lips. "How could this happen to me?"

"How could *what* happen to you?"

"The bit — woman killed me!"

"Well, something had to." The moment the words left my lips I knew they were a mistake. Again I wondered why had I been chosen a celestial detective — obviously not for my tact. "Start at the beginning with your name."

"Stone Girard," he said as if it were a household word.

"Stone?"

"Nickname. Had it for years."

"Because you did drugs?"

God, why did I keep poking at the man? He was hardly the type I could picture sprawled with a hookah or hypodermic. Nor, I gathered from the raise of his eyebrows, and the angry clamp of his jaw, could he. "Never! I never broke the law!"

"Let me remind you where you are, Stone. Up here you are always under oath."

It was a moment before he regained enough composure to insist, "Never once did I knowingly break the law."

"Knowingly? Ah hah!" Having to tell the truth, that's a shock for a lot of them. In some cases it leaves them nothing to say. Stone was being honest, if not helpful. And I could hardly ask him what law it was that he didn't know he'd broken.

"*I* would hardly have broken the law," he insisted as if he'd read my mind. "I was a judge."

In a great show of control, I said nothing.

"And I was running for the United States Senate!"

I couldn't help it; I laughed. I considered whether Stone's protest was indicative of remarkable naivete, and decided that he merely meant a gubernatorial candidate was wise to be circumspect.

Stone clutched a bunch of newspapers and shook them at me. The rustling of the pages grated oddly on my ears. The breeze chilled my bald head. It's so warm up here I'd almost forgotten why the still-living have hair. "I'm not — I *wasn't,*" Stone said, "one of those political idiots who can't keep it zipped." He smacked the papers into my hand.

That he still had the papers didn't surprise me. Death is such a loss. To lose a loved one can be hard. But when that loved one is the one you hold most dear — yourself — it gives *hard* new meaning. Cools come across kicking and screaming and clinging on for dear life. Literally. To calm them, the Sub-Authority offers them a last look below. An invisible box seat at the event of their choice. Some of the Cools who join us in January choose to see the football playoff games. Artists up for awards, scientists in the running for grants often choose to see the ceremonies. Parents opt for views of children's graduations. The occasional charismatic leader needs to see who his followers chose to succeed him.

But far and away the most popular event for a Cool is his funeral — the one time he is the true and deserving center of attention. A Cool may hate the idea of being up here, but the offer of a birds' eye view of his wake is more than most can pass up. Cools love the sobbers and the bawlers wailing as if their old hearts would break. They cherish the priestly eulogies extolling their noble natures, embellishing their wit, exaggerating their generosity. They clutch to their now formless breasts their friends' sincere emotions unspoken in life. Equally do they treasure their enemies counterfeit grief, the 'loving memories,' the panoplies of insincere praise those enemies have no choice but to choke out. Richard Nixon just about fell off his chair in the viewing room. I hadn't realized the man had such a sense of humor.

The Sub-Authority allows that. He doesn't object to the Cool clinging to a newspaper account of the event.

But three papers — that was a bit much.

I looked down at the top one so summarily smacked in my hand. Stone Girard was a well-known man. His death was not an addendum in the obit column. It was front page news.

"Girard Dead at Lovers Leap!" the *Los Angeles Times* screamed in banner headline.

"Girard Found Dead with Mystery Woman," the *San Francisco Chronicle* proclaimed.

"Political Fall: Same Old Story," the *Bay Guardian* shook its printed head. "If Stone Girard had taken stock of himself before he threw his hat in the ring, he wouldn't had felt obligated to toss the rest of himself onto the Great Highway. If Girard couldn't wait till after the election to take up with Olivia Cummings, what his choice tells us is California is left with the better man."

Marc Bellingham, by default the senate-elect presumptive, clearly understood the better part of valor. From the length of the headline article Bellingham was the only one within the Golden State or the United States Senate who did not have a comment on Girard's passing.

I read the coverage in all three papers and every one of the comments.

And while the word 'stupid' was never employed, I doubted there was a euphemism in the English language that had gone unused, nor any two lines that could not be read between. The closest reporters came to censoring the defunct candidate was denigrating his choice of leap, from an outcropping of rock above the Great Highway. If Girard hadn't died in the fall he'd have been crushed by a tourist bus. Stone Girard may have been, as he had insisted to me a minute earlier "not one of those political idiots who can't keep it zipped." But his way of departure was unlikely to garner him the epitaph of political visionary.

"Mr. Girard —"

"Stone."

"Stone, you and Olivia Cummings were found dead, *together*, at the bottom of Sutro Heights promontory."

Girard pulled his tidy form up to his full, if not impressive, height. "Don't even suggest that I was philandering. I am a man of principle. I did not entertain assignations. I wasn't called Stone for nothing."

Repressing a smile, I asked, "Why were you called Stone, Stone?"

"Because, young . . ." Stone assessed my hairless pate, swept his eyes discreetly down the front of my robe, apparently unaware that the soul is without sexual indicators. "My detractors called me Stone because I was sufficiently upright to cast the first one. They aimed to make me a laughing stock, but I wasn't laughing —"

That I believed. I'd yet to see any indication Stone Girard had a sense of humor. He had the makings of the Sub-Authority's right-hand man.

"— I took that name and made it my slogan. Voters want a man they can trust. They want to vote for a man who could cast the first stone. Bellingham may scoff at purity, but I'll tell you, little . . . person . . . these days purity is a plus."

"But, Stone, your body was found with this woman. How do you explain that?"

His jaw quivered. "I don't know."

"You don't know?"

"No, dammit, I have no idea."

I started to retort, then backed off. Maybe he was being truthful. His chiseled face was hewn into an expression of bewilderment. If so, it was no wonder he couldn't come to a decision at his Hearing.

Newly arrived Cools have no memory of the day of their death. Death can be traumatic, and Judgment is no piece of cake either. Particularly for those who've spent their lives pretending they are the Boss' earthly representatives. The Cools have plenty to contemplate without recalling their dying days.

Memory blackout is a good rule, but it was going to make my job harder. "Okay, Stone, for now we'll skip the reason for your presence on Sutro Heights. Tell me about the woman. Who was Olivia Cummings?"

"Nobody."

"Hardly no-body, Stone. Au contraire, not just a body but a *corpus delicti*. Was she an old flame?"

"No, no, no. I barely knew the woman. She was married to someone else."

"Are you sure?"

"Of course, I am. I married her myself."

A grin pulled at my lips.

"When I was a judge, I performed the ceremony. My one and only marriage."

"How come no more?"

He shot glances in both directions of the hallway, then lowering his voice, said, "I wouldn't want this to become public —"

"Don't worry. The old adage that the cemeteries vote democrat isn't true. There are no absentee ballots from here."

He flushed, then his eyes widened in horror. I had the feeling that for the first time he was really taking in the fact that he didn't have to worry about the election.

"You gave up performing marriages because —" I prompted.

"They take a lot of time and a judge can't accept payment for them. California Penal Code section ninety-four point five."

"Why not, so the judge can't be bribed?"

"It doesn't matter whether the payment was intended as a bribe or not. No money, no thing of value. Not before the wedding, not after."

"A judge can't be paid ever?"

"Not unless the wedding is performed on a Saturday, Sunday, or holiday."

"California, Land of Loopholes!" I threw my head back and laughed so hard my wings flapped. I nearly flung myself into the wall.

Stone cleared his throat, magistratively.

"Okay," I said, shifting my wings back in place. "But you did perform this one marriage, Olivia Cummings' wedding. Why?"

"It was a spur of the moment thing. They just called me because I was handy."

"Can you clarify that?" That sounded bland and legal enough for Stone.

"Olivia's father called me because I was spending the weekend in the other half of their cottage in Tahoe."

'Cottage' in this case could be a euphemism worthy of Stone's wake. "How big a cottage?"

"I don't know, three, four bedrooms."

"Who was Olivia's father?"

"Avery Cummings."

"Avery Cummings, the shipping magnate?"

"I don't know."

"Stone, remember where you are. The truth?"

"Cummings owned some ships."

"How many?"

"I don't — The Pan Asia Line."

I smiled to myself. Maybe I *was* cut out for this job. If the cases were all this easy, it'd be a snap. At this rate I would have plenty of time to check up on my own demise. "And so Stone, afterwards Avery Cummings supported your political campaign, right?"

"Wrong."

"The truth, remember?"

Girard jutted out his chin. "Cummings never gave me a dime. Never promised a loan or twisted an arm."

"He supported your opponent?"

"Him neither. Took no sides in politics. Said it didn't matter who won, nothing changed. Sounded like a goddamned radical. Said the best political investment for him was keeping his money in his pocket. And that's just what he did."

Surely not. I tried again, "But he let you use his vacation house."

"Let me *rent* it, at the going rate."

Okay, so the banker didn't go out of his way. But his daughter's wedding — half the money in California could have been invited. A couple of well-placed introductions and Stone could have been set for his whole campaign. "But at the wedding, he did introduce you to his influential friends, right?"

"He introduced me to his scatter-brained daughter, his cotton-headed son-in-law-to-be, and the maid and gardener he called in to be witnesses."

"And —?"

"That's all. No one else was there. They had to drag the maid out of bed. And the gardener. The guy didn't live on the grounds — we're just talking a house here, sizeable, but not an estate. The gardener lived in a cabin ten miles into the woods. Cummings called the guy's brother in town, got him up, convinced him to drive out to the guy's cabin and bring him back."

"Convinced him how?" I said, perking up.

"Financially," Stone said in the tone he'd have used with a particularly dim-witted lawyer.

But I wasn't about to be deterred, not when I knew the consequences of his being recompensed. "Did you hear him offer the gardener cash?"

"It was understood."

"Ah ha!"

"What does that mean?" he demanded icily.

"That you, too, could expect him to make it worth your while."

"I didn't! *He* didn't. Expect it or receive a cent from him. He didn't give me the benefit of his influence. He never once contributed to a campaign of mine. I don't think the man voted at all. And his damned daughter gave a couple thou to Bellingham. In fact, the whole affair ended up costing me."

"Costing you?"

"Right. I slept through a nine a.m. meeting I'd scheduled with Donald Davis, the financier. Davis was a potential contributor. With all the shenanigans connected with the wedding, the miserable affair took half the night. The groom was so drunk Cummings had to throw him in the shower to sober him up. Then Olivia decided she'd made the right decision when she called off the formal wedding — it was scheduled for a couple of weeks later — and flounced off to bed. If I'd been smart I'd have hightailed it out of there."

"But you didn't?"

"No. Big mistake. Cummings asked me to have a brandy with him, to settle us both down after the fiasco of an evening. So he pours the brandy and we're sitting there, and out comes the son-in-law-to-be. By now he's alert enough to realize he's been jilted for a second time and he's prowling the house, moaning like a dog with a churning stomach. I wanted to force some bicarb down his jaw and tie him to a stake in the yard."

I glanced at Stone's face to see if he intended to be amusing. Nothing suggested so.

"I just sat with Cummings, sipping the brandy. Sat silent. Just calming down. Should have kept watch on the son-in-law. Boy must have groaned his way down the hall to the girl's room. Must have made her sorry enough or horny enough to reconsider. Whatever. I was just about out the door when the two of them came racing in, grinning ear to ear, announcing they'd changed their minds."

"What about the gardener?" The question had nothing to do with the answers I needed, but I was too caught up in the story not to wonder about the groggy gardener and his groggy brother and the cabin ten miles into the woods.

"He was still at his brother's. It had started to rain about midnight and he'd decided not to make the trip back to his own cabin. So Cummings called a cab for him. When he got there, I lined 'em up, performed the ceremony — the actual legal necessities don't take long — and was back in my half of the cottage before the groom had kissed the bride." He shook his head. "Got myself so soaked I had to take a hot bath. Probably the reason I overslept, snubbed Davis, teed him off, basically kicked him into the other camp. Almost lost the election because of it. Davis has big bucks." He hesitated, glanced around furtively, then said, "Or at least he did. Dead now. Is he . . . here?"

"They all come through here, Stone. Where they go after I can't say."

"Not in the loop, eh?"

"Can't say," I managed to get out in a neutral tone. Of course, I didn't know what had become of moneyman Davis. The Sub-Authority doesn't report to me on the disposal of souls. But I wasn't about to admit that to Stone. Much less was I willing to show my pique. Up here, they frown on pique.

The smell of brimstone wafted past my nose. I shot a glance behind me, but, of course, there was no fire, not yet. Whatever the source of that evil smell, it did snap my attention back to the vital task at hand. Fail to solve Stone's dilemma and I would have eternity to contemplate the fate of Davis. Maybe he'd be right down there next to me, fanning the flames. "What became of Olivia and her groom?"

If Stone said they had a storybook marriage, topped by three charming children, all Rhodes scholars, I would have been surprised.

I wasn't.

"Divorced. Marriage lasted fifteen years. I would've put money on less than one. I'm not often wrong."

"But you were this time." I grinned.

"True. Figure it took Oren took that long to run through Olivia's money. No pre-nuptial agreement. Doesn't surprise me. They didn't plan anything else, why would they all of a sudden get responsibility and think about that?"

"Surely old man Cummings, a banker, would have pressed for it."

"You didn't know Olivia. Stubborn as she was spoiled and self-centered. Thought the world owed her a living. Figured as long as there was a world she'd go on living high. As for old man Cummings, he must have decided it wasn't worth the fight to buck Olivia on this. He was only in his fifties at the time. He must have figured he'd long out-live the marriage."

"Didn't he?"

"Nope. Heart attack the next year. That's why Oren and Olivia stayed married as long as they did. If they hadn't had her inheritance to go through they would have seen each other in the cold light of dawn a lot sooner. But money and illegal substances can rose-color the worst of situations."

"So they divorced?"

"Three years ago. Oren's a viper, but he's got a certain reptilian charm. Married more money within the year. Lives on an estate in Hillsborough."

"And Olivia?"

"Not so fortunate. High living took its toll. She was one of those chipmunk-faced girls kept from being plain by youth and money. Without either she came to resemble a Basset."

I shivered for Olivia, rolls of skin are more appealing on the face of a dog than a matron. "So what did she do for money?"

"Hit up everyone she knew. It was embarrassing. I mean how sorry can you be for an whiny woman who's run through a couple mill? Oh, some friends of the family helped out. An aunt gave her a studio in the city. A cousin took her by the scruff of the neck and explained the facts of life."

"Like?

"Work! Said he'd pay for her to take classes. Para-legal, it turned out. Olivia made it though a semester, maybe two. But when you expect the world to support you, work isn't part of the plan. Dropped out."

"And then?"

He shook his head. "Heard not a thing about her till she called. Yesterday." Girard paled. "God, just yesterday I was . . . alive.

"Don't think about that! You don't have time. Not now. *Olivia!* What happened after she called?"

She had arranged to meet him at Sutro Heights. Because all that happened the day of his death, he wouldn't remember it. He wouldn't know why he went, or what happened. Maybe she was so enraged he'd gotten her married to Oren in the first place that she pushed him over the cliff. Or perhaps he saw her in a new and seductive light, reached passionately for her and together they slipped into oblivion.

I didn't picture Stone rushing to an amorous tryst with a whiny, vindictive woman who looked like a low-slung hound.. Certainly not the week before the election. No way would Stone Girard set up a clandestine meeting at a lover's leap with a woman of questionable reputation.

Still, he did.

I started to ask him, more pointedly, what possessed him. But before I could speak he faded into the off-white wall.

"Get back here!" I yelled.

No response.

I banged my fist in fury, but it's a waste of time in a room where there's nothing solid to hit.

"Hey," I yelled into the atmosphere where the Sub-Authority was probably lurking, "this is really unfair. If you expect me to investigate, you've got to give me access to my client!"

No reaction at all.

"You know what kind of deal this is? Huh? A diabolical one!" That's a big insult, but not big enough to draw the Sub-Authority out. Clearly, I'd gotten all I was going to from Stone Girard. I hoped it was all I needed.

Once again fetors of brimstone rasped against my nose. No time for anger. I had to think. I coasted back and forth in front of the court room door. Why do people kill? Love. None of that lost here. Hate. Stone and Olivia were too inconsequential to each other. Envy, jealousy, revenge, greed — Ah, greed. Blackmail. One of the few ways of income acquisition left for Olivia. The conclusion quite pleased me.

Until her lack struck me. What had she blackmailed him with? The man had merely done her a kindness. Still, blackmail was all Olivia Cummings had left. But facts I didn't have.

What I did have, I realized, was one chance to peruse the evidence in person. I could choose my scene and go below, back to the time and be there as it occurred. One scene, but only one.

I'd take the minute before he died.

No, I wouldn't. The time he'd blacked out, was blacked out for me, too. I had to travel through *his* memory. Somehow from all the minutes and hours in his life, I had to pick out the key moment. If I didn't . . . But I was already sick of brimstone.

❖

Rain dripped down my neck, soft as if the drops broke their falls just before they landed on my skin, caressingly cool against the warm humid late summer air. The fresh and pure scent of an incense cedar cut the smell of wet grass. In the distance cars accelerated on the dark, empty stretch of road behind Cummings' Tahoe duplex roaring in quickening passion, gasping for breath, for gear change, speeding faster to a climax out of my hearing. Whiffs of gasoline came and were gone. In the shock of silence that followed, the gentle lapping of the lake seemed to pound like tsunamis.

Cummings' house was everything I might have imagined: large, shingled, the living space secluded from roadside eyes. Standing ten feet off the path by the front door, I watched as the portal opened. Stone stalked out. Face pinched, breath heaving angrily, his ire focused on a foot high glass jade plant in his hands. He stalked across the wet lawn toward the other door, *his* door, soft leather shoes squishing in the mud. He barely noticed that, so intent was he on stripping off the small glass leaves of the jade plant, one after another, and pitching them in the bushes. "A leaf for every damned minute!" he grumbled as he tossed the last one against the shingles, and fingered his pocket for the door key. "Some 'thank you'."

He stepped inside.

I could feel myself fading. I couldn't be pulled back yet! I hadn't solved Girard's death, and hadn't even thought about my own demise! I couldn't go back up there with nothing! I curled my toes, trying to clutch the earth, to wrap myself around the smell of the cedar, sound of the icy lake water splatting on the shore. Of earth. I hadn't realized how much I missed it. Greedily I moved my gaze back and forth over the sky, the clouds, the trees, the lawn imprinting them all on my memory. The pull grew stronger, a budding tornado in reverse.

On the road a horn blew.

I slipped behind a redwood, raced to the bushes, stooping low behind them. Sweat coated my neck. I inched toward Girard's front door, hoping he'd been too distracted to lock it. The wind, the *pull*, sucked the fallen leaves off the grass, twisted the fronds of the redwoods. I reached for the doorknob and was inside.

In a vestibule with a closet, mirror, narrow table and a book, *The Perfect Crime*, by Leigh Ward. I grabbed it and slid into the safety of the closet.

❖

The hallway outside the courtroom was empty, no Cools, no staff, no smells, not even a familiar soundless word. Footsteps came down the hall toward me, slowly, from a distance. Stone's steps. When he reached me, we would go into the courtroom, he would turn to me, then he'd have to give his answer.

Stone paused next to me, reached for the double door and we walked in. The great seal gleamed down at us. From under it the Sub-Authority exhaled slowly. "Charles Stone Girard, all is forgiven. Do you accept forgiveness for all?"

Stone turned to me.

I pictured the pick-up driver in the room on the corridor, trying to cut the line, smashing into the railing, getting the ticket, and starting over again, endlessly, blocking out reality with his insistence. Stone was a judge. He should have known what was in the penal code. Laws can be foolish, but only a fool ignores them, particularly if he's running for senate. Only a fool drives into the same railing again and again. Only a fool assumes a jade plant is so insufficient a 'thank you' as to be of no value at all.

I said, "California Penal Code section ninety-four point five." The code appeared in his hand:

> *Acceptance of fee by judicial officer for performance of marriage. Every judge, justice, commissioner, or assistant commissioner of a court of this state who accepts any money or other thing of value for performing any marriage, including any money or thing of value voluntarily tendered by the persons about to be married or who have been married by such judge etc whether the acceptance occurs before or after performance of the marriage and whether or not performance of marriage is conditioned on the giving of such money or the thing of value by the persons being married is guilty of a misdemeanor.*
>
> *It is not a necessary element of the offense described by this section that the acceptance of the money or other thing of value be committed with intent to commit extortion or with other criminal intent.*
>
> *This section does not apply to an acceptance of a fee for performing a marriage of Saturday, Sunday, or a legal holiday.*

"And section ninety-eight:"
> *Officers to forfeit and be disqualified from holding office. Every officer convicted of any crime defined in this chapter, in addition to the punishment described, forfeits his office and is forever disqualified from holding any office in this state.*

It was a moment before Stone groaned, "You mean the fucking jade plant? I could lose the senate seat because of that jade plant?"

I nodded.

His shoulders slumped, he started to sag toward the floor. Then abruptly he pulled himself up. "No wait. That's what she thought, the greedy bitch. But she was wrong. Look back at ninety-four point five: *does not apply to legal holiday*. The wedding was Labor Day!"

I shook my head, "No, Stone. The wedding would have been Labor Day if Olivia and Oren hadn't squabbled and put it off. By the time they got around to marrying it was well after midnight. Late enough to be Tuesday. Late enough to bar you from the senate. She blackmailed you, and regardless of who pushed whom, she killed you."

"All is forgiven, Mr. Girard. Do you accept that?" the Sub-Authority repeated.

Stone hesitated, his face tightening as I'd seen it over the jade plant. Then he surprised me; he nodded.

As he walked through the double doors at the far side of the courtroom I realized how much he had given up losing his senate seat. The man was meant to be a politician; he knew how to accommodate himself. Now he had accommodated himself into heaven.

I walked back into the hall. The vague scent of brimstone had returned. I had succeeded at this job. The Sub-Authority wouldn't be able to commit me to brimstone. Not yet. But he'd never trust me down below again, either.

I had merely extended my stay on the corridor. If I succeeded case after case I could stay here forever, endlessly ignorant of who I was and why I kept myself here. What had been so horrendous, appalling, galling about my own death to make me less willing to forgive than Stone Girard?

I, the celestial detective, had not a clue.

My left wing felt stiff, tense, tired. I pulled out the book I'd hidden under it. *The Perfect Crime.* Stone Girard's death had hardly been a perfect crime.

I looked at the book and smiled.

The perfect crime had to be mine. So perfect I couldn't part with it. But what crime? Victim or killer? How had I — I peered down toward the book but it was gone.

A new Cool shuffled out of the Hearing Room, head down, face pinched in confusion. Up here the authorities have to be fair. They can't offer one Cool benefits and deny them to the next. I moved beside him. "Need a detective?"

This story joins two of my favorite things — creating the afterlife, and revenge.

I'LL GET BACK TO YOU

I'd always thought Purgatory —

Well, no.

The truth is I'd almost never thought of Purgatory. I mean, who does? You hear people discussing Heaven or Hell, but how often do they speculate on the number of eons they may inhabit the lowliest room in Purgatory? *If Purgatory has single rooms, which wouldn't have been my guess.*

If asked, I would have said accommodations in Purgatory were like those of the cheapest traveler's hotel — those coffin-sized chambers in the walls of Japanese airports where businessmen lie abed watching pay TV — roomettes in which suffering could be done in dignified if uncomfortable semi-seclusion. Purgatory would be a shabby place of tedious suffering in which sole souls atone for minor banal sins. If, as in those Japanese airport chambers, the occasional moan could be heard and wriggle felt in the adjoining chambers, so much the more suitable for Purgatory.

But I was wrong.

If I am in Purgatory it's not shabby, not small, not solitary. Maybe this is not Purgatory. It's not like there's a sign in the lobby: *Hotel Expiation, extended stays encouraged.* I can't even find a lobby. What they've got here is just long off-white halls with spongy walls and carpets that are never the solid ground of knowing. I arrived here without warning, without explanation of what offenses I had committed in life, how I'd departed life, or even who I'd been in it. Much less just what this place is or how long I'll be here.

There are, of course, rules — unspoken rules — here, created by the Boss — the *Authority* — enforced by the Sub-Authority with unseemly zeal. (I'd love to know who *he* was in life.)

I don't know who I was in life, but it's clear to me *what* I was, was a rule-breaker. *Don't shout!* the unspoken rule here shrieks. Why not? With no one on the hall but me, who's to hear? *Don't spread your wings in the halls! Don't glide!* Well, I mean, what are halls for? I can't prove it but I'll swear the Sub-Authority, a penguin-shaped spirit, hardens those spongy walls; I scrape my wings on them every time.

Don't open the doors! Don't peer into the rooms! Don't look at the sufferers inside!
Fat chance!

If I hadn't opened a door I wouldn't have overheard the Sub-Authority telling the Boss to get rid of me. I wouldn't know that the only reason I'm still in a place decent as this, is because I'm their 'designated detective.'

The Sub-Authority is not going to put up with me forever. If I don't figure out who I was, how I died, and why I can't remember a thing about my life, or death, I can never accept the Sub-Authority's offer of forgiveness for all involved, and go on to the Glorious Whatever. It's just a matter of time till the Sub-Authority finds a reason to move me out of here. Out and down.

I can't do that up here. The only chance I've got is to sneak some time down on earth while I'm on my official cases.

So, I hang around outside the Court of Final Appeals — sort of a post-mortem ambulance chaser — eager for the next soul who, like me, can't bring himself to forget and forgive.

Usually those souls — Cools, we call them — are huddled in a corner of the court lobby, baffled by their tragic deaths. (They don't have to have been plucked in the flower of youth or skewered while on a mission of mercy. Passing in their sleep at the age of ninety is cataclysmic if the passer was *them*.) They've just come from the Courtroom where the Sub-Authority read out the list of their transgressions; they're shaken and exhausted. The artists and writers have the worst time; they don't mind being branded as sinners, they'd be insulted with anything less. It's the utter banality of their individual transgressions they just can't accept. A few have actually sprained their necks looking around, terrified someone they know is in the room taking notes, eager to recount the damning discovery to their critics. ("As if they haven't known for years," I always want to shout. But I control myself.)

Sometimes Cools are too stunned by their humiliation to even hear the Sub-Authority pause at the end of the sin list, stare them in the eye and pronounce: "All is forgiven. Accept and move on." They don't stop their cervical swivelling long enough to spot his stare, much less agree to his offer of forgiveness for them and everyone involved with them.

Most Cools aren't that dim. They comprehend the offer; they grab it. But there are those who get it but can't bring themselves to accept. Some can't forgive themselves. Without their great and hidden sin what would be left of them? But mostly with the indecisive, it's someone else they can't excuse. Sometimes they don't even know who that person is. My job is not necessarily to uncover their murderer or their victims — whichever they had

— but to get them enough information so they can make The Decision. Ideally, then the Cool moves on to a blissful realm I can only dream of. But some Cools never can accept forgiveness for themselves, much less for their enemies. Even when the facts of their demise are laid out before them, when they are reminded that their enemies will not ruin their lives, because they, the Cools, are *dead!* They're not about to stop pointing the finger even when it means . . . Those Cools settle into their own personal hells in rooms along the hallway here.

It's rather embarrassing to admit I've had *two* hearings in the Court of Final Appeals. The Sub-Authority insists he read my list of transgressions, my extensive — to use the term he all-too-lovingly employs — list, at both of my hearings, but if so, it's too painful for me to remember. I don't remember why I died, how I died, or even who I was. All I know about my life is that it's end is connected with *The Perfect Crime,* a book by Leigh Wright. Leigh Wright could be me. Or maybe the book was *about* me. Or maybe the title is just a hint, a tease, a special torture the Sub-Authority has created for me. I only saw the book for a minute, and that, by snatching a moment on a case when the Sub-Authority wasn't looking.

If I'm going to get out of this place, off the hall, I'm going to have to do better. I'll get one more hearing — the *final* Final Hearing — and I'd better be able to make my decision then.

So I need a Cool who will provide me an easy case I can dispatch quickly enough to leave me spare time. I eye the Cools as they stumble out of the courtroom, heads down, eyes glazed, bodies tense with fear and helplessness. Their lawyers trot alongside reminding them they have only one last chance.

I spot a man across the room, brow wrinkled painfully, fingers moving back and forth as if about to grab an answer just out of reach. Bingo. I moved toward him, careful not to lift a wing, not to indulge in the forbidden glide. I —

"Let me out of here! I have a meeting!" A brisk, brown-haired woman in her early forties strides out of the court room, brushing the worried man aside without breaking stride. Even under her white robe I can tell she's got one of those tight, muscular bodies, the type men covet and women envy. She races forward, legs nearly windmilling, oblivious to the fact she's merely treading space. She is holding a white towel.

Often Cools come to trial still clutching some vital item as if it were a talisman. Not infrequently that item is the picture of a spouse, child, cat. Wizened patriarchs arrive holding the baseball bat with which they hit the winning run fifty *years* earlier! Matrons come clinging to the wedding dress, the pair of jeans, the silk skirt they're still planning to get into again. (When *they* hear about the body falling away, their first reaction is glee.) Executives hold the brass name signs from their office doors.

But the brisk brunette, Tasha Pierce, was holding nothing but her anger. And her towel.

It is a bad sign that I suddenly knew her name. Knowledge comes like that up here. Suddenly you know it, as if you've always known. But you don't know for no reason. I stepped into her path. "You have a meeting, Ms. Pierce? With whom?"

"Selwyn!" Her full dark brows drew low over equally dark eyes. An instant later, when she realized I hadn't reacted to the vaunted name, she insisted, "Selwyn Reed, the C.E.O. You don't blow off a meeting with the C.E.O." She was racing her feet, still clad in white running shoes. If I'd had any questions about her haste to get to Selwyn, I needed only note her shoelaces — untied. I could picture her yanking off the pumps that went with her dress-for-success suit, poking her feet into the running shoes as she leapt from her chair, and racing out the door. She had the look of a woman who assumed the purpose of red lights was self-enhancement: the driver's opportunity to apply make-up, the pedestrian's chance at shoelaces.

As if I had perused her file, I suddenly knew that Tasha Pierce had been Personnel Director. In the home office fifty people had reported to her: the satellite offices under her authority tripled that number. Staffed with her selections, Selwyn Industries "ran like a well-oiled machine," she had announced more than once. Other quotes were: "A company is only as good as the people it employs," and "dead wood means dead sales."

Ah, *dead wood*. Wood that had seen itself as headed toward being a mighty oak, is not prepared for the ax — in trees or personnel. Perhaps Tasha Pierce had conducted one too many termination interviews. I smiled to myself. Her case could be the easy investigation I needed. I just hoped she hadn't thinned an entire forest of potential suspects. Couching my question in the kind of impersonal terms personnel departments love — words like their title, so close to personal as to float the illusion they are concerned about people — I said, "You downsized?"

"Me? No way. I don't do that shit. We've got an out-placement department."

An entire department! Selwyn Industries didn't just thin, they clear-cut! How many people had Selwyn laid off? But that carnage wouldn't have been aimed at my client alone. So much for the easy case.

Still, it looked like someone had done her in. And to say she was unready to forgive her killer was the understatement of the eon. If that person had been lying on the floor she'd have pounded him to dust with her racing feet. "Look, fellow — lady" — she glared at my sexually-ambiguous form — "whatever the hell you are. I don't have time to stand around while you get your act together. Either get the asshole who did this or —"

"Which asshole is that?" I asked with renewed hope.

"How the hell should I know? One minute I'm running —"

"Running where?" I struggled to keep my voice calm. The rule is: Cools don't remember the days of their deaths. Too traumatic, the Sub-Authority says. (Too much bother for him, I say. If they could run that final day's tape, Cools would spend eternity watching, rewinding, and caterwauling. Each time they'd see some new affront — hospital roommates who screamed, snored, or blared the TV, sisters who looked more longingly at their jewelry than them, brothers who stepped out for a smoke at the moment of death . . . The Cools would languish in recrimination long after they should have taken the Sub-Authority's offer and moved on. Gladly would they take up the cudgel in memory of their dying selves and stalk out after that offending sibling or roommate — who might well be right here!)

Much as it's a nuisance to my job, I see the Sub-Authority's point. The rule had never been broken — until Tasha Pierce. If I could just squeeze enough from her memory to pinpoint the 'asshole' who had caused her death. "Running to where?" I repeated, glancing down at those white running shoes with their undone laces.

"Nowhere," she said, shoving my question out of the way with a flourish of hands.

On earth she might have been lying, but here Cools don't have that option. I grabbed her hands, held them down, and tried to elicit what she did know. "Tell me what you saw as you were running."

Her small face tightened; her hands squeezed into fists; she jerked forward.

"Tell me!"

She let out a frustrated snort. "Trees, buses, people, cars."

"And your meeting with Selwyn, where was that to be?"

"His office, of course."

"In the building you worked in?"

"Where else?" Her eyes added: *you idiot.*

"You were running there. So then, Ms. Pierce, what building were you coming from?"

That stopped her.

"The leaves, the trees, the people: what buildings were behind them? Which buses did you see?"

Her forehead wrinkled, and her eyes almost closed. She was peering inward for all she was worth.

And apparently it wasn't worth much. With a shake of the head she announced, "That tack's not working. Look, honey, I'm not a detail person. Was when I started. Had to be. But now, I'm dealing with the big picture. I've got lackeys to sweat the details. You're going to have to come up with something else."

I could have said . . . Instead I pressed my wings tight to my sides and descended halfway through the floor she had assumed to be solid. A figure eight flight would have been more effective, but alas, up here we can do little more than they do in the NBA.

"Hey, Angel, don't think you can blow me off with that collapsing routine. I've seen magicians better'n you."

I shrugged and turned toward the corridor. "I'll get back to you."

"I should live so long. We'll do lunch, right?"

I started to reply, but clearly Tasha Pierce was not one to allow extraneous words, at least ones that weren't hers. "Look, I know all the ways of blowing people off. I'll get back to you means: fat chance. I'll call you *right* back, means 'I'll get back to you.' The great thing about being Personnel Director is never having to bother with that shit. I don't deal with that call 'em back garbage like I had to coming up through the ranks. Then you've got pests bugging you all the time. 'Did you get my resume?' 'How come you haven't called me back about the interview?' 'Do you have any other jobs?' as if I had nothing on my mind but them. Now, thank God, I've got a secretary for that. She holds my calls; I deal with them at *my* convenience. I don't have time for calls and messages; they wait."

And so shall you. For all I cared about her convenience she could spend eternity bitching right here. As long as I didn't have to keep running into her. Only the reminder that I had my own reasons for taking this case kept me from speaking out loud. I tried again. Normally I start with suspects' possible motives, but with Tasha Pierce to know her was to be motivated. Whoever killed her should be wearing a big smile. "Let's talk suspects. Your secretary?"

"On my team. I go, she goes. She's probably back in the typing pool already."

"Assistants, sub-directors, people in line for your job?"

"I'm not a fool. In business you don't have colleagues, you've got subordinates. They rise above subordinate status, you move 'em out the door.

Otherwise you turn around and they're sitting in your chair."

I asked about family: distant; friends: none to speak of; expectant heirs — no will, because it clearly had neither occurred to her that she would die, nor that it's more blessed to give. "Selwyn," I last-gasped. "What about Selwyn? Blackmail, exposure, love, revenge? Any motive at all?"

"Selwyn? Puh-lease! Selwyn Adams is sixty-three years old, biscuit-shaped, and too damned self-absorbed to entertain love or revenge. If the man had done anything worth blackmail I'd have died from shock instead of . . . whatever."

It was with some small amount of pleasure that I said, "I'll get back to you."

But by the time I got back to my corridor that little light of glee had faded. This case was my only chance to check out my own death. There was a reason I'd suddenly known so much about Tasha Pierce. Maybe it was the Boss's plan to help me, or it could have been the Sub-Authority tantalizing me for his own amusement. Whichever, I couldn't dismiss Tasha Pierce.

And besides, I wondered as I glided and thumped back and forth, forth and back through the empty corridor (smacking my head more than once on the Sub-Authority's unnecessarily low ceiling), how had the woman died? New York is a big city and she'd probably alienated half of it. But murder? If guns were shot and knives thrown at all the rude and self-absorbed, survivors would have their choice of cabs at rush hour.

But Tasha Pierce had died — in a way she couldn't accept.

I slowed to a flutter. A door beckoned. All the doors on the corridor beckon. The Sub-Authority views unauthorized entry as kindly as does a hotel dick. If he catches me again — But I'm careful. It's an addiction, peeking into these rooms, I know that. On earth I'd be grist for twelve-step, but here, what's an addiction going to do, kill me?

One little peek. It'd take only a minute.

I checked to my left. Hall empty. To my right. Clear. Then I grabbed for the handle, and pushed open the door.

Inside is a well-appointed dining room. Dinner is over, coffee cups are nearly empty, brandy snifters still half full, the brandy line is still at the neck of the bottle despite the eight glasses poured from it. (That kind of thing — candle oil that burns overlong, multiplying loaves and fishes is commonplace here. The celestial answer to recycling.) I focus on the man at the end of the table. You'd think the man would be smiling — well, you'd think that if you'd been here a lot less time than I have. In these rooms nobody smiles.

He is shouting and slamming his fist on the table as he makes his point.

His muddled words echo off the walls. And the echo infuriates him. His face reddens. He shouts louder. He glares down the table, grabs his brandy snifter and swallows too much of the honey-colored liquid, coughs loudly — so loud no one can interrupt him.

But no one will interrupt him — because he is alone. If he lifted his eyes from his snifter, if he took the slightest break from planning his verbal assault or delivering it, he would realize that. The silence of the empty room would reverberate if, just for an instant, he would listen.

That, he is forever unwilling to do.

I shut the door, turned.

And gasped.

The Sub-Authority was rounding the corner. Had he spotted me peering into one of the forbidden chambers? I didn't wait to find out.

I flew down the corridor with feet racing about six inches off the floor as if that would speed me out of danger, and ended up back in the courtroom lobby. Not the best spot to hide out. In fact, there was only once place I could be sure of escaping the Sub-Authority. Earth.

Here's the deal: Cools are not the most reliable witnesses. At best, they remember selectively; at worst they conceal. The Sub-Authority understands innate duplicity (in fact it was he who first proposed Original Sin). So he realizes I can't count on my clients to be honest about their former lives. I have to do leg work in the field. The field below. I can choose to visit any time in the client's life or the week thereafter.

But like I said, the Sub Authority understands conniving, he sees evil intent in all actions, particularly mine, so I'm limited to one visit. Usually I interview the client at length, weigh the possibilities, and choose the most potentially most valuable scene.

Usually.

Now I just skidded to a halt in front of the elevator and hit DOWN.

❖

It wasn't a skyscraper. (There aren't really skyscrapers. If there were, my trips down wouldn't end with such rude bounces.) The first bank of elevators only went down to the seventy-second floor and there I had to change to get to Selwyn Industries offices on the thirtieth, thirty-first, and thirty-second. I pushed 31, the car shot down, and when the doors opened I was facing a glass partition that announced:

SELWYN INDUSTRIES
Personnel Department
Accounting

Inside on the reception desk were two almost-tastelessly-huge bouquets with big black ribbons draped around their white wicker baskets. There were pale pink roses, white carnations, blue and violet irises, shoots of orchids in varying pastels, and exotic blooms I couldn't name. Conspicuously absent were lilies. Between the two displays I recognized a photo of Tasha Pierce draped in black. Had the flowers been brought from her memorial service? Or were they office memorials, from her subordinates, or the esteemed Selwyn himself?

I stepped back to contemplate that. Invisibility is great, but it does have a down side. People can't see me, but I do have form. I have to be careful they don't run over my toes with their supply carts, smack me with their tossed packages, or, worse yet, back into me, panic, and end up calling everyone in sight to feel around for the soft, cold body they can't see.

As if I had suddenly turned the *volume* to ON, I could hear the laughter. Twitterings, giggles, great rolling guffaws from voices too sweet and delicate-sounding to be associated with those great rumblings of glee. Behind the desk the receptionist had to pause to control her laughter before she answered the phone. "No. I'm sorry," she said, her poorly-muted chuckle belying her words, "Ms. Pierce is no longer with us." She barely got the phone disconnected before she proclaimed, "Tasha pushed her way out," and burst into giggles.

I expected her to look around the seemingly empty reception area with a mixture of guilt and relief, but the woman showed no remorse at all. She spotted a middle-aged man coming down the hallway and called out, "Pushed her way out!" and both of them dissolved in laughter.

"Gotta say," he said, leaning an arm over her desk, "couldn't happen to a more deserving woman."

"Danger of the fast lane, huh?"

"And the slippery world of periodical publishing."

At this they doubled over. Three more people joined them. A brown-suited man was smacking his fist on the desk as he guffawed.

"You know what they always tell you," a woman in green forced out. They all doubled over again. Fists pounded, sides shook.

I had no idea what they were talking about. I had assumed Tasha Pierce would not be widely mourned, but this! Marley's Ghost drew more tears.

The same thought must have crossed the mind of a woman in gray. She put a hand on the speaker's arm. "Maybe we should cool it. Who knows who's around. I mean, even Selwyn could walk up, and the way we're going, we'd never hear him."

"Selwyn?" the guy in brown said, "you think Selwyn would care that she's dead. He's probably out celebrating over a piece of chocolate pie."

"Two pieces!"

The burst of chuckles was muffled and the laughers glanced uncomfortably behind them. Clearly in Selwyn Industries derision was best aimed at the dead.

"He's probably just relieved never to see her again race into his office, plop that liter bottle of spring water next to the desk and bark out her choice for his secretary, his driver, or his —"

"— wife?"

Any attempt they made at control failed. Hands were slapping, arms swaying so much I had to jump out of their midst.

"I heard he tried to put her off an hour earlier," a woman in yellow said. "But, of course, her secretary told him she was on her way."

"Was she?" a blue-suited guy asked.

"Who knows? Even if she weren't she wouldn't have taken the call. She hadn't answered any others this week. I wonder if she's busy telling Saint Peter she'll get back to him."

"Enough!" the woman in gray warned.

"No," I screamed. "Don't stop!" But no sound came out.

"We really ought to watch what we say," she insisted.

I wrinkled my forehead and concentrated on transmitting the thought: Gossip is a *good* thing.

They hesitated. The women in yellow and gray were starting to leave when the blue-suited man asked, "But what is the official word? I mean the cause of death."

"Smothered in her towel." And that sent them off again.

The towel. That white towel she'd been clutching. I'd thought it was a strange talisman. Now it made sense. So she'd been smothered with her towel.

No wait, smothered *in* her towel. Not *with* the towel, or *by* the towel, or even *under* it. But *in* it. How does one smother in the towel? She'd have to have been face down to be *in* it. Was she attacked, and slammed down? But that wouldn't smother her; she'd still be able to breath through the towel. Unless her assailant wadded it up around her nose. But that would be being smothered *with*. Not *in*.

Go on, I urged. Alas, discretion, the scourge of detection, had taken hold, and one by one Tasha Pierce's co-workers wandered off.

I had come in looking for a notice of a memorial service. I guess I'd heard the real thing.

I did have one more stop, just to confirm my suspicions, but that would take an instant.

Which left me a few minutes leeway for my own work.

But the Sub-Authority was watching me. Maybe not every moment but . . . Would he realize I had solved this case? I couldn't take the chance.

I followed the man in brown through the lobby door into the DOWN elevator. I got out in one of those faux marble lobbies, followed the man out to the sidewalk and found myself, as I'd suspected, in Midtown New York.

Sleet was pelting down, so thick I could barely see in front of me. It bounced off the sidewalk and the inadequate women's pumps, men's leather shoes, ubiquitous running shoes. People turned up collars, reached in pockets in hopeless search for gloves. Clearly this day had started out many degrees warmer. These days were the worst, the ones that made you understand why people moved to the suburbs where their cars stood waiting for them. To a one, people here were shivering.

But not me. Death does have its advantages.

Pedestrians raced past me, sliding on the slick sidewalk. A man scraped my side with his briefcase. A woman grazed my nose with her elbow as she raised a manila file over her head in vain effort to save her hair.

I had to get out of there. But where to? Movie theater — across the street!

I ran in front of a double-parked truck and was nearly picked off by a car squeezing around it. Invisibility has its drawbacks. And what's the point of being dead if you can't even fly high enough to clear traffic! But, I was safe now.

It was a moment before I realized I couldn't just sit here. I might be out of the way of the pedestrians, but *safe* I was not. Not from the Sub-Authority. He'd know the difference between investigating and watching — what was on the screen? *The Return of Raffles,* the black letters on the gray white background announced, as the opening credits rolled — watching an old black and white movie about a cricket-loving thief. Not much could be farther from Tasha Pierce. Or me, for that matter.

Was I sure about that? I wasn't. In fact . . . But I couldn't stay here a sitting duck for the Sub-Authority.

I edged out of the theater, pinballing my way between the rushing workers, smacking into the wall, rebounding into a nun, bouncing back into a fat man with an umbrella. Enough! I lowered my head, hunched my wings forward and steered through the stampede, oblivious to whom I tossed where.

And when I spotted glass doors, I didn't worry about what reaction viewers would have to their opening apparently by themselves. I yanked one open and flung myself in.

Into, it turned out, the lobby of the Hotel Melbourne. I tossed myself into an empty stuffed chair amidst the decorative wrought iron railings that separated each clutch of chairs. Wrought iron was at the top of walls, too. And while the chair had the heavy look of a British men's club and the carpet was oriental, there were enough palm trees around to suggest the south seas.

Ah, the Hotel *Melbourne*.

This would do fine as a place to gather my thoughts, make my plan. And a gin and tonic would hit the spot. I raised my hand for the waiter.

It was only after three waiters passed without a glance that it occurred to me how distracted I was. I lowered my invisible hand.

A waiter put down his tray of drinks by the four men and women in the next chair cluster. I reached over and grabbed the nearest glass, and then with a scintilla of good sense, moved behind one of those potted palms to drink it. Who knows what liquor traveling down the esophagus of an invisible dead person would look like? Maybe it would be invisible too. Maybe.

"Where's my drink?" a woman who could have been Tasha Pierce's emotional double, demanded of the waiter. "It was a Singapore Sling."

Suddenly I was aware of my feet. They felt light. Ominously light. As if they were merely grazing the top of the oriental rug. The soft brush of it tickled them. I tensed. I knew that light-footed sensation. The pull from the Other Side. Desperately, I grabbed a red book off the table next to me and ran for the door, zigzagging as if I was avoiding gunfire.

The street was still packed, but this time my momentum, coupled with fear, hoisted me over the pedestrians and across the street in two leaps. I raced back inside Tasha Pierce's building, checked the information listing, and pushed onto the UP elevator smacking two startled executives against the back wall. The red book dropped to the floor, landing partially behind one of the men's feet. *Raffles* was all I could see of the title. Before I could make a grab for it, I was out the door at 3, and into Tasha Pierce's Health Club.

Women in bright blue and green sports bras and tights with sports briefs over them, or shimmery red leotards with matching headbands, sat poised on nautilus machines, pushing the black padded machine arms toward each other. Others straddled pads with their thighs, grunting softly as they forced the pads together on one machine, apart on another. The carpet was a red plaid, the walls yellow. Everything in the place screamed: Faster! All around me women panted and grunted. Weights lifted and banged down, shaking the floor like a 6.0 on the Richter scale.

But for the first time since I'd left Selwyn Industries I was relaxed. Here I had legitimate reason to be — getting the final piece of Tasha Pierce's puzzle. I started across the floor.

But my feet were lighter!

"No," I yelled. "Not yet! I still need —"

Headbanded heads swiveled toward me.

Could I be heard down here? I looked around, unnerved, but the heads had turned not toward me, but at the treadmill. Just where I was heading myself. I moved faster, but the tug was stronger. I grabbed the railing on the side of the treadmill. Behind me someone was calling, "Jennifer, treadmill! Jennifer, you're next on the list for the treadmill."

A woman jumped onto the treadmill and started the belt, ignoring the call from the sign-up sheet. She had the mill; possession is 9/10th of the law; Jennifer be damned. In a bright green lycra unitard, she ran on the moving belt, glancing down at the machine's changing display: time elapsed, mileage covered, speed, on the rib-high digital display shelf. A towel hung over the bar on the front of the display shelf, and she almost pulled it loose as she bent, still in stride, to grab her water bottle from the shelf below.

The Sub-Authority's pull was fierce. My feet were off the ground. I grabbed the machine's side bar-railing and held on for dear life.

"Jennifer! Treadmill!"

"I'm Jennifer," a gray-haired, remarkably un-Jennifer-looking woman said bewilderedly as she eyed the occupied treadmill.

My hands slipped. Life, dear or otherwise, was no longer mine.

❖

"So?" Tasha Pierce demanded. We were in front of the courtroom door. "Who's the bastard who killed me?"

"I could tell you," I said, still catching my breath. That pneumatic suction's a killer. "But I think this is one case where they'll let us roll the tape. Right?" I said aiming my demand at the Sub-Authority.

In an instant I was standing beside Tasha Pierce watching a tape of two women panting on treadmills and one gathering her belongings and stepping off the third machine; it was so real I could have been in the Health Club.

I thought of the epitaphs Tasha Pierce's co-workers had given her, ending with: "Smothered in her towel."

The tape grabbed my attention. Tasha Pierce let the Health Club door bang after her. She ran in, pulling her blouse over her head, slowing to unbutton her skirt and let it drop to the floor, around her untied running shoes. Now in standard health club attire, she put her clothes in her tote bag and made a bee-line for the untenanted treadmill, ignoring the sign-up list and the sign posted at the end of the treadmill. With awe-inspiring speed, she plopped the tote bag at the end of the treadmill behind her, the water bottle on the lower shelf, set her Walkman and magazine on the display deck, draped the towel over the bar, and turned on the machine.

The woman on the next treadmill muttered: "Sign-up sheet!" but by that time Tasha had her earphones in place and her tape blaring traveling music. Without a glance, she pushed "faster" and the belt picked up speed. She was past the power walking stage and into the jog.

The woman next to her stepped off her machine, adjusted her turquoise unitard, and tapped Tasha's shoulder.

Tasha hit *faster*.

The woman shrugged, checked the list, and called out: "Annie, treadmill!"

To Tasha, the deceased Tasha next to me, I said, "You knew you'd cut in line, didn't you?"

"Yeah, sure. Look, I've got half an hour to be in and out of the gym. I don't have time to wait while every housewife and secretary climbs on the treadmill before me."

I shook my head. If they're not remorseful up here, where?

On the screen the turquoise-clad woman wandered off camera but we could still hear her call, "Annie, treadmill! Annie!"

On her own treadmill, the not-yet-dead Tasha ran at sprint-rate. The water bottle shimmied on the lower shelf; the magazine quivered on the display deck; with each step Tasha's knees hit the hanging towel. Sweat ran down her forehead, glistened on her shoulders, coated her back. Her legs moved faster. And faster.

She stopped pushing the *faster* button.

But the machine continued to pick up speed.

For a minute she seemed not to notice. She was running full out.

"Couldn't bring yourself to admit it was going too fast for you, huh?" I asked, unkindly.

She didn't interrupt her rapt watching to answer.

On screen she hit *slower*. The machine speeded up. Her face was red, sweat soaked her headband, poured down her back. She was panting in split-second breaths. The treadmill belt was snapping with speed. Sparks came off the sides. She couldn't keep up. Her feet fell farther and father back away from the read-out deck. She grabbed for the bar.

Missed.

Her shoelace caught under the treadmill; it knocked her forward. Her arms flailed; her head hit the bar; the Walkman and magazine flew off the display deck, onto the belt, and smacked up against her tote bag at the far end. The caught shoelace pulled her leg crooked; she grabbed again for the bar, caught the towel by mistake, dropped it, as she fell, twisting to the racing belt.

Here, the tape slowed almost to slow motion, and we watched the towel clump at the end of the belt, catching the Walkman. We watched Tasha fall, her head hit the radio, the belt thrust her face tighter and tighter into the wadded towel. She flung her arm out, trying to get purchase, but her hand fell on the slippery magazine, caught at the outer edge of the towel. The big, heavy, water bottle flew off the shelf delivering the final blow.

The women around her were staring wide-eyed. But if they had any impetus to help her the sparks flying off the machine kept them at bay.

The video tape speeded up. I had assumed it would end there. It had covered all I'd gleaned of the case, but it continued while they pulled her dead body off the machine, while an employee tried CPR as another called 911, while the medics carried Tasha out. Then the employee who had given the CPR turned to the stunned exercisers and shook her head. "We posted a sign that the machine was out of order," she said in plaintive annoyance. "It was right at the end of the treadmill. She couldn't have missed it."

"She *chose* to ignore it," a woman muttered.

"We called every treadmill 'regular,'" the employee insisted. "I phoned her office myself, early this morning. I left a message to call us." She shook her head. "She just never called back."

❧

Tasha Pierce was given her final chance to accept forgiveness for all concerned. In her case all concerned was, of course, only her.

I found myself back in the beige hallway. I stomped down it. I was only an employee, a cog in the greater set of wheels, but, dammit, I had done the work on this case and it was a petty bureaucratic move on the Sub-Authority's part to shift me out of the court room before she made her decision. Maybe my whole detecting shtick *was* just for his perverse amusement. I stomped harder, not that it had any effect on the spongy carpet.

"Raffles," I thought, trying to distract myself. "The Melbourne Hotel, a

Singapore Sling, and *The Return of Raffles*. No, just *Raffles*. What could all that have to do with me and my demise? Had I been a thief who traveled to Melbourne and Singapore? A witty, debonair Raffles-like cricketer? If so, death had really changed me.

I paced more slowly down the hall. And back again.

The Perfect Crime. Raffles, Melbourne, and Singapore.

I paced.

Perfect crime. Singapore, Melbourne Hotel, Raffles.

And back.

After the fifteenth circuit I gave up in disgust, and as much to spite the Sub-Authority as to appease myself I flung open the first forbidden door I came to.

There stands Tasha Pierce, hand on phone receiver, foot tapping.

That didn't surprised me. What startled me were the words coming from the phone: "Yes, this is the Authority's Office."

The Authority's office! No one gets through to the Authority. You don't just pick up the phone and call the Boss! If He took calls from everyone who felt they had a problem the poor Entity would be swamped. No one calls Him direct — not Popes, not Bodhisattvas, not heads of the Altar Guild.

But there is Tasha Pierce, brash as life, shouting into the receiver: "I'm being detained here. I need to speak Him right now."

"Certainly, Ms. Pierce. He's away from the altar right now, but I'll give Him your message and He'll call you right back."

"Yeah, right!" she snarls and bangs down the receiver. "I should live so long!"

It doesn't occur to Tasha Pierce that the Boss doesn't blow off supplicants. The Authority does not lie. But we all judge by our own standards.

She will, of course, fume, holler, rage until she grabs the phone and again demands to speak to Him, slams down the receiver again, stalks off again, fumes . . . eternally.

Hell hath no fury like a woman scorned, as they so sexistly say.

I shut the door on Tasha Pierce and glided slowly down the corridor. The walls seemed not so much off-white as gray, the carpet not spongy but swampy. I had failed. It wasn't my fault my investigation hadn't helped Tasha Pierce, but it hadn't helped me either. I was no closer to getting myself out of here than before. I had failed. I could picture the Sub-Authority's flabby form bent over in laughter, his pear-shaped posterior, spread across his chair as he penned a report on my transgression. How soon would he convince the Boss to shove me in the elevator and hit DOWN?

Up here there's no place to hide. I trudged on down the corridor. I was almost to the end when I realized: The Perfect Crime, in the Raffles Hotel! In Singapore!

I had died in Singapore! The perfect crime, *my* crime, had been committed in Singapore!

I half-ran half-flew to the court room lobby to find a newly dead traveler in need of a detective.

ASSORTED STORIES

There is no obvious common thread connecting these stories. Au contraire. *My preference in reading a volume of short stories is variety. So I have put these in an order that I hope will allow you to read one after the other and get a slightly different view or taste with each.*

If there is any connection, it is that these stories are the most extreme, each in its own way. "Double Jeopardy" was my first published piece and is a straightforward mystery story.

"No Safety" is the most serious; there is not a humorous thought or aside in it. "Check-out" is the most frustrated, "A Worm in the Winesap" the only time I've been asked to include a recipe with a story, and "A Surfeit of Deadline" most true to the writer's life.

Still, the real reason they are grouped here is that I thought you'd enjoy them most in this order.

This was my first story published. It was the 'first story' entry in a 1978 Ellery Queen Mystery Magazine, and was called "Death Threat." The version here is a bit filled out — the same story, but more description — and as such was in Women's Wiles, *edited by Michele Slung.*

DOUBLE JEOPARDY

"Don't give me excuses. Do it right, damn it! What do you think I'm paying you for?" Wynne slammed down the phone.

I stood in the doorway, still amazed at my sister's authority, despite the fact that she had controlled situations for nearly forty years.

Even now, lying in the hospital, she continued to play the executive. But, after all, she was the first woman in the state to have become senior vice president of a major corporation. I wondered if it was Warren, or some other harried assistant, who had felt the sting of her tongue this time.

As she looked at me, her expression changed from irritation to concern. "Lynne, why are you lurking in the doorway? You're shaking. Come in and tell me what's the matter."

I walked in, a bit unsteadily, and sat on the plastic chair next to the bed. "It happened again."

"What this time?"

I took a deep breath, holding my hands one on top of the other on my lap, trying to calm myself enough to be coherent.

The room was bare — hospital-green curtains pulled back against hospital-green walls. The flowers and plant arrangements had been sent to Wynne's apartment when she had first taken sick leave months ago, but by the time I arrived in the city, they were long dead. Funny how I hesitated to change anything in her apartment, where I, for however long it might be, was only a guest.

Wynne sat propped up on the hospital bed, her hair black and shining, not a hint of gray.

I looked at her face, at the deceptively fragile smile that had always been strong. Our features were so similar, almost exact, yet no one had ever mixed us up. And Wynne's compact body had always looked forceful where mine had merely seemed small.

She'd changed suddenly when she'd become ill. It was as if her underpinnings had been jerked loose, and she had sped past me on the way to old age.

"Lynne, I'm really worried about you," she said with an anxiety in her voice I hadn't heard in ages. "What happened?"

"Another shot. It just missed my head. If I hadn't stumbled . . ." My hands were shaking.

Wynne leaned forward and reached out with her hands to my own, steadying mine with her own calm. "Have you notified the police?"

"They're no help. They take a report and then — nothing. I don't think they believe me. Another hysterical middle-aged woman."

Wynne nodded. "Let's just go through the thing again. I'm used to handling problems — gives me something to think about when I'm on the dialysis machine."

It sounded cold, but that was the way she was now. We'd been apart since college, and emotionally longer than that. Really, I could hardly claim to know her any more. Our twin-ness had never had that special affinity — secret baby language, intuitively shared joys and apprehensions. In us, the physical resemblance had merely served to point out our very different traits. I had wound up teaching in our home-town grammar school; she, more determined and ambitious, had made her way up in the world of business.

"So?" she said impatiently.

"Someone shot at me three times. If I weren't always tripping and turning my ankle . . ."

"And you have no idea who it might be?"

"None. Who would want to kill me? Why? Really, what difference would it make if I died? Who would care?"

"It would matter to me." She pressed my hands, then drew away. "You're all I have. I wouldn't have asked you to come if you weren't vital to me."

I bit my lip. "There are things . . . I want to say before . . ." But I couldn't say, *you die*, and Wynne, for all her lack of sentimentality, didn't seem to be able to supply the words for me.

Instead, I said, "Wynne, you shouldn't cut yourself off like this."

"I have you. I need someone away from the company."

"But why? Why not let Warren come?"

"No!" She spat out the word. "I can't let him see me like this."

She looked all right to me. Better than I was likely to look if I didn't find out who was shooting at me.

Wynne must have divined my thoughts, for she said, irritably, "You don't show someone who's after your job how sick you are. I've never told any of them that I'm on the dialysis machine." She shook her head as if to dismiss the unacceptable thought. "I told them it was just one kidney that failed, that I was having it removed." Her face moved into a tenuous smile. "I know all the details from your own operation. So don't say that you never did anything for me."

I didn't know how to respond. Could Wynne really hide the fact that she was dying? Warren had been her assistant for ten years. He had taken over her job as acting senior vice president. I had assumed they were friends, but I guess I didn't understand the nature of friendship in business.

Brusquely, Wynne gestured for me to go on.

Swallowing my annoyance, I reminded myself that she was used to giving orders, and now she had no one but me to boss around.

But before I could answer, a nurse came in and with an air of authority that dwarfed even Wynne's, motioned me away as she drew the green curtain in a half-oval around the bed.

I walked to the window and looked out, but I didn't want to see the parking lot again. I didn't want to search each bush, behind every car, looking for a sniper. Instead, I turned back toward the room — this small private room, so very impersonal. Even Wynne, with all her power, hadn't the ability to stamp any image of herself onto it. It was merely a holding cell for the dying.

"Just another minute," the nurse called out.

I nodded, realizing as I did so that she couldn't see me behind the curtain.

I wondered if this room held the same horror for Wynne as it did for me. Or more? Or different? Would I ever see this mind-numbing green without thinking of the day I arrived in the city, unnerved by Wynne's sudden insistence that I come, after years of increasingly perfunctory letters. That first day. I'd sat down and she said she was dying. No, wait, not *dying*. She had never used that word. It was her doctor who said, *dying*.

It had been bright and clear that day, too. The sunlight had been cut by the Venetian blinds so that pale ribbons sliced across the green wall. And when he told me, the light merged with the green and the numbing green shone and the wall seemed to jump out at me and I couldn't focus, couldn't think about anything but the wall.

Time softens things, but that moment remained hard and bright and brittle.

"Lynne, you keep staring off in the distance. Ar you sure you're all right?" The nurse was gone. Wynne was looking at me, her lips turned up in the hint of a smile, but the eyes serious. "Are you still seeing the doctor?"

"Doctor? You mean the psychiatrist at home?"

"Yes."

"Wynne, I wasn't seeing him because I was crazy. It was just therapy. I needed some perspective."

"On?"

"Us," I answered. She looked truly surprised, and I couldn't help but feel stung to realize once more that she, who had influenced every part of my life, was so unaffected by me.

"You were saying, before the nurse came for my spit and polish, who might want to kill you? It's so hard to believe."

I shifted my mind gratefully. Still, where to begin? I was too ordinary — a middle-aged first grade teacher — to make enemies. If it had been Wynne . . .

"Well," she said, tightening her lips, "we'll have to examine the possibilities."

I shook my head. "I don't have any money, no insurance other than the teachers' association policy."

"And that goes to Michael?"

"Yes, but Michael's not going to come all the way from Los Angeles to shoot his mother so he can inherit two thousand dollars and a clapboard house."

"I didn't mean that." She looked momentarily confused, and hurt. "I was just listing the possibilities. You have to do that. You can't let sentiment stand in the way of your goal. I had to learn that long ago. There are plenty of people who have wanted me out of the way."

"But they weren't trying to *murder* you!"

She shrugged. And she watched me.

"Wynne, I'm the one they're trying to kill. No one would kill you now. What would be the pont? I mean . . ."

Her face turned white.

"Wynne, we don't have much time! Either of us. Maybe we can't find out who's shooting at me, but at least we can feel like sisters." I paused, then went on. "When you asked me to come here, after all these years, I thought you wanted to close the gap between us." I smiled, but heard my voice breaking. "Frankly, I was surprised it mattered to you. It was a shock to realize how much it mattered to me. I . . ."

Her eyes were moist. She looked away. But when she turned back there was no sign of the emotion that had passed.

Startled, I began awkwardly brushing at my hair with my hand, rather than reaching toward my sister, as I'd instinctively wanted. I forced my attention back to the question under consideration. Suppose no one did know Wynne was dying. Warren at least had been kept in the dark, or so Wynne thought. I was beginning to wonder if she had accepted it herself. "You're not working," I said. "You don't have any connection with the company now. How could *you* be a threat to anyone?"

The lines in her face hardened. "I know things. When I get out of here, I'm going back. I'll see who's been out of get me. I'll take care of them! I'm too valuable for the company to just forget."

"You what!" I stared at the green wall. Wynne had shoved the death threat to me aside, finding it of less importance than interoffice grudges. I looked at her, wondering what we really meant to each other. In many ways we were so alike. I felt helpless in the face of her bitterness.

"Who, particularly," I asked, "would want to kill you?"

"Me?"

"I mean who might mistake me for you? An old lover?"

She half-smiled, surprised. "What do you know about me?"

"Only what you've wanted me to know, like always. The lover was just a guess. After all, you're forty years old and single. There must have been men, maybe married . . ."

"You make it all rather melodramatic." She continued to look amused.

"Shooting is melodramatic!"

She didn't reply.

"What about Warren?" I persisted. "Would he kill to keep your job? Would he mistake me for you?"

She looked at me in amazement, as if the possibility was too fantastic to believe. "Lynne, anyone — Warren in particular — who would take the trouble and risk involved in murder, would be a bit more careful than that."

"Maybe they don't know you have an identical twin?"

She sighed, her jaw settling back in a tired frown. "They know. When you've held as important a position as I have, believe me, they know." She paused, then added, "But if you really think that someone is mistaking you for me, maybe you should move out of my apartment. Take a hotel room. I'll pay for it, of course."

I shook my head.

Fingering the phone, she said, "Lynne, you haven't made much of a case for this death threat. I don't want to sound unsympathetic, but the truth is that you've always leaned on me. Are you sure that this death thing isn't just a reaction to my own condition? It does happen in twins."

"I think not," I snapped, finally exasperated. "I've been through years of therapy. Our bodies may be identical, but my mind is all my own."

She sat silent.

The awkwardness grew. "Listen Wynne, I know you've got business to take care of. I interrupted your phone call when I came in. I'll see you tomorrow."

She nodded, a tiredness showing in her eyes. But I wasn't out of the room before she picked up the phone.

As I walked down the hall, I thought again, what an amazing person she was. Dying from kidney failure, and she was still barking at subordinates. I wondered about Warren — did he allow her to run things from her hospital room? Did he believe Wynne's story about her condition? Could he think I was she, coming in for treatment? Not likely. If Warren were anything like Wynne, by now he would have a solid grip on the vice presidency. He would have removed any trace of Wynne, and she'd have to fight *him* for the job.

Still, I stopped by the door, afraid to go out.

If Wynne wasn't giving orders to Warren or some other subordinate, who was she yelling at? "What do you think I'm paying you for?" she had demanded.

She wasn't paying anyone at the company. She wasn't paying any expenses — I was handling those. There was nothing she needed.

Or was there?

My hand went around back to my remaining kidney.

This is the last of the stories I think of as 'early ones', along with "Double Jeopardy," "A Burning Issue" and "Hit-and-Run." I rarely use San Francisco as a setting. But in "No Safety," the San Francisco of the times is as important an element as Berkeley would become for me later.

NO SAFETY

Jeremy Coughlin should have known. It was the one thing upon which everyone involved agreed.

When he was seven, Jeremy saw his father shot. An attempted hold-up. Only momentarily did he think his father dead. He stared in horror, disbelief. And for the first time he felt a hollow sense of loss. Years later he would be able to describe it as feeling like all the air had been sucked out of his chest and his ribs were about to burst inward. But the seven-year-old just stared at the gun with hatred.

Determined to make the world more peaceful for any son he might have, Jeremy became a pacifist, one of the few who achieved legal status during the Vietnam War. He spent those years sweeping the floors in Agnews State Hospital, walking softly on the violent wards, sitting softly with those patients whose depression robbed them of vitality and visitors, patients whose conversations wandered in sharp cornered circles, and had no point other than to try to reclaim a tenuous connection with the human race. Jeremy sat on the cold metal folding chairs, forcing himself to listen as the disjointed words tumbled out, the laughter, the screeches that accompanied them unconnected with their meaning. When he could no longer give credence to the words, he could *appear* to listen, to provide the illusion of the bond the patients sought. He was good at it.

The early seventies came. A good time to be in San Francisco. A good time to marry, to rent the first floor of a Victorian in the Haight, half a block from the Panhandle of Golden Gate Park.

He and Anne sat on their garage sale wicker sofa, in those days, their feet on the sill of the open bay windows. They smoked a joint and watched the pony-tailed man in a tie-dyed T-shirt, the woman in an ankle-length Indian skirt, and the blond toddler with the star-shaped birthmark above his temple, as they jumped down from their crimson and purple converted school bus across the street and meandered along the broad sidewalk toward the lazy twang of the guitars in the Panhandle. Sometimes after a second joint he and Anne followed them onto the green strip of the Panhandle. He sprawled against the thick trunk of a eucalyptus, letting the music flow through him like Pacific waves. The acrid smell of marijuana mixed with the tang of the eucalyptus. And in those moments he could believe that he belonged there in the narrow green land of the lotus eaters.

Or almost believe. Ah, to climb on that crimson bus and leap down wherever it stopped! To have no plans past the next song. To never have to sing a chorus!

He felt that familiar hollowness inside his rib cage. The freedom of the bus family cost more than he could afford. Jeremy ran the hose over the soapy top of his Volkswagen and watched the white water erase the muddy marks of their bare feet on the sidewalk. He never could be one of them. But he could talk to them, listen to them, and he could go with them when they battled the welfare or the health department or the police. He could make life more peaceful for them and their children. He could be their advocate. Yes, Advocates of Peace would stand with them.

With the years, the flowers wilted in their hair; mellow warped to manic. The San Francisco winters became grayer, colder, the rain more leaden. Those who would protect the innocents were replaced by the keepers of the purse. The posters from peace demonstrations frayed; he taped them back together. Once or twice a year the crimson and purple converted school bus turned up across the street from the Coughlins' house, its festive colors ever dingier. The soapy stream from the Volkswagen hood washed over bare feet that walked woodenly beneath drug-vacant eyes.

But Jeremy's dreams of peace and justice were not washed away with it. As the government moved to the right, he, in the name of Advocates of Peace, became stronger. With that same feeling he had sitting on the cold metal chairs in Agnews or leaning against the eucalyptus in the Panhandle, Jeremy listened to the stories of men whose eyes no longer focused and convinced them that he understood. And when he sat on a hard wooden chair, presenting his proposals for those needs to the mayor's aide, he let his tie and jacket speak of his commitment to The City.

Demonstrations outside city hall edged into violence; Jeremy Coughlin was called to mediate. Representatives of fledgling groups asked his advice.

The chairman of the Mayor's Subcommittee on Individual Rights sold out, and was forced out. MSIR needed a man of integrity, a man of peace.

As Jeremy pulled a metal chair up to the long table, he scanned the committee members, representatives of street people, the homeless, the drug burnouts. In the audience, he spotted the family from the crimson and purple bus. Gone were their bright clothes, their easy smiles, the buoyant freedom Jeremy had envied. They looked like ice-sculptures slightly melted. The boy, eight or nine now, was no longer blond, but that star-shaped birthmark was still discernible. Only he responded to Jeremy's smile. Behind the table were the mayor's aide, a sheriff, a police sergeant. And between the groups, himself. How had *he* gotten here, he wondered. But as he looked out into the audience, at the family, as he called the meeting to order, that hollow feeling in his rib cage dissipated, and *the chairman* began to speak. By ten p.m., he had achieved consensus. On a small point, admittedly, but consensus nevertheless.

Amazed at his magical achievement — a miracle of peaceful agreement, the mayor's aide called it — he shook hands with the city reps., pressed hands with the street group reps. He looked for the family, suddenly anxious to share this moment with them, but they were gone — back to their crimson and purple bus parked on another street in the city, no doubt. Perhaps tomorrow it would be across from his own house again. He called goodbye to a priest from the Council of Churches. Then, still buoyant, he drove to the beach.

There were no stars in the January sky. Fog rested on the hills and caught on the tall bolls of the sequoias and the fronds of the date palms. Like a soaked goose-down comforter, it sagged onto the beach, creating a charcoal gray unity of air, wet sand, and Pacific whitecaps. Only the most desperate of the homeless or the deranged huddled on the far reaches of the beach, against the thick cement wall. At night only the foolish walked alone, close enough to hear the breakers splat onto the sand.

No other time would Jeremy Coughlin have considered it. But tonight he felt as powerful as the breaking waves, the icy blanket of fog his protective shield. He skirted close to the water, letting the salty spray hit his ankles, stepping gently as if to avoid being jolted back to the reality of himself. He relived the events of the evening more with wonder than pride.

Only when the fog had seeped into his clothes and penetrated his skin did he start back across the beach, moving quickly now, before that familiar hollowness inside his rib cage could catch him.

The gun was near the cement wall. The streetlight shone on its black barrel as it lay half concealed by sand. He glanced at the men and women huddled a hundred yards down along the wall. He couldn't leave that gun here for one of them to find. He picked it up.

Later, he would agree that he should have known then.

He held the gun in the light, staring meditatively at the long thin barrel, at the wooden stock with the cross-hatch marks, at the S and W cut into the metal above the trigger. The cold black metal stung his fingers. He closed his hands around the stock. The gun looked surprisingly delicate, not like the fire-spitting handguns on the cop shows his daughter Meggie had become enamored of. It seemed quite odd that this gun, with its crafted wooden stock, should be an instrument of such violence.

Pocketing it, he headed home. He would drop it at the police station in the morning. It probably wasn't even loaded. But he felt an odd attachment to it, as if it were a commemorative symbol of his evening's triumph. He smiled at the levels to which fantasy had taken him.

But he wasn't illogical enough to take the gun in the house, not with Meggie there. He'd leave it in the old empty tool box, locked. He closed the garage door, turned on the light and opened the tool box. Then he pulled the gun out. Sand still clung to one side. There was sand on his hands. Here in the light, the gun seemed shorter, thicker, more powerful. Not the delicate imposter it had before. More manageable. He felt a shiver flow down his spine as he touched it, this manifestation of the violence he had fought against, and that shiver filled the hollow within him. Tomorrow he would leave it at the police station.

"You're late," Anne called as he walked in.

"The meeting time ran over, but it was worth it. We're onto a new kind of working here. We formed a consensus."

"You brought those guys together? Hey, kiddo," she said, flinging her arms around his neck, "you know, you really are something." Her kiss silenced his protest, and he let himself feel the warmth of her body against him, and the warmth of the illusion she believed, the fullness he still held.

After they were in bed, as he lay listening for that moment when her shallow breath sunk into the deep, husky exhalations of sleep, he remembered the gun, and thought how odd it was that he had forgotten to mention it to her. Perhaps that was the moment when he should have known.

The weekend came before he realized he'd forgotten to take the gun to the police station. By then, it was too late; he couldn't do it without answering lot of questions he didn't have answers for. Who owned the gun? Had it been stolen? Used in a crime? He closed the garage door, unlocked the tool box, and lifted the gun out. The sand had dried. It flitted away at his touch. He checked the bullets. There were only three. Had the others been shot at a hold-up victim like his father? Had they been pumped into the heart of an errant wife? Or had they been aimed at empty chili cans on a fence? What kind of person had owned this gun? He stared down at the gun, and at his sandy palm. But neither gave an answer. He put the gun back in the tool box, locked it, and hung the key back under the work bench.

"Police Raid Abandoned Building in the Haight.   Thirty Squatters Evicted," the headlines proclaimed.

"Free Needle Clinic Picketed."

"Disabled Demonstrate for Bus Access."

Advocates of Peace thrived. Jeremy found himself on call day and night. He rushed through the garage to the car, ever almost late for an appearance before the Board of Supervisors, to give a workshop on peaceful disagreement, or chair a meeting between the university hospital directors and the neighbors whose land they coveted. At one a.m. or two, more nights than not, he drove back in, too tired to worry whether the bond he created was real or another illusion, too tired to deal with the nagging hollow feeling. He patted the old tool box as he passed. The intention of turning in the gun had faded. There was no reason for him not to have it. He wasn't going to shoot someone with it. No danger of that. He rarely had time to take it out of the box.

And yet, it was there in his mind. He wondered how it would feel in his shooting hand. He tried to imagine what his father's assailant had felt as his pointed his gun. Sometimes, when Jeremy stopped home between afternoon meetings, when Anne was out, he stood in the garage and held the gun. He flicked the safety on and twirled the revolver like an Old West gun fighter, all the time listening for footsteps, afraid his foolishness would be seen. But Anne never caught him. Only Meggie saw him. And she was delighted.

He found himself zeroing in on the handguns on Meggie's detective shows. Did Rockford, or Rick and A.J. Simon use a Smith and Wesson like his? He watched the detectives' moves, the way Rockford shot through the open window of his truck, or Cagney and Lacy braced their feet and held their guns out with a two-handed grip.

Meggie liked the company, and Anne was relieved that he hadn't refused the girl permission to watch her shows. "Who am I to imagine I can control a twelve year-old mind?" he'd asked, laughing. "After all, I can't make her the one kid in the sixth grade to watch only Masterpiece Theater." And he had to admit, it was interesting to see how the private eyes viewed life. He found, to his surprise, that he could understand them. As an advocate, it was important for him to understand.

After a while he rarely looked at the gun. He rarely unlocked the tool box at all. When he wandered down the stairs from the dining room into the garage, it was to get in the car, or more rarely to wash it.

❖

The August fog was just beginning to roll in when he drove the old Volkswagen out onto the sidewalk and headed back into the garage for the hose and bucket.

He could have taken the car to a wash or even hired someone. But there was a reassuring certainty to rubbing the soapy water over each section of faded metal. No magic here; half a cup of soap, two gallons of water, and forty-five minutes of soaping and hosing down invariably yielded dirt-free red paint and shining chrome.

He was soaping the hood when a hand hit his shoulder. "Hey, man, get your fucking car out of the way!" The guy wasn't big. Neither were the other two. He'd seen them ambling along Haight Street before. One time they'd been banging angrily on the crimson and purple bus. Their eyes stared vacantly now, their fingers flitted as if they were working invisible cat's cradles.

Slowly, Jeremy put down the bucket. "I'm almost done," he said in the peaceful tone that had become his trademark.

"Almost! Bullshit!"

"I just need to rinse the soap off the hood. Otherwise, it'll be a sticky mess."

"Bullshit!" The speaker lurched toward him.

Behind him he heard Anne's panicked call, "Jer!" He grabbed the hose, and aimed it at the three. "Beat it!" he yelled. They stared, looking more surprised than angered, as if the water had washed away the last few minutes. Shivering in the afternoon wind, they moved on.

Still holding the hose, Jeremy turned. Anne stood, arm around Meggie's shoulder. "Are you okay, Jeremy?"

"Yeah," he said. "Sure."

"You showed 'em, huh, Daddy?" Meggie pulled free.

"Yeah," he said, looking back at Anne. "Don't let them upset you, Hon."

"It's not them," she said slowly. "I've never seen you react like that."

He nodded slowly. "Odd, isn't it? You know, I could have talked them down. That's my specialty. And these guys, they weren't hard cases. I could have done it. I just didn't. Of course, they didn't know my vaunted reputation. Alas, a prophet gets no honor on own his soapy sidewalk." He shrugged; glancing into the garage, he said, "On the other hand, I didn't wave a gun at them."

Meggie opened her mouth, then slammed it shut. But not soon enough.

He hesitated, then said, "Out of here, you two. I've got a soapy hood to deal with."

But he wasn't surprised to find Anne in the garage when he finished. And he wasn't surprised when she demanded, "What's this gun business?"

He hesitated only momentarily before getting the key from the under the work bench, and opening the tool box. "I found it on the beach."

Silently, she stared at it, waiting for the rest of the story. And when he had finished, she asked, "You are an Advocate of *Peace*. Why have you kept this weapon?"

"I don't know. I'll never use it. But, there's something comforting about having it down here. It's like the ocean. We'll never swim in it, but it's good to know it's there."

"Jeremy, get that gun out of here!"

He put it back in the box, and locked it.

Her voice was high and brittle. "If you don't get rid of it, I will. We have a child to consider."

"I am considering her. I want her to be safe. The neighborhood isn't what it used to be. Those guys weren't bussed in here, you know. We've already had two robberies."

"Break-ins, you called them then," she insisted, her voice quivering. "They didn't take much. You said yourself it was probably kids."

"Still —"

"Still, what? You'd rather have shot them?"

His breath caught. For a moment he stood staring at her taut, pale face, and the fearful hunch of her thin shoulders. "I wouldn't shoot anyone. You know that. I've never considered using the gun. I don't even think of it as a weapon. It's more like a talisman."

"The police have no-questions-asked turn-in days."

He nodded. "Okay. You're right. You know," he said, looking back at the sidewalk, "those guys, I could have talked them down. I just didn't bother."

Anne patted his shoulder.

He should have known then. Anyone would have. He should have gotten rid of the gun. Anyone would have.

❖

The burglar didn't come till spring. Jeremy never knew how he got in. He was just there, in the back of the dining room when Jeremy brought Meggie home that Saturday night. The boy must have been so nervous, so drugged up that he hadn't heard, or didn't compute the garage door opening, the car pulling in, hadn't heard Jeremy's feet on the stairs, didn't notice the door sliding back into the wall. Jeremy was halfway through the door to the dining room when he spotted him.

"Hey!" he yelled. "What are you doing?"

The boy spun toward him. He was only a couple years older than Meggie, maybe fifteen, but big, with long, wild hair. His eyes were pinpoints, his skin pimpled. He reached in his pocket and pulled out a knife.

Jeremy stepped through the door, shoved Meggie back and slid the door shut. He took a slow step forward, his eyes never leaving the boy's face. He could see the boy fighting to concentrate; he could see the panic that that losing battle brought. Jeremy felt his body tense. He didn't have a hose this time. And the gun? No time to slide the door open, run downstairs, snatch the key, unlock the box, and get it.

He looked back at the boy, seeing not the street-tough facade but the adolescent fear beneath. And the hollowness when the facade hangs too loose.

The boy planted his feet, tightened his grip on the knife. "You got a kid. I can cut her."

Jeremy's breath caught. He didn't need the gun, he told himself. The boy's talk was bravado. The boy would be glad to have his decisions made for him. He was just a boy. Using the peaceful voice that had worked so well, so often, he said, "Nothing has happened yet. I'd like you to leave now. The door is past me, to your left. You'll need to turn the dead bolt first, then the knob."

Sweat covered the boy's face. His T-shirt clung to his chest. His fingers tightened on the knife.

Jeremy watched him, feeling that familiar sensation of hollowness.

The boy took a step forward. "Give me your money, man."

Jeremy nodded. "My wallet is in my back pocket. I'm reaching for it." Slowly he extricated it, and slid it across the floor.

The boy picked it up, yanked out the cash and stuck it in his pocket. With a toss of the head, he flung his hair out of his face. And Jeremy spotted the starshaped birth mark.

Jeremy reached toward him.

"Hey, get back!"

"You used to live in the converted school bus. Your folks parked it right across the street a couple times a year, for years. I've seen you around since you were a toddler, a little blond toddler going down to the Panhandle with your parents to listen to the guitars. Remember?"

The boy's hand tightened on the hilt of the knife. Panic was clear in his eyes. "You're making a mistake, man. You don't know me."

The words, the look seemed to ricochet off the inside of Jeremy's rib cage. How could he have made such a dumb move? He had been distracted, thinking of the gun.

He thought he knew then. And the swirling fear within him scratched against his brittle facade. All these years? What had his work been for? This was the boy for whom he was going to make life better.

The boy looked around at the television, the VCR, the computer. But he made no move toward them.

Jeremy forced himself to concentrate. In his own hollowness, he could read the boy, see his indecision. "A lot of trouble," he said, surprised at the calm of his voice, "when you can just walk past me and on out."

The boy hesitated. Then he turned toward the door. Jeremy sighed; he had won. He hadn't saved this boy, but he hadn't lost him either. The boy could be okay. He could help him. The swirling slowed, and he felt solid.

The boy started forward, carefully keeping a distance between himself and Jeremy as he neared the doorway.

The shot resounded through the room. The boy grabbed his chest. The second shot was louder. And the third louder yet. The room smelled of burning. The boy's eyes opened wide. Then he dropped to the floor, on his side. The starshaped birthmark lipstick red against his bloodless skin.

Jeremy turned slowly around. Meggie stood on the step beneath him, feet braced apart, the gun held in both hands, in front of her.

The hollowness in his rib cage burst through his skin. It encompassed Meggie, and the boy, and the room.

And then he did know. But it no longer mattered.

This story brings together two themes that run through my many of my stories: personal faults, the afterlife. It provided me a great deal of pleasure-in-grumbling as I wrote it, and I was delighted when it was awarded both the Anthony and the Macavity.

CHECK-OUT

There's probably not one of you who doesn't have some expectations of the afterlife. Some of you ponder it more than others, of course. But I'll bet most of you are like me: you think of eternity as little as possible, and never as a reality. And yet, even you, if pressed, would come up with some picture of it.

But few of you would have the right one. I sure didn't.

Let me backtrack here, so you know who you're dealing with. I had no particular religious attachments — I'd flirted with a lot, in an academic sort of way, so if indeed there were many mansions in Heaven, I could have described a lot of the rooms (like a post-mortem version of one of those tacky vacation inns with the Beethoven Bath, the Schubert Suite, the Liberace Lounge.) I wouldn't have been surprised to come across a newly painted white hallway with a bright light at the end and a helluva suction. A clutch of departed Tibetan monks ready to lead me on a side tour through the Bardo of the Book of the Dead for forty days before dispatching me into my next incarnation would have given me little more than a moment's surprise. Finding nothing at all wouldn't have shocked me . (Well, really, how could it? What would it have shocked?)

I had considered and altogether dismissed any Final Judgment — sheep baa-ing smugly at disgruntled goats.

Even so, had I discovered myself eye-to-eye with Saint Peter, I would have been prepared to become wing-to-wing with the heavenly host, or fork-to-pitchfork with guys advertising ham spread. Cartoon heaven, I understood. But I never, ever expected this.

Dead. I was definitely dead. And where was I? No white hallway, no glowing Saint, wizened monk, or prodding devil. I couldn't make out my surroundings at all. I didn't know where I was, but what I was doing was standing in line. Standing in line, of all miserable things. I could have done that alive. I *had* done that alive. It had driven me crazy, queuing up in the bank behind ten other people, squatting down, checkbook on knee, trying to fill out the deposit slip with each check number and amount. All the time I'd be watching for the line to move, and when it did I'd madly scoop up my half-done checks, and duck-walk forward trying to keep the checks from flying (not to say bouncing) all over the bank. I'd perform the whole thigh-killing gymnastic exercise to avoid standing blankly in the line for half an hour with two thoughts slapping at me: not only was I wasting time here (1), but (2) I'd shot ten minutes before I got here writing out those checks.

But forewarned is not forearmed. If I had ten checks the line moved like lightning and I got to the window with every one unsigned and unnumbered and the teller silently berating me for holding up the line. (I never stopped to consider what the people behind me thought. I'll bet they could have killed me.)

Killed me? Had they dispatched me into the Brinks funeral cortege? I was, after all dead. But you don't die because you delay the bank line. If you did CitiCorp would put in a mortuary next to the vault.

In any case I didn't want to waste time pondering how I died. Dead was dead. And I had more pressing problems: these damned lines.

Lines! Lines everywhere! I really did hate waiting in line. And not only in the bank. But the airport. All flights east from California leave at 7:00 a.m., as if there were one big gust of air per day off the Pacific. How many sag-eyed 6:15 a.m.'s have I spent behind thirty people accompanied by suitcases with wheels, pull straps and expandable sections in all directions. They had backpacks, shoe racks, cloth sacks, kiddie strollers, bags of crullers, giant umbrellas. And three carry-ons apiece, each the size of a moose. And every single item was without the name and address labels the agent insisted they spend five extra minutes filling out. They inched forward to the two ticket counters, herding their luggage like flocks of sheep that multiplied as they moved. Our communal 7:00 a.m. departures grew closer. Behind me travelers pressed in tighter, as if at the moment of truth proximity to the counter would count. Ahead of me the Bo Peeps, tickets between teeth, thrust their heads at the airline clerks, and when he'd pulled the sodden tickets free, insisted the entirety of their luggage would fit in the overhead compartments, demanded window seats and a list of the nightshades and crucifers in the vegetarian meals. "Every seat lands at the same time," I told them, perhaps a mite more curtly than I intended. If they'd paid attention and moved along, they wouldn't have forced me to actual rudeness. But did they ever appreciate my good sense and concern about expediting everyone's wait? Not hardly.

I know some of them could have killed me; they told me so.

I paused again. I had tickets for New York in my purse right now. Had I died at the airport? But no, no matter how irrational the rest of those travelers were, they weren't likely to miss their planes just for the satisfaction of offing me. Even if it would have meant freeing up a window seat and a special fish plate lunch. No, much as they might have liked, they hadn't done me in and tossed me on the luggage conveyer to eternity.

Anyway, no point in worrying about that now. I didn't care how I died. What I wanted was to get out of this damned line. Lines, always lines; lines, life's penultimate example of stillness in motion.

The airport is bad, okay, but it's nothing to the true Purgatory: the California freeway. How many hours had I spent waiting in line just to get *on* the freeway, standing behind car after bus after truck, waiting for that red light to turn green and admit the next vehicle to the slow lane? Enough people to populate Albania were driving on my freeway, and there was no need for them to be there! They weren't all going to work. Why couldn't those non-9-to-5'ers show a little consideration and stay home at rush hour? They had the whole rest of the day to dawdle on the road. It was bad enough to find the freeway jammed; I'd gotten used to that. I'd learned to force my way into traffic; it was a sport of sorts, eyeing the line of cars, "making" the drivers by how slowly they hit the gas, how far they dragged behind the car in front, how much wax and chrome adorned their own vehicle, and how much they'd give up to keep from getting it scraped. Before they could blow their horns I'd spot the weak link and cut in front with half an inch to spare and brakes squealing. And I'd heard enough hollers, seen enough clenched fists, and digital birds flying to know what those weak links would like to have done to me.

Could I have been driving to the airport when I died? Rush hour starts before dawn on these freeways. Had I misjudged and cut in front of a truck without brakes or a lunatic with a rifle? But no. If there's one thing you can count on in rush hour — no one's going fast enough to rear end you into the hereafter. And freeway snipers don't snipe when they'll be stuck next to your corpse in traffic. No, indeed, my funeral cortege was not a first-gear-only affair in the diamond lane to Judgment.

Why was this question nagging me? It was like having a chatterer right behind you in line — one of those infuriatingly cheerful people who was sure everyone was doing their very best and there was a good reason why we were kept waiting. I silenced the thought with the same icy stare with which I'd squelched them.

But neither the bank nor the freeway held the line I hated most. I took a breath and listened. The air was chilly. I wished I'd died with a sweater on. My feet hurt. Why couldn't I have died in running shoes, or even sandals? It was like I'd just rushed here on the spur of the moment and stumbled onto line. I hadn't expected it to turn out to be *this* line. I couldn't quite make out the surroundings. Undertakers don't bury you with your glasses on, so in the hereafter reality is a bit fuzzy. Music I couldn't quite place played in the distance. I strained to hear, but the melody was too bland to register. Then it stopped, and a voice said over the loudspeaker, "Attention shoppers."

Oh no, I was in the most infuriating line of all, the *9 items or less* line in the supermarket! Nine items to eternity! The loudspeaker still slapped at my ears but I blocked out its words, a skill I'd mastered in life. Instead I focused on the mob in front of me. Clearly, this was not the Lucky's Markets of eternity where they'd open a new line if more than four people were waiting. There were at least 12 people ahead of me, and some of them were not holding little plastic baskets, but leaning on full-sized grocery carts. Fuzzy-eyed or not, even I could tell there were more than nine items in those carts. I glared at the miscreants. Would there never be justice? How many times had I called for a bolt of lightning to crash down and strike gluttons just like these with 10 different edibles in their carts! (Were we too high up for lightning now? Not yet. And I was not likely to be unless long-suffering was the Heavenly criteria.) The check-out clerks know when customers plunk 10 items on the counter. You'd think they'd send them packing to the full-cart line. If those gluttons got tossed out a couple times, they'd learn. Which was just what I told a few of them (the ones I couldn't shame out of line. A good, loud voice can pique humiliation in the most callous lout, and the rest of the cowards in line behind are willing enough to form a chorus once they know they're not in danger.) The shamed louts sputtered; they glared; a couple have even waited for me outside —

Surely, I wasn't murdered there, not in the supermarket — and dispatched in a cortege of grocery carts. But no, the louts wouldn't have dared, not in public, not and take the chance of someone walking off with their groceries.

Dammit, why did my mind keep coming back to that useless question? My foot was tapping, my blood boiling as it had so many times in lines just like this. There was nothing to do but stand and fume. And glance through the magazines and stick them back in the wrong holders. It had always pleased me, I remembered, to page through those periodicals for free. And here, to my left, was a copy of *Time* (*IS UP*). It looked just like old earth's *Time*. How many copies had I fingered through, glancing at the articles, checking the letters for well-known names, looking at the Milestones to see who had married, given birth, or died. Died!

I gave up. I sighed mightily and turned to the Milestone page and, skipping the happy occasions, moved right to the deaths.

I don't know what made me think I'd find my own passing there. I wasn't famous. But, in fact there it was: DEATHS: Ann Thompson, 42. That was all! No mention of what I'd done in life to qualify for an obituary there (well, obituary was overstating it) and more irritating yet, it didn't say how I died.

I slapped the *Time* (*IS UP*) back in the rack in front of a stack of (*DEAD*) *People*. Well, dammit, how did I die?

I pulled free a copy of *Life* (*NO MORE*) and turned to the index. Ignoring articles on "Pestilence, familiar and unexpected," "Plague, the common scourge," "War, tried and true," "Famine, the familiar favorite," I came upon one headed "New service at Final Check-out. p. 45."

When I turned to p. 45 I almost stumbled back into the cart behind me. Page 45 and 46, the centerfold, sported a picture of this store, this checkout counter, this very line I was in. And me in it! I turned to the next page. "Shoppers, are no longer surprised to find new services available at the check-out," it proclaimed in big, black letters. "They've long since become used to price scanners, check cashing, and charging their goods on credit. But never before have they been as eager to be rung up and handed their receipt! And why? Because it's not the receipt they're used to. It's a new, exciting game your grocery is offering just for you, our valued customer. A game so engrossing it's heart-stopping! Just guess the answer at check-out and you walk away free and clear. (Free and clear, indeed. I understood what that meant, in the eternal sense.)

And if I failed to answer the question? But of course, in true marketing fashion, they didn't spell that out.

They also didn't spell out what was the question to be answered. But I could guess.

I picked up a copy of *Conde Nast Traveler* (*STYX RIVER SPECIAL*). This time I didn't have to consult the index. The cover article was "How did you Die? Win a free trip to Heaven." As quickly as possible I scanned the rules. (Why hadn't I worn contact lenses; the undertaker might have slipped up and buried me in those.)

"Present your check-out clerk with one item and one item only. You have the whole market to choose from."

"What do they want, one carton of milk or gallon of ice cream to signify how I died?" I demanded of the crowd in front of me. But the line that had been twelve somnolent slugs had suddenly dwindled to four beavers busily organizing their few items on the conveyor belt. They didn't have time to be bothered with me.

And I certainly didn't have time to waste on them. Frantically, I looked around for some clue. How had I died? What could possibly symbolize that? A knife from the cutlery department? A pack of cigarettes (even though I didn't smoke)? The aerosol hair spray from the display behind me? A can of cherry cola — that was as close to poison as I could think of.

How could I possibly choose if I didn't even know how I died? Dammit, this was like every contest I'd ever entered — astronomical odds and no way to beat them. Just like the lines — once you queue up, they've got you. Then they don't care how long you cool your heels.

Furiously, I looked around. My eyes lighted on a copy of *Country (NO LONGER) Living*. I open it to a picture of the road — a two-laner in the wine country. And on it was me. The page before was also me, three pictures of me. Me having had to wait for a table for brunch at the Tortoise Winery; me drumming my fingers while the waitress made her eleventh trip to the kitchen before she brought out my Mimosa and Eggs Mercury, me slamming in my chair and stamping my foot till she finally brought the bill. The caption said: "Already half an hour late. Can make up the time on the way back to the city."

I stared at the picture of the country road. The two lane road.

There were only three people ahead of me in the check-out line now. Had this still been life, my two predecessors would have had twenty-seven items each; they would have insisted on paying with out-of-state, third-party checks; they'd have scratched their heads, stroked their chins and pondered the earth-shaking question: paper or plastic. The man in the business suit would have looked over his array of currency and finally settled on the hundred dollar bill that would force the clerk to get change from the next aisle. The woman with the purse the size of a watermelon would have poured every last coin into her palms and begun sorting out pennies, counting them, trying to figure out how many she could get rid of here, all the time explaining to the clerk the curse of carrying around too many copper coins. Now, the one time I would have welcomed any of those maneuvers, the man in the business suit slid his credit card through the slot, grabbed his bagged food, and loped into the parking lot.

That left me only two people ahead, and the picture of the country road in my mind. The two lane road nearing the intersection. The intersection with the last four-way stop sign between me and the city.

Suddenly the minute of my death was clear. The intersection was a meeting with another two-laned road. As I neared it, I could see the cortege moving forward. I could see the beginning but not the end. The damned funeral line extended to eternity. And those corteges never let anyone through, as if their getting to the cemetery late would hold up the corpse. If I stopped I'd be here forever. But the stop was a *four-way* stop. I stepped on the gas. A four-way stop is a fools's stop. Four people stop; they sit; they wait. No sense in that, especially not when you're in a hurry. And with liveried drivers like the hearse driver too many traffic tickets mean unemployment — they obey the laws. Some might have said I'd be cutting it close (some of my former passengers) but I knew there was plenty of time.

The woman with the watermelon purse smiled at the clerk and held out exact change. There was only one person between me and the final check-out. I didn't have time to reminisce about my demise. I had to choose the symbol.

I needed to think, but there was no time. Flinging the magazine down, I raced out of line — I could always cut back in — but I knew if my turn came and I missed it that was it for this line, and for me. There would be no chance to stare down the timids behind me and demand to cut back in. And I certainly couldn't go to the end of the line — no such luck this time.

I raced past the aerosol display behind, ignoring the pictures of cheery green turtles with shiny, lacquered shells, past the deli counter where the egg salad had been laid out longer than I had, and skidded to a stop at to the meat counter. There was a special on hamburger. People were lined up three deep for it, blocking access to every other item in the cooler. Was hamburger somehow the answer? Was that why they were all here?

I shoved forward, pushing past lamb chops, pork roasts, filet of flounder. Panic grabbed me; I began to sweat. This was a very ordinary supermarket. Maybe they wouldn't even have my item.

But no, there it was. I grabbed, shoved, raced, and plopped it on the counter just as the clerk was about to set my basket, my empty basket, aside.

"Fowl," the check-out machine read.

The clerk looked at me questioningly. "Are you sure? We've got a special on —"

I hesitated, seeing the rest of my penultimate moment of life. The two lane road. The four-way stop. My foot moving toward the brake then hitting the gas. I'd been in the intersection before I remembered that funeral corteges don't stop for red lights or stop signs. Before I realized how big a hearse was, I'd been spinning out of control. My car was splintering before I realized how flimsy it, and I was.

She who hesitates is last. I stared down at my item on the counter. I'd made my choice, there was no time to second guess now. "Sure." I ran my credit card through the scanner.

The clerk punched in the code.

I looked down at my item. It was dead as me. It didn't even quack. After all, when that hearse hit I'd been a dead duck.

The check-out buzzer blared.

The clerk shook his head. "I'm sorry, Ma'am, your card has been rejected."

Panic filled me. "Rejected? What do you mean rejected? A dead duck, what's more appropriate than that?"

The clerk looked down at me with the scorn he might have shown a shoplifter. "A dead duck, indeed. Rather banal, don't you think? You could have come up with the right answer — you could have won — if you just taken the time to look around — if you hadn't been in such a hurry."

From the customers behind me came a murmur of agreement.

Chiding is never pleasant, and decidedly less so at a time like this.

"Shall I show her the right answer?"

The murmur grew louder.

The clerk stepped around the register and took three steps behind me, and plucked from the display of smiling, shiny tortoises a cylindrical can with a plastic snap on lid. I looked at it in bewildered disgust. "Hair spray?"

The clerk shrugged, displaying his disbelief and disdain. "Hare spray."

"Hare spray!" I screamed. "Splattered like a dead rabbit, is that what you mean? The tortoise and the hare? I can't believe my whole eternity depends on a silly pun!"

Behind me the glossy, grinning turtles stretched their glossy green necks and smelled the roses. The clerk nodded and smiled.

"Talk about banal!" I yelled. " 'Tortoise and the hare!' 'Stop and smell the roses!"

Furious, I grabbed for his throat, but the clerk and the counter disappeared and I found myself at the tail end of a long snaking line. I was ranting at, grabbing for the ghostly customer in front of me.

Exhausted, I let my hand drop. It was too hot for such histrionics. Better I should see what this line was for.

"Take a number, please," the loudspeaker demanded.

I reached up to the dispenser beside me and pulled loose 100. I was an expert on lines; I knew how to handle this. Now that I had my number I could relax and see what we were waiting for in this line. I stretched my head forward (like the damned turtles), but the sign was so far away I could barely see. The whole place was steamy hot. Already my "100" slip was getting damp in my hand. I stretched as far forward as I could, and squinted. Now I could make out the sign: *99 Fans for Sale.*

When Nancy Pickard asked for a story for her anthology, Mom, Apple Pie, and Murder, *I wanted to include all three in a story. And so I have 'modernized' this family and their problems. The recipe was part of the deal.*

A WORM IN THE WINESAP

"*Whopper Rooter: We shoot your wad.* Good morning."

"It's afternoon, and hardly good."

"What's your problem, clogged pipe?" There was a sudden pause, then the dispatcher asked, "Is this Eve, again?"

Eve groaned into the phone. It was not a good sign, being on a first name basis with the sewer rooter men. "Yes, it's Eve. The whole system's clogged. Send out the big truck."

"Eve in Eden Township, right?"

"Right. Your guys know the way. Hurry."

"We'll get someone out as soon as possible. At least now" — the dispatcher paused and before he could control his snicker sufficiently to go on, she guessed what was coming — "At least you don't have to worry about a flood!"

She hung up. She would have slumped down on the couch if she hadn't already been sprawled there, a brown shepherd pup at her feet, a tan shepherd pup wedged between her shoulder and the sofa back, chewing contentedly on the cushion. Eve gazed at her Whopper Rooter Club card — all ten holes punched. Who would have thought she'd be eligible for her free root so soon?

Anyone who knew her sons, that's who.

This was a fine way to spend Mother's Day.

All she'd ever wanted was to be respectable. With a sigh, she pushed herself up, stepped over the white pup gnawing on the carpet, grabbed her eight-year-old son by the scruff of his decidedly scruffy neck and shoved him into his bedroom. "You can stay there till you're ready to apologize to your older brother. If I were you, young man, I'd apologize sincerely enough to make him forgive you. You know your brother's temper." She shut the door with restraint, not that that would make a difference. Both her sons could think till Christmas and the concept of personal responsibility wouldn't enter their cerebrums. They each had their own obsessions. They were, after all, their father's sons.

Their father, of course, was all too aware it was Mother's Day. He was presiding in the kitchen of his beloved restaurant, *Adams' House of Ribs*. From all over the state families came to claim their much coveted reservations, and were now lining up in the lobby under the *Adam's, the Original Rib House* sign, eager to cram into the dining room and chow down in honor of Mom.

Adam's was always crowded. His ribs were known all over. He easily could have franchised, opened second, third and fourth Houses of Ribs. His operation could have spread out like ribs from the breast bone, but, alas, he lacked the foresight. "Branch out, Adam" — she had urged him time and again — "include pie, or cobbler, or pan dowdy, we've got the apples." That, of course, was before one of the boys denuded the tree, flushed the apples, and the Whopper Rooter man punched whole number three. With one phone call she could have bought apples — Golden Delicious, Red Delicious, Red Junes, Red Melbas, or Red Spies. A couple of e-mails would have scored her Jonathans, Kings, Pippins, even Newtown Pippins. Or Cortlands or Arkansas Blacks . . . but it didn't matter. Adam had no head for apples. Adam was obsessed with ribs.

How had her life come to this — married to a man whose life was in ribs. To say he had tunnel vision was to credit him with a depth of perception beyond the rim of the sauce pot. Adam, alas, was the personification of stodgy. *Chances* were not items Adam took. To Adam, chances were slippery slopes. Twenty years ago when she stepped down off the bus in Eden Township she was too young to understand what stodgy meant. Twenty years ago when she stopped in the restaurant for take out, she had been awed at Adam's renown, impressed by his status. She was just about flattered out of her mind when Adam himself offered her one of his ribs.

Adam was looking for a hostess at the restaurant and she had beaten out nine other girls for the job. Then she'd figured her victory was due to her chipper smile, her long blonde hair, her A in Algebra. It was only after she started at *Adam's House of Ribs* that the other waitresses kidded her about being chosen for her name. "Oh no," she'd assured them. "How silly. Adam is a businessman; he's tight with the guys in power, the mayor, the governor, and all. No way would he be so superficial as to pick a stranger off a Greyhound and install her as his hostess just because her name is Eve. He's a chef of renown, a force in the rib world. All over town, lips lick at the very thought of his barbecue sauce. No, no. He chose me because I'm a great hostess, not because I'm Eve."

She had been a great hostess, the best, Adam said. She had loved figuring out which table suited the mayor's party, and how to handle things when the governor came and the mayor was already ensconced at the best table. She knew what to do when the governor's wife and ex-wife arrived in separate parties, and the governor was already there, eating with his girlfriend. She knew good and evil, and how to seat them at opposite ends of the room. Adam kept saying he didn't understand how she managed it. Of course he didn't; forethought and discrimination were not Adam's focus. Ribs were.

Adam may not have known how she managed to charm the customers, but her skill at it certainly charmed him. She was the only woman for him, he vowed. Theirs would be a marriage made in heaven. A rootless eighteen year old, she had been awed at the prospect of becoming the wife of such an important man, such an upstanding family man who would never humiliate her in public. She had had a father who philandered and a boyfriend who strayed; she knew all too well what it was like to have the neighbors uncover their humiliating secrets and the whole family be disgraced. Never again would she huddle behind closed doors while the neighbors smirked. But with a man like Adam such an abhorrent possibility was out of the question. Adam was everything good, trustworthy, and oh so respectable. For all that, stodgy was a small price to pay. And after the whirlwind trip to Reno and the Paradise Wedding Chapel (gown and tux provided) she had loved driving home into her garden in Eden and standing proudly at the gate with Adam. She loved walking through Eden with Adam; she loved it when Edenites greeted her smilingly because she was Adam's wife. The ridiculous idea that he might have been attracted by her name, she dismissed as easily as she brushed her thick blonde hair away from her big blue eyes.

She had been wrong. How wrong, she didn't understand until the birth of their first child, Cain.

"Cain?" she had shrieked. "I thought we were going to call him Dwayne, or Derek or Kyle. What about a middle name?"

But Adam would have none of it. Cain, just Cain, the boy was. Adam adored him, adored his own status as a father and even more firmly settled pillar of the community. "We'll be having us another," he took to saying, "like with ribs from *Adams House of Ribs,* you can't stop after just one."

Eve could have stopped. Cain was a fractious child. Eve's blonde hair and blue eyes and experience at seating the governor's wives at opposite ends of the restaurant were not great preparation for child rearing. She knew better than to repeat her mistake.

But Adam was adamant. "Little Cain needs a brother to rough house with," he said night after night. *Monday* night after Monday night, when the

House of Ribs was closed.

"Little Cain needs a brother," he insisted while the boy was battering at the sides of his ant farm.

"Little Cain needs a brother," he said as Cain pushed a playmate off the jungle gym.

"Cain needs a brother," he intoned, as they headed to Eden Acres Elementary School to get the boy reinstated after he backed up the plumbing and flooded the school.

"Cain is a natural born farmer. What he needs is a little brother to help him out," he said as the boy worked off the debt to the school board cultivating Adam's oregano plants.

"Cain needs a little brother," Adam insisted as they got Cain from Juvenile Hall after the sheriff found his own 'oregano' patch.

How many times had she dreamed of leaving Adam? Lots more often than she considered producing a second son. But leave him she could not. There was Cain — decency forbade her to leave the boy with a father who was never home. Decency and everyone in town forbade her. Cain was not an appealing child, an endearing adolescent or an attractive teenager. Still she was his mother and she couldn't abandon the boy. But she wasn't about to take the little ruffian with her. And there was the restaurant where she'd hostessed away her best years. After Cain's birth, she did all the ordering, threatening, permit-getting, inspector-bribing, and anything else not directly rib-connected. So there would be no danger of Adam's important friends wondering why he couldn't afford to hire an administrative assistant, she created that identity for herself. No supplier suspected that it was Eve ordering vinegar, no health department inspector guessed Eve was sending his payoff. As far as the neighbors, the mayor, the governor and their wives knew, Eve was lounging in the garden with Cain. Between Cain and the restaurant work she'd barely ever gotten out of the garden. If she left Adam, she'd never be recompensed for all her work. She was Adam's wife and she wanted her half.

Even so, she might have waited till Cain was collared again, cut her losses and filed for divorce, but she had nowhere to go, and no friends in town to help her. "Family first," Adam always insisted. "When you've got a family you don't needs friends coming by, filling your ears with gossip." With a respected man like Adam, what kind of case could she make for divorce? Inadequate, that's what. She could hardly protest that Adam was stodgy, boring, totally without imagination. Adultery was grounds for divorce, stodgy was not. And she had to admit, though it didn't make her think better of herself, she did love being the respected wife of a pillar. She wasn't about to humiliate him, and herself, in public.

It had been too infuriating to think about, and so she didn't.

She had no decent explanation why after ten years she'd let herself get pregnant again — maybe just the wish for a daughter. Adam was ecstatic. He created a new tomato-less sauce in honor of "Cain's impending brother." No amount of suggestion would convince him babies come in two sexes and by the time her due date arrived Eve knew within herself that he was right. Cain would have a brother. She did the only thing she could — bribed the birth certificate clerk, and named the baby Dominick. Adam, of course, was furious.

"You won't be happy till his brother kills him, will you, Adam?" she said.

But Adam's life was complete and he was happy. He built a gazebo and now on Monday evenings he sat there with Cain and Dominick watching Monday Night Football.

The rest of the time he was cooking ribs. Cain occupied himself by growing marijuana and picking on his brother. Cain didn't share his father's belief that he needed a little brother. Eve felt so guilty about poor little Dominick that when he asked for a dog she could not refuse him.

Not quickly enough did she realize the danger in giving the boy twenty dollars and sending him to the pound. By the time she remembered the pound's motto, "It is more blessed to give than to receive," little Dominick's German shepherd had a litter of ten. Little Dominick petted them lovingly. Cain fingered them suspiciously. When Adam put his hands beneath the pups ribs . . . well, it didn't make her think better of her husband.

How had her life gotten to this state, she asked herself as a brindle pup teethed on her hand. She would have washed off the slobber if she'd had more ambition, *and* if she'd had water. Where was the Whopper Rooter man? He knew the way here as clearly as to his own house. She thought longingly —

The knock on the door was so soft she almost missed it. The Whopper Rooter man? But no. Wayne, the Whopper Rooter man used the front door. This knock was on the back door, the favored entry of Cain's "clients."

Only this morning she had walked in on Cain as he packaged leaves and seeds and said, "One of these days, you're going to get yourself sent away for good."

"Nah, I won't." Cain twirled the pigtail left after he'd shaved his head. "Dad's got friends in high places."

"That's your father, not you. You don't make yourself likeable, Cain."

Cain had shrugged, then spotting one of his brother's dogs, kicked at it as he had a dozen times before.

"Hey, Crutch, lay off!" little Dominick whined, knowing that the hated nickname would set his brother off every time. Then, usually, Cain lunged, Dominick sidestepped and ran, furniture suffered.

But this morning when the scene replayed itself little Dominick had said nothing; just stalked out of the house. And it wasn't till the toilet backed up that Cain had realized his crop had gone down river. Cain had screamed: "I'm going to kill you, you little bastard!" He'd uttered this same threat time and again without interruption of originality — he was, after all, his father's son. But this time was different. This time she believed him.

Now Eve cocked an ear to hear what Cain was telling this disappointed customer. But before she could distinguish a word, the front door bell rang. She pushed herself up, threaded through shepherds and pulled the door open. Dog hair flew. The Whopper Rooter man would be a relief in more ways than one.

But when she opened the door there was no familiar brown-uniformed man holding a snake. On the stoop was a tall redhead wearing a boa, a feather boa.

"Adam here?" The woman was years older than she, but beautiful, voluptuous and dressed like no one Eve had ever seen in the burg of Eden. Her flowing beige ensemble looked cool, comfortable and likely to drive men wild. And her snake skin boots were made for stomping. There was a jiggle to this woman, like she was an engine idling, an engine too busy to take time to stop and start again. This was a press the gas and go gal. "Adam? Is he here or what?"

"No, of course Adam's not here. It's Mother's Day. He's been at his ribs since four a.m."

"Oh, the rib thing," the woman said with a laugh. "You know if we were talking anyone but Adam I'd give you my friend's card. My friend is a shrink in Vegas; deals with fetishes. But Adam —"

"Adam's *cooking* ribs, at his restaurant, *Adam's House of Ribs*. You must not be from around here if you don't know about *Adam's House of Ribs*. Who are you, anyway? And what do you want?"

The insistent woman shifted her weight on her stiletto heels and tossed her boa over her left shoulder. She was tapping her toe, ready to move on. "I used to live here. Just passing through on my way back to Vegas. Haven't heard from Adam in thirty years, not since I left. Just figured I'd stop in and see how the old bird was doing, you know?" She shifted her weight back, blinked her mascara'd eyes and stared at Eve. "Who are *you?*"

"Me? I'm Adam's wife." She would have demanded an answer from the woman but the woman was laughing so hard, her whole body shaking, her boa fluttering like a flock of flamingos. She was laughing so loud it set the dog barking, the pups whining.

"Adam scored another wife?" the woman managed to squeeze out between paroxysms.

"*Another* wife, what do you mean another wife? We've been married for twenty years. We've been together since the day I arrived in Eden. I've hostessed in his House of Ribs, I've borne his sons, I am Adam's wife, his only wife. Adam and Eve. Our son is Cain," she added defensively. For the first time, she felt a pang of regret at not having named her younger son Abel, as if that would have clinched her argument and cemented her status as Adam's wife, a pillar-ette of the community. She glared up at the beautifully-coiffed stranger. "Who the hell are *you*?"

The redhead swallowed hard. It took her three swallows and one more toss of the boa to get herself under control. Still she didn't answer.

"*Who are you?*"

"I'm Lilith, of course, Adam's first wife."

First wife! Eve stumbled back against the door. There were a hundred questions she could have asked, but she knew none of them would change anything. She wanted to scream at the woman: "Liar!" but she knew as sure as God made little green apples, that this woman, this Lilith was telling the truth. Lilith had been married to Adam.

Eve squeaked out the most pressing question, "Did you lived here?"

Lilith shrugged, the kind of careless off-hand response more suited to a question like "Do you want more peanuts? "Oh, yeah, I lived here, in this house, which I gotta say was in better shape back then. 'Course the town wasn't called Eden Township then, wasn't incorporated. I'll tell ya, Hon, the burg was so dead back then that Adam looked good. The only time I wasn't bored was when I was pissed off."

"And so you got a divorce?" Eve asked hopefully.

"Divorce? Hell, no. One night I took a good look at Adam and what I saw was — well, you put up with the guy for twenty years, you gotta know what he's like. Stodgy; everyone in town knew that. I'd had it, Hon! Enough; you know what I mean? You don't live forever — just seems like it when you're in Eden and bored outa your skull. So, I up and lit out of here. Never looked back."

The damn woman was missing the point. "So Adam divorced you, then?"

"Never served me with papers. Coulda. I'm in the book in Vegas. Lilith's

Realty." For the first time she stopped moving. Her alligator purse bounced against her hip and settled, the boa hung limp. She put an exquisitely manicured hand on Eve's shoulder. "Listen kid, I'm sorry if I upset you. I'm sure your life is fine here in Eden. Excitement, independence, they're probably overrated anyway. A life of your own isn't for every woman. You got a nice house and garden, all those lovely apple trees. So what if Adam is stodgy; you hadda know that when you moved in with him, right? I mean everyone in town knows that. Hell, I told 'em all before I left. What do you care if all those dullards are laughing every time you're introduced as Adam's wife. But, listen, Sweetie, forget all that. You just put me out of your mind. Here," she added, "for you."

Before Eve could open her drooping mouth, the boa was around her neck and the woman was climbing back into a white stretch limo Eve hadn't noticed before.

"First wife!" Eve stormed out of the house, jumped in the *Adam's House of Ribs* delivery truck and headed for the *House of Ribs,* muttering as she went. "Damn you, Adam. I knew you were stodgy, but at least with stodgy you expect honest. But you, damn you, are stodgy and dishonest. Damn you."

❖

Adam's House of Ribs was built to resemble ribs, curved, red plaster cascading to the ground. She entered through the breastbone and stalked back to the heart of the operation. Adam was standing beside a huge stew pot he could almost have drowned in. Years ago he had succumbed to the occupational hazard of the chef and now for all Eve knew he might have given away all his own ribs. Certainly none of them showed. He was an apple of a man — red, round and, with his clothes off, dead white underneath. Now he looked up at her furious face, smiled and said, "I'm trying a new recipe, want a tas —"

"You were married before?" she demanded.

"Before what?" He gave the long wooden spoon a turn.

"Before me, that's what. You had a first wife!"

"Oh, that."

"That! Why didn't you tell me?"

"It was a long time ago. Before I met you. Before I even got the idea for *Adam's House of Ribs.*" He stirred the pot twice around. "Lilith wasn't into ribs." He stirred a third time. "This sauce, I'm using flax powder and cardamon, see and —"

She yanked the spoon out of his hand and slammed it to the floor. "So Lilith just left, right? Did she divorce you?"

Adam stopped the spoon. "I don't know."

"How can you not know?"

"I don't know. Gone is gone. I didn't have time to worry about her. I had ribs to cook, sauce to stir," he said pulling himself up righteously to his full five and a half feet.

"I could go, too, just like she did."

Adam fished another ladle out of a drawer. Then he laughed. "You? You, Eve? Where would you go? You haven't spent a night out of Eden since we've been married. And how would you support yourself? The only work you ever did was hostessing here, and surely you don't expect a reference from me."

"I could get a different kind of job."

"What, Eve? As a housekeeper? *Our* house looks like a kennel. Or maybe you could apply as a governess. Tell them what a great job you did with Cain."

"Cain is your son, too." But she knew that protest would change not one mind. For once Adam had thought more clearly than she. Of course he'd had years to prepare for this moment, ever since he spotted a potential second wife.

Questions and accusations lined up in her brain, but she didn't bother to voice them. She was too depressed. She drove slowly home, suddenly seeing every corner as Lilith must have, as a spot with four roads leading out. This is what her life had come to: married to a stodge, laughed at all over town, and what was the best she could hope for? That the Whopper Rooter man had arrived at the house and cleared her pipes.

But he hadn't. When she pulled into the driveway she saw not the hoped for rooter truck, but three motorcycles. The front door ajar. In the house deep-voiced men were swearing, dogs barking, howling, and whining, and little Dominick screaming as if his life depended on it.

"Cain!" Eve yelled as she flew through the door. "Cain, don't you slay your brother!"

But Cain was nowhere to be found. The three hulking muscle-shirted men she recognized as Cain's customers were stalking from room to room. Little Dominick was howling. Three little shepherds had knocked over the cookie jar and one was regurgitating on the sofa, while the rest of the dogs ran in circles, kicking up fur. The only word she could make out in the melee was "kill."

"I'll kill him. Where is the bastard?" one of the men demanded.

"Out!" she commanded. "Out of . . ." But it wasn't her house, was it? It wasn't her furniture. Outside, it wasn't her garden. The clothes she was wearing, legally were they even hers? She fingered the only thing that was unquestionably hers — the feather boa. Cain's three enormous and irate customers stalked toward the door. One of them was holding a Gravenstein. *Her* apple? Without thinking she grabbed it out of man's hand. The behemoth scowled, did a double-take and kept moving.

Eve held the Gravenstein in her hand and stared at the light shining off its shiny red skin. Now, she realized the truth in Cain's customer's question: *Where is the bastard?* Cain was, indeed, a bastard, spiritually and genetically. Cain was a total bastard. Adam, whose interests spread no farther than the rib cage, had, of course, never bothered to divorce his first wife. Not his *first* wife; his *wife, period*. And she, Eve, what did that make her? She was not his wife at all. She was his concubine, his mistress, his woman of the night, his whore and his dupe. She was astonished, furious, and most of all humiliated. How could she ever again stand at her garden gate and face the upright people of Eden? She felt totally exposed, in fact, naked. The Gravenstein was still in her hand. Without thinking she took a bite.

Before she could swallow, little Dominick raced up to her, squeaking, "Crummy Cain tried to poison my dogs. Mama Dog she went after him and he ran. That way!"

Calming herself she said, "Dominick dear, where is the poison?"

"In the dog food, Mother."

"How do you know it's poison, dear?"

"Because crummy Cain poured it from the bottle with the skull and crossbones," he said nodding his little head sincerely. "I always watch over the dog's food. Sometimes I even taste it. Cain doesn't like my shepherds and Cain might —"

"But you're not sick, are you Dominick? If there was poison —"

"The black puppy got to the bowl before I could get there. I grabbed him around the middle and made him throw up."

She glanced at the small shaking dog and the mess around him. He was an empty dog, and she could tell he would survive, though the couch would not. She took a necessarily shallow breath to calm herself and asked little Dominick, "Does your bother know you taste the dog food?"

"Of course, Mother. I made sure of that. So he knows he can't kill my dogs, see?"

She grabbed the phone and dialed Adam.

"Adam's House of —"

"Put Adam on." The fury that filled her like extra hot sauce must have steamed out of her mouth. The present hostess at the *House of Ribs* didn't ask who she was or what she thought was important enough to interrupt the chef in the act of creation. She must have run for the kitchen. In less than a minute Adam was at the phone. "Eve? What do you —"

"Cain tried to kill Dominick."

"How could —"

"He put poison in the dog food he knew Dominick would eat."

She could hear the horror in Adam's thick intake of breath. She'd never heard such outrage from him. Perhaps she had misjudged him as a father. He took another labored breath before he could speak. "My son eats dog food?" Adam croaked out. "*My* son eats dog food? I'll be laughed out of the barbecue business. How could you let this happen? You have no responsibilities, Eve, except to maintain our place in Eden and you can't even do that. Every chef in town is going to be laughing in his sauce. Eve, you've got to hush this up. You've got to —"

She slammed down the phone and turned to little Dominick. "Pack your dogs, dear." Grabbing the poisoned dog food, she herded little Dominick and the shepherds into the Rib truck and drove to the *House of Ribs,* to the back door. She left the engine running.

For once the kitchen was empty. Adam was nowhere in sight. She looked at the great steel pots. She stared at the kitchen of this restaurant to which she had tied her security, for which she had endured two decades of boredom, with neighbors nodding knowingly behind her back, for which she had endangered the life of her younger son, not to mention his shepherds. This kitchen was not half hers. It would never be half hers. The new sauce boiled, sauce that was not hers. This sauce was Adam's alone, and when he died it would be the sauce of his legal wife and his sons, plural, if Dominick evaded his brother that long. Never would it be hers. Fans rattled, sauce boiled. She looked at the sauce. She looked down at the dog food in her hands. She poured.

❖

Evelyn, as she is known now, sat on the veranda of her new home. It was a rental, but Lilith had gotten her a good deal on it. "Here Spot. Here, Blackie. Here, Whitey. Here, Tan-o." (Dominick was a nice child, but not a whiz with names.) She smiled as the dogs dropped *The Eden Township Sentinel, The Tribune, The Wall Street Journal, The New York Times* and *The Washington Post* at her feet. Front page on all five. She picked up the *Sentinel* and smiled at the headline: "Local Chef poisoned by own sauce. Scads of Edenites get the runs." The *Tribune,* after insisting it was not its policy to speculate, noted that Adam's wife, or more accurately long-term mistress, and younger son were missing and some of the ribs in *Adam's House* were of questionable origin.   The *Times*, after insisting it was not its policy to speculate, alluded to Adam's notorious first wife, and to his infamous son Cain. *The Wall Street Journal*, after insisting it was not its policy to speculate, commented that while Adam had been beyond reproach the same was not likely to be said of his beneficiary, his remaining son, Cain.   And *The Washington Post* noted that Cain had fled the saucy scene of the crime and had been spotted in Nod, a sleepy village east of Eden before vanishing.   But authorities had distributed flyers with his picture and they insisted they expected little difficulty in capturing him. Cain was, after all, marked.

The other dogs arrived, papers in mouths, but Evelyn had to put off reading them. She was in a new town, in a new state, and this was her first day as pastry chef down at the New Jerusalem Pie Shoppe.

She planned to make a name for herself with apples.

❖

EVELYN'S APPLE RHUBARB PIE

Pastry for nine inch pan:
2 Cups sifted flour
½ t. salt
1 cup shortening
6 T. very cold water
Mix salt into flour, cut in shortening; gradually add water till you've got a workable paste. Too little will leave it like dry dog food (see above). Divide in half. Form into ball. Chill thoroughly Roll out, 1/8th inch thick, and line pan. Reserve other half for top crust.

Filling:
1/4 cup brown sugar
2 apples, sliced thin
2 lb. rhubarb, cut in small pieces
Spread rhubarb on pie crust (already in pie pan) as bottom layer.
Spread apples as next layer.
Sprinkle sugar over apples.
Place reserved top crust on top.
Bake at 450 degrees for ten minutes, then 350 degrees for 40 minutes.
Find snake to serve it.

Toward the end of writing a book, life becomes frenzied. Fiction blends into life, it washes over life, it drowns life. And that's at the best of time. This story was written for an anthology about writers. For the inspiration for non-writer character, I am indebted to Barbara D'Amato and her bathroom remodeling.

A SURFEIT OF DEADLINE

I'm not that kind of writer. Really.

Not that my agent or my editor believes that. Okay, so I've missed a few deadlines. Well, every deadline. But I have had excuses. Well, not great excuses. But what kind of tyrants would demand that I come up with a great excuse when I'm madly trying to finish a book?

I used to have great excuses, but I've gone through them by now; that's what makes my position so difficult. "When you said September, naturally I assumed you meant the *end* of September, not the first." My editor and my agent had both heard that one before. (Actually, it was my virgin offering to the sacrificial pyre of publishing deadlines.) A real daughter's wedding, that would be a lock for a month's extension. For the first time, I was sorry I didn't have children. Earthquake? Great for eliciting sympathy, but hard to fake. The flu? Too temporary. Broken arm? Too much hassle, and besides I'd already used that twice. Dying grandmother, lover, Labrador retriever?

I sighed. I had fabricated so often, nothing short of death was going to get me an extension from my editor. But suicide seemed a bit extreme, and it was too late to fly to New York and do him in.

I sighed again and contemplated the remaining eighty — that's eight-oh — pages necessary to complete my contractual obligation. Necessary in order for me to get paid. Knowing how close to the financial edge I live, my editor and agent cooked up a Machiavellian deal to 'encourage me to deliver the manuscript in a timely manner.' My 'payment upon delivery' sat in a checking account. As soon as my agent authorized its release I could write a check for it — and cover my expenses for the trip to Paris I'd arranged to reward myself (not to mention the house payment, and my tab with the grocer, the dentist, and six credit card companies.)

So, I had to get the book done.

September 1 was Friday. Friday evening I would be on a plane to Paris. And my manuscript had to be on its own UPS plane to New York. Perhaps I would even pass it in the jet stream. Five hundred fifty pages of magnificently plotted prose, sporting devilishly clever characters, diabolical deeds, and a beats-the-devil denouement. The threads of those misdeeds would be winding in and out, creating a Gordian knot of danger, deception, doubt, and dubiety, until my detective, the suave and prescient Cerai, skillfully unraveled it, thread by slick, colorful thread. By page four hundred he'd be chasing after danger, by four seventy-five he'd stare death in the face, till, around five four-three, give or take a page, he'd skewer the murderer on his own petard.

Well, clever characters had done their job. They had tied the plot in knots tighter than any I had managed in any novel before. Cerai appeared stumped.

Cerai *was* stumped. He couldn't spot the murderer or his petard, much less impale him.

It was now Monday, August twenty-seventh. In the next five days I had to write those eighty pages, pack for Paris, figure out who the killer was, and how he or she did the dastardly deed. Even then my editor would ask, "How come Cerai, so flummoxed for five hundred pages, suddenly, out of nowhere, cottons to the truth?" But his question was weeks away. I wouldn't have to deal with that till after I got back from Paris. By then I would have found the answer. (Answers, like fine wine, love, and inspiration flow more freely in Paris. All writers know that.) For now it was just a question of fingers flying and nose to the computer, a tortured posture at the best of times. I had turned off the phone, canceled the newspaper, and wouldn't have answered the door had it not been for the handy man who needed to redo the tiles on one wall in my studio shower which he had botched in the remodel last week. Hassling with Fred, the handyman, was the last thing I had time for, but I knew Fred. If I let that repair go till after Paris it would never happen. When he was on the job, it had taken all my carrot and stick abilities to get him through his allotted work each day before he settled on my step outside for his afternoon break, which invariably meant a couple of beers and cigarettes and the denouement of the work day.

I have only myself to blame, of course — not that that makes any situation better. The same Fred patched my still leaking roof, installed a used stove on which the burner flames go out after two minutes heating, thus threatening me with carbon monoxide poisoning every time I brewed a cup of tea, and constructed a deer fence low enough so it wouldn't block my view, or, as it soon became obvious, deer. He had promised to rectify all those mistakes. I was still waiting.

Those problems I had decided to live with. After all, it was the dry season, and I could be careful with the stove, and deer really were preferable to gardens anyway. But the tiles were a different issue — row upon row of eyesores. If they stayed on the wall a week they'd be there forever. I knew Fred.

"Fred," I had said Friday afternoon when I saw the 'champagne' colored tiles, "those tiles are green!"

"Champagne."

"Fred, champagne is golden. Those are seaweed."

"Champagne." He had pointed to the tile box.

"I know champagne when I see it. I've drunk it, not as often as I'd like, but I've held a fluted glass or two in my time. I've watched the bubbles bustle to the surface and dance into the air. I've felt the frisson of liquid excitement as I lifted the glass to my lips. I've —"

He jabbed a stubby finger at the box. "Champagne."

"Bilge water green."

"Champagne."

"Pus."

"Champagne."

"Cash."

"Cham —" Fred stared, confounded.

Perhaps he thought I had merely raised the vulgar level of my replies to one more ladylike, if less aptly descriptive. I have not been a writer for years for nothing.

I was still sitting at my desk out here in my garden studio. I looked past the beige computer monitor, across the ersatz pine desk, past the stove and the tiny refrigerator that turned milk to white bricks, through the never-quite-closed French doors at the slate step on which Fred stood, like an oversized plaid-shirted garden gnome. Smoking a cigarette.

Smoking was why he was not inside the studio here, planted on the other side of my desk, poking his paw into the tile box as he gave forth with chorus after squeaky chorus of "champagne." He wasn't standing outside from courtesy, or due to concern that the stench of smoke would linger in my rug, chair cushions, much less my own clothes and hair. He had no conception of that; he'd long since burnt out his olfactory mechanisms, which may have explained why he now assumed showering to be an unnecessary indulgence. No, it was not the danger to my lungs that touched him. It was our contract. I had written into the contract an escalating penalty for each time he crossed my threshold with a lighted cigarette. He had already accrued the five dollar fee, and the twenty-five two days last week. (I could tell by the telltale stench, he trotted in here smoking every time I was gone, but evidence of those breaches was too circumstantial to fine him.) Even so, he knew that one more step forward now would cost him $625.

So he kept himself outside.

And in doing so, he reminded me of the power of the contract. My editor and agent had taught me only too well the tyranny of contractual agreement. Like my publishers, I had paid Fred a third of his fee in advance, with two thirds due upon completion on the job. I said, "Until those *green* tiles are replaced, Fred, the job is not complete."

He grumbled. He muttered. He waved cigarette in air. But in the end there was nothing for him to do but accede.

It was a moment so sweet I would almost have put up with the green tiles for it. Sweeter yet that I got to have my cake and watch him eat my green tiles too, so to speak.

"I got to get more tiles from the store. Store'll be closed by the time I could get there. I can't get to this here till after."

I nodded, willing to be magnanimous after so grand a victory. "So, I can expect you Monday morning, then."

Fred stubbed out his cigarette on the sole of his work boot.

"Monday, the twenty-seventh," I reiterated.

"Yeah. No problem."

"Good, it's settled then," I said, suddenly panicked that I would have to write Fred a check Monday, long enough for it to bounce before Friday when I got paid.

That only showed how unused am I to being on the 'proprietor' side of the contract. I have good reason. I've only owned this house for a year. Before then I never had the money to even think of buying a house. And, in fact, I should never have taken the leap then. The payments took every penny of my advance. And this studio, which clinched the deal for me that bright hopeful day last August had proven to be icy in winter, clammy in summer, leaky in rain, and a curse every time I needed coffee or toilet (major hobbies in the writer's day.) And when my book was done, my money in the bank, I would replace . . .

When the book was done.

But at least now, I'd have my lovely bathroom. As I pondered Cirai's escalating dilemma, I could stare lovingly through the bathroom door into the depths of the muted golden tiles. By noon next Monday, I thought then,

I could stare lovingly.

❖

Monday morning as I sat in my studio watching the fog unroll exposing the land (and my studio) to the August sun, I waited for Fred. Had it not been for the problems with my book, probably I would have overlooked his tardiness (after all, we hadn't specified an hour. I had just assumed he understood that first thing Monday morning meant eight a.m.) Had it not been for the plodding plot, I wouldn't have been sitting here to contemplate Fred at all. I'd have been out at brunch celebrating with Crepe Suzettes and, of course, champagne.

Instead my eyes were making a circuit from the computer on which Cirai was slowly, painstakingly interrogating the murdered woman's adulterous husband, to the clock on which the minutes till my Friday, September 1st deadline ticked away, to the tiles that grew ever greener.

You say, Mr. Montgomery, that you were out sailing on your yacht the afternoon when your wife was murdered. Alone?" Cirai raised a bushy eyebrow.

9:45
Lime green.

"I wasn't alone."
"Really?"
"Really."
Cirai pulled a pen and pad out of the pocket of his plaid shirt. "Then you must let me speak to the person who can vouch for you."
"No."

9:48
Algae green.

"This is a matter of life and death."
"No!"
"Mr. Montgomery, save us both time here. You got a mistress. You spent that afternoon with her there on your yacht, right?"

9:51
Pond scum green.

Montgomery's lips tightened. He was avoiding Cirai's stare.
Cirai stepped forward, jabbing his finger in the adulterer's fa —

Damn! I was so caught up in the time and the tiles I had turned my suave and clever detective into Fred, the handyman!

This had to stop. I barely had time to finish the book, much less go back and correct this kind of mistake. I had to deal with this problem now.

I picked up the phone and dialed Fred.

It rang. And rang. And rang and rang. I was just about to put down the receiver when the message tape activated. "Fred D'Amato. I'm out on a job. Leave me your number and I'll call you as soon as I get back. No problem."

Out on a job! A job for someone else! The tiles pulsed slime green. It embarrasses me to admit how long it took me to realize that Fred, the handyman, was not out working for someone else. Fred, the handyman, was still in bed.

I turned the phone on and called back. "Fred. You were supposed to be here at my studio this morning replacing those green tiles. I'm waiting. Call me right away." I resisted the urge to slam down the receiver. But I couldn't keep myself from staring at the offending instrument as it sat, blithely not ringing.

The phone rang. I grabbed it. Too quickly.

"Good morning, Jeffrey Hammond here." *My agent!* "So, how's that manuscript of ours coming?"

"Just putting the final touches on it," I croaked out.

"It's going to be the full five hundred fifty pages?" There was a touch of wariness in his smarmy voice, as if he hadn't quite believed me about those final touches.

"Easily."

"You're sure that —"

"Jeff, Jeff. No problem." Jeez, now *I* was talking like Fred, the handyman. "But if you expect me to finish up, you've got to let me get back to work."

"Uh . . . huh."

I knew better than to question what exactly that *uh huh* meant. "Okay, bye now." I hung up, guiltily turned back to the computer and began to type.

Cirai stepped forward, pointing his slender, elegant finger in the adulterer's face.

10:01
Bile green.

"It is past the time when lying will help you, Mr. Montgomery. It's already ten oh two and the tiles behind you are the color of school room walls."

Damn! This was ridiculous. What I needed was tea. A nice soothing cup of Assam tea.

But the tea was all the way across the courtyard in the house. I didn't want to miss Fred's call. This phone line rang only out here. But it was audible that far away. Surely if I ran I would be back here before it stopped ringing.

I headed over the lawn. It was still wet from the night time sprinklers. By the time I reached the kitchen door my shoes were muddy. No time to scrape them off. I'd deal with the muddy footprints later. I pulled open the cabinet door. I'd always meant to straighten up the jumble of tea boxes in there. People give them to me — peppermint, camomile, Morning Thunder, Evening Slumber. Now the Assam was nowhere in sight. I could take another, I reminded myself. But when you're already grumpy the wrong tea will not make things better. I reached behind the Pleasing Peach, pushed aside a box I'd gotten to accompany an ill-fated diet — Rose Hips for Large Hips — dug under two boxes of Lemon Spice, balancing them on my arm to keep the entire wall of tea boxes from collapsing and forcing me to excavate again to unearth the Assam.

The phone rang.
I spotted the Assam.
The ringing stopped.
I tunneled.
The phone rang again.
I grabbed the Assam.
The second ring stopped.
I yanked the box free, sending rejected boxes hang gliding onto the kitchen floor. I spotted one as it landed in a blotch of mud. Leaping over it I ran for the door as the third ring commenced. I raced across the wet lawn like a hare. Well, more like a bear. As I neared the slate step to the studio my feet slipped on the slick grass. I could "see" my head striking the sharp edge of the stone, my skull splitting open, my brains spewing onto the lawn. The *green* lawn.

I scrambled mightily to keep my balance, feet racing in place, arms circling fast enough to qualify me for a helicopter license. My hand squeezed the Assam box. Tea flew like confetti. But I succeeded: my head was uncracked, my brain still an *in*terior organ. I slumped down on the doorstep and sighed loud enough to be heard at the airport.

That's when I realized the phone had stopped ringing.

I sprang up, raced across the room, grabbed up the receiver.

No one there.

No beep indicating message.

Didn't matter. Fred couldn't have gotten more than a couple feet from the phone. I dialed.

It rang. And rang. And rang and rang. "Fred D'Amato. I'm out on a job —"

"Fred," I yelled over the message, "I know you're still there. Fred! Fred?"

The message ended. Silence continued. I glared at the clock. 10:12. "Fred, it's now nearly ten-thirty. I don't have all day. Call me."

Fred didn't. He didn't call; he didn't come. Not Monday morning, nor Monday afternoon. Nor Tuesday, Wednesday, Thursday. Tuesday my agent called; I had finished the manuscript itself and was merely redoing the dedication page, I reassured him. Wednesday my editor called and I swore that I had just this minute recalled a possibly libelous comment and I was going through the manuscript to exorcize it lest the publisher be sued. Thursday when my agent caught me again I was so depressed with the sixty remaining unwritten pages I went blank on excuses and almost 'fessed up. But years of experience in fiction rushed to clamp the hand of rationality over my mouth. When I had regained my senses, I said, "I just need to go out and get a mailing envelope. The book will be ready for the UPS pick-up in the morning. No problem." But from Fred, the handy man, I heard zilch. He might have forgotten our appointment for first thing Monday morning, but he couldn't have overlooked his need to call me. I had left him two more messages Monday, another Tuesday, four Wednesday, one every hour on Thursday.

I had a business card with his address, but he didn't live close to me, and with my deadline looming tighter every day, I hardly had time to go searching for a workman's cottage in some town across the hills. What was the matter with the man? Was he so irresponsible that he had forgotten not only about my tiles and his promise to replace them, but about the payment he wouldn't get until he did?

If we writers comported ourselves like workmen there would be no literature at all.

I was stumped. Just as Cirai was stumped. Here it was a dank, gray, fog-covered Friday morning, September 1st. I hadn't packed. I still had fifty pages to create and Fred, the handyman, had shoved Cirai and his petty fictional problems out of my mind. How could I concern myself with Mr. Montgomery's mistress' admission that while she was on the yacht she couldn't corroborate Montgomery's alibi because they had a kinky affair and she had been blindfolded? How, indeed, when the bile green tiles were glaring at me.

What I needed was a miracle. Two miracles, actually, one for Fred and the other for Cirai.

Miracles are not highly thought of in detective fiction. But in life they are quite fine. And just as I was about to give up entirely, I got my miracle. It was 10:06 Friday morning. I was dialing Fred for the who-knows-how-many-th time. I pushed in the final number. I could hear the phone mechanism connecting me.

Then nothing.

Then "Hello?"

It was Fred.

There, at home.

In that instant I knew he would never have answered my call. But my chance — by miracle — before the ring started he had picked up the phone to dial out. I could 'see' him standing by a mortar-scarred phone, wiping his hands on his plaid shirt, cigarette poking out of his mouth.

"Fred, it's me. I want those tiles changed and I want it now."

"Oh, hi. I've been trying to reach you."

"I've been here all day, every day."

"There must be som't'ing the matter with your phone."

For a moment I almost believed him. Later I would wonder if he had this conversation so often, with so many different clients that it began to take on a certain truth for him, the way we give validity to a religious chant in a foreign tongue even though we really have no idea what the words mean. But for now, I recognized the smokescreen. "You were supposed to be here Monday morning."

"Oh yeah. But, you know, I was down at the shop trying to get the tiles you wanted. But they were out. They said they'd have them in the next morning, so, see, I figured I'd just pick them up then and come on out to your house right after like. But when I got to the store Tuesday —"

"Fred, do you have the tiles now?"

"Oh, yeah."

"Then come on out now."

"That's what I was planning. I was halfway to my truck when you called."

"So you'll be here when?"

"In an hour. No problem."

"By eleven o'clock then."

"What? Yeah, sure. No problem."

I sighed in triumphant relief as I put down the receiver. So Fred had told a few lies? So he hadn't tried to call me, he probably hadn't called the tile store, and he certainly hadn't been halfway to his truck when the phone rang, *because* the phone had never rung on his end. In two hours he'd have been here and gone. My tiles would no longer be compost green, but sparkling gold. Cirai would no longer be digging himself deeper in the bilge of Montgomery's yacht but pulling together all the clues, muttering "Aha" and charging on to his penultimate danger.

Fred didn't come in an hour, nor by at eleven.

Not at noon.

Cirai was still on Montgomery's yacht trying to coerce a confession from Montgomery's mistress' accountant's incestuous sister's dachshund trainer.

I stared at the computer.

I scowled at the tiles.

I glared at the computer screen, not the words but the page number.

I glowered at the tiles, the phone, the computer, the crisp new mailing envelope that was clearly not going to get filled with my manuscript by the end of the day. I slumped back in my chair.

I had to admit it, I was defeated. The only fiction I had been creating this week was telling my agent, my editor, and myself that I would meet the deadline. No way would I be able to do it. I couldn't even *type* fifty pages in an afternoon, much less create them. There was no more chance of my doing that than there was of Fred, the handyman, turning up with my champagne tiles. Even for the remainder of my publisher's payment I couldn't do it. Even for double the payment. Or triple. And no excuse I could create would be good enough. From me they'd heard them all. With them I had milked dry the cow of sympathy.

Depression had relaxed my face so that I wasn't glowering any more, just staring dully at the tiles. I would simply have to get used to that awful green. It didn't matter about Fred any more. It was only a matter of time till the bank called him to announce that the initial check I gave him last week, postdated to yesterday, had bounced. Then I would have to promise him double his fee just so he didn't sue me. Fred was nothing if not greedy. He'd told me often enough about the other much better-paying jobs he normally worked. I hadn't believed him, of course. Why would anyone willing to pay more put up with unreliable, dishonest, smelly Fred. But I did believe in his greed. Double his fee? Even he would haul himself over here for that.

Suddenly the curtains of fog split and bright golden sunshine poured through onto my studio, onto me, onto the phone which I picked up and dialed. I waited till I heard Fred's message ending — "I'll get back to you. No problem" — and said, "Fred, I've been thinking. This tile job is really important to me. I absolutely have to get it done today. I know you've got other, better paying jobs, but if you can finish mine today I'll" — I started to say *double*. But in for a kid, in for a goat — "triple your fee if you can do it today. I'll be home for half an hour then I'll be in and out, so if you can call me —"

"Hey, Fred here. I just walked in from the tile store and heard your voice. I got tied up in the tile store or I would have called you sooner, see. When I asked them about the tile —"

Another time, just out of professional curiosity, I would have let him go on so I could see where his story line ended up. But now there was no time. "No problem, Fred. How long will the job take you?"

"Half an hour max. If you're in that big a rush I could probably get the green tiles out and the champagne ones up in . . ."

He was still talking, but I wasn't listening. It didn't matter what lie he was giving me. I knew he'd never take the old tiles down nor put the new ones up. What mattered was that he'd known all along he'd installed the wrong tiles! It made me feel better.

Still he was talking. "So, like I said, I can be at your place in an hour, as soon as I go by the tile shop. The thing is those champagne tiles are going to cost you more than the green ones."

I didn't say *so that's why you installed the cheap green ones to begin with.* Or shout *on top of your triple fee?* "No problem, Fred."

"But see, the tile shop —"

"I said it was no problem. Listen, Fred, I'm going to be straight with you, and I expect you'll be straight with me." Fat chance. "I know you've got other jobs and you're not going to get here this afternoon. And in fact I've got too much work to do here this afternoon to be interrupted for the tiles. So here's the deal. I'm leaving for the airport at seven this evening. I will put the check on my desk then. You can do the work any time this evening. But my housesitter" — housesitter, that was a laugh. If I'd been organized enough to find a housesitter, I'd have been organized enough to finish the damn book — "my housesitter is coming in late, around midnight and I'm leaving him a note telling him to go to the studio and if he finds an envelope with a check in it, tear it up. Clear?"

"Yeah. I'll be there this evening."

"After you've had a couple of beers, huh?"

"Hey, listen —"

I sighed a mite too loudly. "You're right, what business is it of mine if you arrive half-sotted as long as you do the work? So you will be here this evening?"

"Yeah, no problem."

❖

I hadn't lied to him about needing all the time I had before my seven p.m. pick-up. There were clothes to wash, clothes to iron, a quick trip to the store for ointments and potions to fill all those essential little jars in the travel cosmetic bag. And there was the manuscript to print out. Those last fifty pages stumped me for a while until it occurred to me to print out the first fifty again and simply change the page numbers. I was being overcautious, of course, but I have had years of training in planting all the clues and tieing up all the loose ends.

It was a bit after four when I plucked the last page out of the printer and pushed the manuscript into the mailing envelope. I called UPS and arranged for a morning pick-up tomorrow.

Then I dialed my agent.

"Jeffrey, it's done! It's in the envelope. UPS is coming tomorrow morning."

"Great, my dear. I'll release the money as soon as it gets here."

I had expected that, of course. This wasn't the first time I'd told him the manuscript was in the mail. Once I'd even said I had just gotten back from the airport after dropping off a friend who was hand carrying it on the red eye. "Jeffrey, I'm leaving for Paris tonight. Do you expect me to sleep on the street there, Rue de la Pennyless?"

"My dear, we have a deal."

"I know, I know. But Jeffrey, what good would it do me to lie to you now? If the manuscript isn't in your office by noon the day after tomorrow you'll know it. You've got my address in Paris; if I lied to you about this —

oh, yes, Jeff, I know you think I would lie about it — you would simply make my vacation hell. So what would I gain by lying? If I hadn't finished the manuscript, which, of course, I have, wouldn't it be easier for me to beg for a day or two's indulgence rather than give you a lie you're bound to see through?"

"My dear, your past record —"

"I know, Jeffrey. I am ashamed. What can I do to convince you? My plane leaves in a few hours. There's no way — No wait, I could fax it to you. Do you have a fresh box of fax paper?"

I could picture Jeffrey picturing himself canceling his Friday night dinner reservations so he could stand by the fax as five hundred fifty pages chugged out. Maybe he would have to race to an all-night supply store for more paper, or blacken his hands changing the ink cartridge. All for a commodity that would be redundant when the UPS man arrived.

"Well, my dear, I don't —"

"Would you like to call UPS to confirm the pick-up? You can do that; I'm sending the package as a bill to."

He was silent for what seemed eternity. Finally he gave one of those little chuckles of his. "Well, my dear, what you say does make sense. All right. I'm releasing your money. Have a great vacation. We'll talk about the book when you get back."

"Right, Jeffrey, I'm sure we will."

I heated water for my last cup of tea here in the studio, poured it, shut the door with relief, and walked across the lawn to the house. Then I really had to scurry to get to the bank before it closed, to get back home, do all the last minute things you have to for a long trip, culminating with dragging my suitcases down to the end of the driveway so the van driver didn't have to come up here knocking on doors for me.

At the last minute, I left the luggage and ran back to the studio, smacked a *Don't Smoke in Here,* sign on the French door where Fred couldn't miss it, and raced back down the drive.

There were three other passengers in the van, a couple headed for Detroit, and a women who had been out here on business now going back to Houston. The driver grumbled when I asked him to turn off the radio, but it was an hour's ride to the airport and you can't be too careful. If there was one thing I trusted it was that Fred, the handyman, wouldn't get to my house right away. But, like I said, you can't be too careful, and so we rode in a silence broken only by those snippets of pre-travel conversation. The others were intrigued that I was a writer, that I had just finished a manuscript this very day. Wasn't I nervous, one of them asked, leaving it home awaiting the UPS man? No, I assured them, everything was taken care of.

❖

I was in my pension on Rue de La Guerre when my hometown police called transatlantic to notify me of the explosion in my studio, and the unfortunate fatality. Fred they had identified as much from his truck in my driveway as his remains. "Guy's a mess, Ma'am. Everything was blown to smithereens, pardon me for saying so. But just scraps all over." Even an ocean away, I could 'see' the cop shaking his head. "Can't imagine what would possess a guy to light a cigarette and open the door to a place filled with gas. Had to've been drunk."

"Officer, I told him time and again not to smoke in there. The stove has a gas leak, but he knew that, he's the one who installed it. I don't know what more I could have done, Officer, I even left a sign on the door."

"Terrible shame. Must be awful for you, Ma'am. If there's anything we can do, you just ask."

In any other circumstances a woman who had killed a man the day before would be uneasy talking with the police, but I had not one twinge of worry. I had plotted well, laid in a school of red herrings and left the police to follow them. But that was not what gave me such easy of mind. No. Suppose the worst did happen and I was arrested. Suppose I came to trial before a jury of my peers. Suppose the wiliest district attorney in the state presented his most compelling evidence that I had premeditated and murdered. Upon hearing of Fred's unanswered calls, all the times he did not show up, hearing that the gas-leaking stove Fred himself had installed and never repaired had ignited from his own cigarette, which of those twelve of my peers would not sympathize with me. I defy anyone to find twelve American citizens who would not declare my act justifiable homicide.

So, it was with calm heart and a clear conscience that I said. "This is going to sound strange, Officer, but would you do me a favor and call my literary agent and tell him about the explosion? I wouldn't want him to hear about it and worry. Would you call him and tell him that the studio and its contents were destroyed, but everything else is okay? He'll be concerned about my manuscript — agents are so venal — so tell him that I've got a back-up disk in the house that has all but the last fifty pages on it."

A SUSAN DUNLAP CHECKLIST

BOOKS

Jill Smith Series:

Karma. Raven House, 1981; Severn House, 1991
As a Favor. St. Martin's 1984; Robert Hale, 1986
Not Exactly a Brahmin. St. Martin's, 1985
Too Close to the Edge. St. Martin's, 1987
A Dinner to Die For. St. Martin's, 1987
Diamond in the Buff. St. Martin's, 1990
Death and Taxes. Delacorte, 1991
Time Expired. Delacorte, 1993
Sudden Exposure. Delacorte, 1996
Cop Out. Delacorte, 1997

Vejay Haskell Series:

An Equal Opportunity Death. St. Martin's, 1984; Robert Hale, 1986
The Bohemian Connection. St. Martin's, 1985; Robert Hale, 1987
The Last Annual Slugfest. St. Martin's, 1986

Kiernan O'Shaughnessy Series:

Pious Deception. Villard, 1989
Rogue Wave. Villard, 1991
High Fall. Delacorte, 1994
No Immunity. Delacorte, 1998

Short Story Collection:

The Celestial Buffet and Other Morsels of Murder. Crippen & Landru, 2001

Anthology:

Deadly Allies II, edited with Robert J. Randisi. Doubleday, 1994.

Short Stories:

[★=stories in *The Celestial Buffet*]
★"Death Threat," *Ellery Queen's Mystery Magazine*, March 1978 [collected as "Double Jeopardy"]
★"A Burning Issue," *Alfred Hitchcock Mystery Magazine*, April 1, 1981; *Sisters in Crime 5*. Berkley, 1992
★"Hit-and-Run," *Criminal Elements*. Ivy, 1988
★"No Safety," *Sisters in Crime*. Berkley, 1989
★"The Celestial Buffet," *Sisters in Crime 2*. Berkley, 1990
★"Ott on a Limb," *Mistletoe Mysteries*. Mysterious Press, 1989
★"Death and Diamonds," *A Woman's Eye*. Delacorte, 1992
"A Good Judge of Character," *Deadly Allies*. Bantam, 1992
★"Check-out," *Malice Domestic 2*. Pocket Books, 1993
★"Bad Review," *Deadly Allies 2*. Bantam, 1994
★"Postage Due," *The Mysterious West*. HarperCollins, 1994
"What's a Friend For?" with Margaret Maron. *Partners in Crime*. Signet,1994
★"All Things Come to He Who Waits," *Dast Magazine*, 1995
★"A Contest Fit for a Queen," *Crimes of the Heart*. Berkley, 1995
★"The Court of Celestial Appeals," *Guilty As Charged*. Pocket Books, 1996
★"I'll Get Back to You," *Women on the Case*. Delacorte, 1996
★"An Unsuitable Job for a Mullin," *Funny Bones*. Signet, 1997
★"A Surfeit of Deadline," *Mystery They Wrote 2*. Boulevard Books, MCA, 1998
★"A Worm in the Winesap," *Mom, Apple Pie and Death*. Berkley, 1999
"Family Surgery," *Mary Higgins Clark Mystery Magazine*, 2000
"Eight Lives," *Ellery Queen's Mystery Magazine*, November 2000
"A flaw in the Plan," *MightyWords.com*, 2000
"Away for Safekeeping," *Crimes of the Heart, vol. 2*. Berkley, 2001
"People Who Sit in Glass Houses," *Malice Domestic 10*. Avon, 2001
"A Tail of Two Cities," supplement to the limited edition of *The Celestial Buffet*. Crippen & Landru, 2001.

THE CELESTIAL BUFFET

The Celestial Buffet and Other Morsels of Murders by Susan Dunlap is printed on 60-pound Glatfelter Supple-Opaque (an acid-free, recycled stock) from 11-point Aldine. The cover painting is by Carol Heyer and the design by Deborah Miller. The first printing comprises two hundred fifty copies sewn in cloth, signed and numbered by the author, and approximately one thousand softcover copies. Each of the clothbound copies includes a separate pamphlet, *A Tail of Two Cities: A Jill Smith Story* by Susan Dunlap. The book was printed and bound by Thomson-Shore, Inc., Dexter, Michigan, and published in April 2001 by Crippen & Landru Publishers, Norfolk, Virginia.

CRIPPEN & LANDRU, PUBLISHERS
P. O. Box 9315
Norfolk, VA 23505
E-mail: CrippenL@Pilot.Infi.Net
Web: www.crippenlandru.com

Crippen & Landru publishes first edition short-story collections by important detective and mystery writers. Most books are issued in two editions: trade softcover, and signed, limited clothbound with either a typescript page from the author's files or an additional story in a separate pamphlet. As of April 2001, the following books have been published:

Speak of the Devil by John Dickson Carr. 1994. Out of print.

The McCone Files by Marcia Muller. 1995. Signed, limited clothbound, out of print; trade softcover, fifth printing, $15.00.

The Darings of the Red Rose by Margery Allingham. 1995. Out of Print.

Diagnosis: Impossible, The Problems of Dr. Sam Hawthorne by Edward D. Hoch. 1996. Signed, limited clothbound, out of print; trade softcover, second printing, $15.00.

Spadework: A Collection of "Nameless Detective" Stories by Bill Pronzini. 1996. Signed, limited clothbound, out of print; signed overrun copies, $30.00; trade softcover, $16.00.

Who Killed Father Christmas? And Other Unseasonable Demises by Patricia Moyes. 1996. Signed, limited clothbound, $40.00; trade softcover, $16.00.

My Mother, The Detective: The Complete "Mom" Short Stories, by James Yaffe. 1997. Signed, limited clothbound, out of print; trade softcover, $15.00.

In Kensington Gardens Once . . . by H. R. F. Keating. 1997. Signed, limited clothbound, out of print; trade softcover, $12.00.

Shoveling Smoke: Selected Mystery Stories by Margaret Maron. 1997. Signed, limited clothbound, out of print; trade softcover, third printing, $16.00.

The Man Who Hated Banks and Other Mysteries by Michael Gilbert. 1997. Signed, limited clothbound, out of print; trade softcover, second printing, $16.00.

The Ripper of Storyville and Other Ben Snow Tales by Edward D. Hoch. 1997. Signed, limited clothbound, out of print; trade softcover, $16.00.

Do Not Exceed the Stated Dose by Peter Lovesey. 1998. Signed, limited clothbound, out of print; trade softcover, $16.00.

Renowned Be Thy Grave; Or, The Murderous Miss Mooney by P. M. Carlson. 1998. Signed, limited clothbound, out of print; trade softcover, $16.00.

Carpenter and Quincannon, Professional Detective Services by Bill Pronzini. 1998. Signed, limited clothbound, out of print; trade softcover, second printing, $16.00.

Not Safe After Dark and Other Stories by Peter Robinson. 1998. Signed, limited clothbound, out of print; trade softcover, second printing, $16.00.

The Concise Cuddy, A Collection of John Francis Cuddy Stories by Jeremiah Healy. 1998. Signed, limited clothbound, out of print; trade softcover, $17.00.

One Night Stands by Lawrence Block. 1999. Out of print.

All Creatures Dark and Dangerous by Doug Allyn. 1999. Signed, limited clothbound, out of print; trade softcover, $16.00.

Famous Blue Raincoat: Mystery Stories by Ed Gorman. 1999. Signed, limited clothbound, out of print; signed overrun copies, $30.00; trade softcover, $17.00.

The Tragedy of Errors and Others by Ellery Queen. 1999. Limited clothbound, out of print; trade softcover, $16.00.

McCone and Friends by Marcia Muller. 2000. Signed, limited clothbound, out of print; trade softcover, second printing, $16.00.

Challenge the Widow Maker and Other Stories of People in Peril by Clark Howard. 2000. Signed, limited clothbound, out of print; trade softcover, $16.00.

The Velvet Touch by Edward D. Hoch. 2000. Signed, limited c
out of print; trade softcover, $16.00.

Fortune's World by Michael Collins. 2000. Signed, limited clothbou
of print; trade softcover, $16.00.

Tales Out of School: Mystery Stories by Carolyn Wheat. 2000. Signed, lim
clothbound, out of print; trade softcover, $16.00.

Long Live the Dead: Tales from Black Mask by Hugh B. Cave. 2000. Signed,
limited clothbound, out of print; trade softcover, $16.00.

Stakeout on Pages Street and Other DKA Files by Joe Gores. 2000. Signed,
limited clothbound, out of print; trade softcover, $16.00.

Strangers in Town: Three Newly Discovered Mysteries by Ross Macdonald, edited
by Tom Nolan. 2001. Limited clothbound, $37.00; trade softcover,
$15.00.

The Celestial Buffet and Other Morsels of Murder by Susan Dunlap. 2001.
Signed, limited clothbound, $40.00; trade softcover, $16.00.

Kisses of Death: A Nathan Heller Casebook by Max Allan Collins. 2001. Signed,
limited clothbound, $42.00; trade softcover, $17.00.

Crippen & Landru offers discounts to individuals and institutions who place Standing Order Subscriptions for all its forthcoming publications. Each Standing Order Subscriber receives at the end of a year a previously unpublished story in a limited edition. Please write or e-mail for further details.